PARTYING WITH PIXIES

HAVEN EVER AFTER - BOOK THREE

HAZEL MACK

COPYRIGHT

Editing - Mountains Wanted

Proofreading - Marcelle | BooksChecked

Cover - Anna Fury Author

Cover Art - Linda Noeran (@linda.noeran)

❀ Created with Vellum

THIS BOOK WAS WRITTEN BY A HUMAN
HUMAN GENERATED
I DON'T SUPPORT AI BOOKS OR ART

AUTHORS ARE NOW FACING AN UNPRECEDENTED CHALLENGE - ARTIFICIAL INTELLIGENCE (AI).

AI-based "books" , which are computer written, rather than human, are flooding the market and reducing our ability to earn a living wage writing books for you, our amazing readers.

The problem with AI as it stands today? It's not capable of thinking on its own. It ingests data and mimics someone else's style, often plagiarizing art and books without the original creator or author's consent.

There's a very real chance human authors will be forced out of the market as AI-written works take over. Yet your favorite authors bring magical worlds, experiences and emotions to life in a way that a computer can't. If you want to save that, then we need your help.

LEARN MORE ABOUT THE HARMFUL EFFECTS OF AI-WRITTEN BOOKS AND AI-GENERATED ART ON MY WEBSITE AT WWW.ANNAFURY.COM/AI

SYNOPSIS

ALO

A good Protector is focused on one thing—duty. That's been my guiding mantra since I came to the hidden monster haven of Ever. My roles as Protector and father come first. But I've got a secret—I'm desperately obsessed with the beautiful, kind, mischievous pixie who lives across the street.

Miriam Saihem invaded my mind first, building a rock-solid friendship I've come to rely on. But my heart demands something more, someone to make it beat again. I don't want to have to choose between her or my child, responsibility or love. I'm selfish-I want them both.
When Miriam learns about a human holiday centered entirely around candy, she asks for my help making Halloween come alive. It's the perfect chance for me to get closer to her and finally make the first move.

But when an evil warlock sets his sights on Ever, those I love are in danger. I've got to find—and eliminate—the threat or I'll never get the chance to make Miriam mine.

GET THE FREEBIES

CONTENT NOTICE

While this book is very sweet and lighthearted, there one specific heavy theme that might upset some readers—on-page mention of an unplanned pregnancy that results in parental split where the father takes the child and the mother has no further involvement.

If you have any particular questions, feel free to reach out to me at author@annafury.com!

CHAPTER ONE

MIRIAM

"Let me get this straight." I cross my arms and sit back in my chair, trying to understand what my soulfriend is telling me. "You carve scary faces into the pumpkins, and then you put them on your front porch, and they just *sit* there?"

Wren scoffs and opens her arms wide, looking to her troll mate, Ohken, for assistance. "Well, yeah, Miriam. It's meant to be *creepy*. The whole night is creepy but fun."

I look at the enormous bridge troll sitting to her left. "Humans are so weird. Do you get this Howl-O-Ween holiday?"

Ohken laughs, a deep rumble that causes Wren to nip at her lower lip. "It is 'Halloween,' my friend. Not 'Howl-O-Ween.' And yes, but only because she brought me a book with detailed illustrations. I can give it to you, if you like?"

"Yes, please." I snort. "Who ever heard of scaring people with pumpkins?"

Wren's emerald eyes spring gleefully wide, and she lifts her arm to point at me. "You know what? I haven't gotten to the

1

best part. And you're gonna love this part. This part is right up your alley."

I flutter my wings, shifting forward to pay attention. Wren appears utterly delighted about whatever she's about to share.

"The best part," she chirps, "is each house prepares candy and treats for the kiddos, and they go from door-to-door yelling 'trick or treat!' and you give them candy!"

"Trick or treat?" Ohken looks skeptical.

Bright joy fills my chest. "Candy, you say?"

Candy I can do.

Wren sits back and slaps her hand triumphantly on the table. "Yep, a shitload of candy. The holiday had far different origins, but the candy is kinda the main thing now for your average human. That and dressing up like monsters and characters from movies and such."

I cock my head to the side. This human holiday seems to have a never-ending litany of rules. Glancing over at Ohken, I drum my fingers on the table. "I'll take that book, friend."

Ohken laughs and shoves back from the table, turning to head into the depths of his cave.

Wren watches him go, her expression wistful. "I swear, he's got the best ass on the planet. Look at that thing, Mir."

Dutifully, I follow her gaze, but all I see is a male who isn't the one I want. Big bouncy troll asses aren't my thing.

High and tight gargoyle muscles? Violently beautiful claw-tipped wings? Fingers as thick as sausages? That's what I want. I compare everyone to Aloitious Rygold. He's fucking perfect.

Wren snickers. "You've got the sappiest look on your face, Miriam. Lemme guess, you're fantasizing about Alo's ass?"

I rub my wings together to dissipate the kaleidoscope of butterflies that rocket around my belly. It's no secret I've got the world's biggest crush on one of Ever's two gargoyle protectors. I've known Alo for five years, since he left another haven and came to live here with his newborn son, Iggy.

"It's complicated," I mutter, the usual irritation swirling low in my stomach.

Wren's expression goes soft and understanding. "I know he's just as nuts about you as you are about him, Mir. He stares at you all the time. I wonder what holds him back?"

Duty.

His child.

Not wanting to ruin a stellar friendship.

I don't say any of those things, though. Wren's only lived in Ever for a month or so. She hasn't watched me pine over Alo for five entire years. She still thinks there's a chance we'll end up together. I'm starting to give up that hope. No matter what I do to show him I'd be the perfect partner, he doesn't reciprocate.

The blue leather band around my wrist vibrates, and a name hologram pops up just above it. I groan when I see it.

"Ugh," Wren mutters. "Ezazel?"

The head of my pixie order is my least favorite monster in town. But he's in charge of ensuring we stay on track with pixie dust production, and we fell behind after a recent thrall attack on the community garden. There is nothing more important than making pixie dust. Without it, we can't power the wards that keep Ever safe from the outside world.

I direct the watch to answer him.

"Miriam?" Ezazel's voice is as gruff as always.

"Yes, I'm here." I roll my eyes at Wren, whose brows furrow. She doesn't care for Ezazel's brusque manner, especially when he directs said brusqueness at me.

"You're on the schedule to stir the dust this evening. See that you're on time."

I hold back a snappish comment. "I'll be there, Ezazel."

Without another word, he clicks off.

Wren scoffs. "Jesus, he's condescending."

It's on the tip of my tongue to remind her how important pixie dust is to maintaining the protective wards that form a bubble around Ever. But Wren's well aware. When she and her sisters arrived, they accidentally punched a hole right through them.

I rise from my chair. "I've got to stop by the shop and check on a few things before my shift, so I'd better go. See you tomorrow, soulfriend?"

Ohken emerges from a back hallway with a book in his hand. He hands it to me with a smile. "*On the History of Halloween in America.* Wren confirms it's an excellent primer for the nonhuman among us."

Laughing, I take the leather-bound book and tuck it under my arm. I gesture around with my free hand. "Thank you for the lovely breakfast, friends. And your renovations to add plants to the living area are genius. Now Wren can be thinking about plants during all your activities instead of just in the bedroom."

Wren groans and throws a hand over her face.

Ohken's auburn brows travel up to his hairline. "Thinking about plants during activities, huh? Hmmm." He strokes his chin thoughtfully. "I suppose I'll have to try harder to keep your focus on me, Miss Hector."

He grins devilishly, and that's my cue to leave. They're newly mated, and they're still in the fawning-over-one-another phase. Although something tells me they'll be fawning for a while. I love it for them, but I'm also very, very jealous.

Wren stands and rounds the end of the chunky wooden table, opening her plump arms wide. Hugging all the time is such a human thing. I sink into her arms, squishing our cheeks together as I hold her tight. Wren's heartbeat is a steady, comforting thud, her chest pressed to mine. We hold the hug for a long minute before she steps back.

I've decided I love being hugged. And I think I love it because there's no other physical interaction in my life. Pixies aren't huggers. Nobody wants to accidentally touch wings and be awkward. It's a mates-only thing.

Wren walks me up a few stairs and out their first door, following me up a long hallway lit by glowing blue troll glyphs. Ohken's cave was always beautiful, but she seems so happy now that he has Wren. The glyphs never glowed before Wren came along.

She presses her hand to the wall just inside the cave door and grins. "I can't wait to hear all your questions once you read about Halloween. It's the best holiday ever. It's Thea's favorite too!"

I smile at her mention of one of her triplets. Thea mated Alo's brother, Shepherd, not that long ago. She is wonderful—bubbly and hilarious and just so lovely.

Also, I'm incredibly jealous of the Hectors and their relationships. They've been in Ever for just a month, and two of the three girls are now mated to monsters. The third sister isn't mating anyone anytime soon, but that's another story entirely.

The bridge entrance's black stones crack and slide out of place, tumbling to the ground outside. I wave one last time at Wren, then step out, emerging under the troll bridge. The creek is quiet at this time of day; the mermaid minnows who use it to get to school have already done so.

Sighing, I soak in the sounds of the verdant-green forest. It's quiet and peaceful here by Ohken's bridge. I duck out from under the aged stones and head along the river before taking a right onto the path that leads back toward Sycamore Street. With Wren's book in hand, I can't switch to my small form and zip back to the garden—the book will be too heavy, and I don't have any dust with me to tiny-fy it.

I walk quietly along the forest path, flipping the book open. It's a lot of small-print words, causing my eyes to immediately glaze over. I've always had trouble reading, so I'm grateful when I flip a page and there's an illustration. A woman wearing striped stockings, a black tattered dress, and a conical black hat with a wide brim, smirks at me from the page. In one hand, she holds an upside-down broomstick. In the other, a vial of purple liquid.

Small text below the image indicates she's a witch ready to go flying on Halloween and steal children.

Oh my word. Witches don't steal children. It's preposterous. Witches are protectors. Don't humans know anything about us from myth? There was a time before the monster haven system was put into place when monsters lived in hiding. Surely the humans had enough random interaction to get some parts of our lore correct?

I flip through a few more pages as I walk. When I come to a page with a black cat staring into a cauldron as a "witch" dumps toads in, I cackle aloud. By the time I reach the end of the path and Sycamore Street, I've made it through all the book's illustrations and come to one conclusion—human Halloween in its current form is utter nonsense. Absolute made-up shit.

Hooking a right on Sycamore, I head for Main Street. By the time I get there, my brain buzzes like it often does when I ingest new info. Ideas come to me, floating lazily inside my mind like fireflies.

Main Street is busy this time of day. Like always, there's a line of monsters out the door at Higher Grounds coffee shop. Two centaurs meander down the sidewalk hand in hand. As I head toward my store, Miriam's Sweets, I wave to Richard, the pack alpha of the shifter pack in Ever.

"You're not usually in this part of town." I laugh and clap his muscular shoulder. "What brings you to Main Street?"

Richard smiles, pearly white fangs glistening in the midmorning light. "Meeting with the Keeper and protector team." His smile falls a little. "After a lot of arguing from the Keeper, Hearth HQ agreed to *consider* not sending us a secondary Keeper, but they're sending a hunter team sometime this week."

My happy mood falls flat as a pancake. I lift my hand to nibble at my thumbnail, then lay it back down. "Do you think they'll bring hellhounds?"

Richard nods. "Absolutely they will." He runs one hand through perfectly slicked-back salt-and-pepper hair. "I haven't told the shifters yet. They won't be pleased."

Hellhounds and shifters have a sordid history. I'm not surprised he's anxious to have the creepy dogs here in Ever.

"On the other hand," he continues, "Wesley has attacked us three times in the last month. Something's got to give— he's too powerful a warlock to allow himself to continue what he's doing. The Keeper's job is to keep Ever safe. He can't be expected to go out and hunt Wesley, but someone needs to."

I nod, but I'm lost in thought. Richard notices, intuitive shifter male that he is. He rubs my shoulder before striding past me.

I've lived here for a long time. I've never felt unsafe until the last month. Even now, I don't feel unsafe necessarily, but I do feel like we're in a spiderweb of Wesley's making, caught and struggling, and he's crawling across the web to wrap us up for dinner.

Shaking my head to ward away the jittery sensation in my chest, I walk past Scoops Ice Cream and shove my key in the lock at my store. The glossy red wood front always brings me peace. Well, most days it does. When I step inside, the scents of spun sugar and vanilla fill my nose. My shop always brings a smile to my face.

I freaking adore candy. More than that, I love making people smile. And my candy does that. Most of it is just plain candy, but I've got a few magical candies that make things happen—like turning your hair another color or making your voice go high and squeaky.

The store doesn't open until lunchtime, but I'm rarely on the shop schedule myself. My work with the other pixies making dust is too important. The sweets shop has always come second. And it's been successful despite my torn focus. I'm really proud of that.

I walk through the customer area toward the back. Two of the four walls are floor-to-ceiling jars of various candies. Walking past the glossy red checkout counter, I enter a short hall and turn left into my office. We aren't teaching any candy-making classes tonight, so thankfully I don't have to get the classroom ready. I don't have enough time for that before my shift.

Breathing out a sigh of pleasure, I look around my office. One whole side is a long storage area with candy ingredients. My desk sits opposite to it. It's where I get all my best thinking done.

I set the Halloween book down then round the desk and drop into my chair. There's a stack of paperwork from my assistant Celset. She's a harpy and fairly reclusive, so she comes in to do the books and paperwork overnight. On the mornings after she's come, there's always a neat stack of papers on my desk awaiting my attention.

I glance at my comm watch. It's nine forty-five a.m. Evertime. I've got forty-five minutes until I need to be at the factory. Plenty of time to sort through this stack of purchase orders and send them to my supplier in Vizelle. The Swiss monster haven is the very best place for recreational pixie dust. Most dust is used for ward protection, but Vizelle has developed a type specifically meant to enhance pixie magic.

Grabbing a pen, I get to work, but I'm still distracted by what I saw in Wren's Halloween book. The inklings of an idea that came to me earlier stretch and move in my mind, forming into a full idea so tangible and exciting, I can't help but grab a sheet of paper and start jotting everything down.

Lost in ideation, I sketch and draw and make myself notes. With a triumphant purr, I sit back and stare at the paper.

The Hectors' birthday is coming up soon in human-world time, and I don't want them to miss it simply because Ever works on a different timeline. I'm going to recreate Halloween for the Hector triplets. Yes! It's going to be amazing.

My comm watch pings, and I notice it's nearly eleven a.m. Groaning, I slap myself on the forehead, not bothering to answer Ezazel. It'll be another sermon, and I'm too excited about Halloween to deal with it. Snapping my fingers, I transform into my small form and zip out of my office, through the store, and out the small pixie hole next to the door handle.

CHAPTER TWO

ALO

T flap slowly through the sky, keeping my movements steady and unhurried. Iggy scrambles next to me, his legs moving like he's running while his far-smaller wings flutter wildly behind his back.

"Easy, kiddo," I caution, holding a finger out for him. "The Keeper just reinforced the wards with pixie dust, so the wind bounces off the ceiling extra hard. It'll be more difficult for you to take off and keep your flight path straight."

My five-year-old's brow furrows, and he stops trying to run in the air.

"You look frustrated, Iggy. Talk to me."

He looks up at me, brilliant blue eyes narrowed angrily. They're his mother's eyes, that vivid shade of blue that's even brighter than the sky.

Not that we talk about her at all. She's not in our life anymore—he knows very little about her. But maybe that's a mistake. Maybe I should have been telling Iggy all about her for his whole life. I've just never wanted to answer the question of why she doesn't live with us in Ever.

"How come we haven't seen Miriam in a week?"

His question surprises me. The reality is he's been more silent than usual, more irritable, and I've been trying to be around for him as much as I can.

I dig into his comment a little further. "Are you missing your friend? Miriam's really nice, huh?"

More than nice. Miriam is pixie perfection wrapped up in a lithe, powerful form with a dash of goofiness topped with powdered sugar.

"I love her," Iggy announces, stabilizing his wing movements. "I want her to be my girlfriend because she makes my heart feel"—he pauses as he hunts around for the word— "fluttery."

I cock my head to the side. "Fluttery? Your heart won't beat until you find a mate, kiddo. You'll be all grown up before that happens."

Iggy shakes his head. "Nope. It's Miriam. Why else would I wish she was here all the time?"

I clench my teeth to avoid telling him he's too young for this sort of feeling, that he won't feel the desire to find a mate until he comes of age, and he's got a full decade before that happens. Who am I to tell him what can and can't happen? He's drawn to Miriam.

Join the club, buddy.

He darts forward and slaps one of my horns with the spade-shaped tip of his tail, then takes off. "Gotcha! You weren't paying attention!"

My child loves a chase, so I let out a fake-angry roar and stretch out long, catching the air currents. But he's getting stronger and picking up how the wards affect the air currents really fast. He bullets up into the blue sky, stopping just short of the faintly shining green ward. He slaps it with his tail too and darts off right as I snatch at his leg.

"Got to tell the Keeper good morning," he shouts. I

imagine all sorts of alarms going off at the monitoring system at the Keeper's castle.

"Yeah, I'm sure he loves a good early morning alarm," I mutter.

Iggy's too far off to hear me, whooping as he spins and dives, grabbing the current that'll take us across downtown toward Shifter Hollow where Ever's single school is located.

I let my son stay ahead of me, getting close enough to grab at his tail a time or two, but he's smart and wraps it around his ankle so I can't quite reach it.

Five playful minutes later, I'm flying upside down underneath him, making goofy faces as he tickles me and tries not to forget to fly.

We land in the school's courtyard, and Miss Cross clip-clops across the aged flat stones with a slow clap. "Well done, Ignatius!"

Iggy flares his wings wide and makes a point to land gracefully. He gives his teacher a wink. "I figured out who my mate is this morning. Wanna hear all about it? It's Miriam from the sweets shop!"

Miss Cross's purple eyes flick to mine, and she suppresses a grin. "Is that so? And how does your father feel about that?"

I cross my arms, grateful for the dark gray skin that hides my blush.

She gives me a knowing look but holds a hand out for my son. "Iggy, why don't you come in and tell me all about it?"

Iggy crawls up my leg, flapping until he can throw his arms around my neck. "Love you, Aloitious Noctis."

I snort. He's just started calling me by my full name sometimes. I don't remember doing that to my father, but it cracks me up.

"Love you too, Ignatius Zion."

Iggy gives me one final slap on the horns and then glides over to Miss Cross's broad back, settling himself there. His pixie friend Kevin shows up and joins him, and they ride on the centaur teacher up to the front door, slapping each other the whole way.

She throws me a wave as she goes into the school. I stand in the courtyard for a moment, grateful Iggy has friends and a wonderful teacher here in Ever. He wouldn't have had that if we'd stayed in Vizelle. And he certainly wouldn't have had that if I'd followed Keira to Hearth HQ for a job.

The elusive headquarters haven is too political, too busy, and definitely too full of assholes for my liking. Or, as Iggy calls them, Hearth-holes.

Shuddering against painful memories, I press off the stones and climb up to the current that'll take me to the Keeper's castle. I swoop over Ever, my adopted home haven, admiring Shifter Hollow from above. Treehouses spiral out from the businesses at the center of the hollow. It's almost a second downtown, especially considering the shifters don't come to Main Street all that often.

The landscape passes in a blur as I grab a current westward and head for the castle. The Keeper, Ever's de facto mayor, is waiting for my brother Shepherd and me to discuss the ward monitoring system and the recent spate of thrall attacks.

The castle comes into view, all black curves and dark windows. It suits the Keeper's austere personality, although the inside was a little bit of a surprise the first time I saw it. It's a mishmash of architectural styles ranging from Gothic to an ultramodern kitchen that looks straight out of a human decorating magazine—which I only know because he showed one to me.

Landing in the stone courtyard, I wave at the castle as she opens the double front doors for me. My brother appears inside them, grinning like a fool with his big arms crossed over his chest.

Like always, there's utter joy on his face and a godsdamned sparkle in his eye. I don't think he's stopped smiling since the Hector triplets arrived and he identified Thea Hector as his mate. Now they're fully mated. He's getting snuggles every night and carving memories into the headboard of his nest.

And I am really fucking jealous.

I'm happy as hells for him—I really am. I've always wanted him to find his person, but gods, I want that happiness for myself too.

But then Iggy's adorable face pops into my mind, and I remember that, when I learned Keira was pregnant but didn't want a child, I knew I'd put that child before everything else, including my personal life. He's growing up with a near-perfect childhood, and that's because I made the choice to give him that. I'll never stop, because I want him to have the same sort of childhood Shep and I had in Vizelle.

Our parents adored and spoiled us, but we trained hard and grew up to be powerful gargoyles. House Rygold is well-loved in the protector community. I'm proud of who we are, and I want Iggy to be proud to carry on the Rygold name.

Shepherd cocks his head to the side, his easy smile falling. "Your scowl is worse today than usual, brother. What's eating you?"

I laugh. "Is that another one of Thea's sayings?"

He matches my laughter and shrugs, running one hand through short black waves. "Yeah, I guess it is. Humans have so many fascinating and weird sayings. I'm defaulting to human-speak, I suppose. Makes sense though. Your sour face looks like someone's eating you, and not in a good way." He winks.

I groan.

Because my helpful brain supplies a vision of Miriam on top of me, her pretty lips sucking at my cock, which goes hard at the mere thought. But I've got to stop having these thoughts about one of my closest friends. She wants me. I want her. But I shouldn't have her because I can't give her all the attention she deserves—I've got Iggy to think about.

"How's Ig?" Shepherd's voice goes quiet.

Like me, it enraged him when the Hearth leader, Evenia, mentioned Keira in front of Iggy last week. It was unnecessary and resulted in a shitload of questions about my ex-mate and where she is. Iggy's never been too interested in his mother's story, and I've tried really hard to be both parents so he never feels like he's missing out.

But when Evenia mentioned Keira's "important" work at Hearth HQ, well, that prompted questions from my son.

"He asked me a lot of questions about Keira, and he's been moody since, but he seemed okay this morning." I don't know why I open the next can of worms, but I do. "He thinks Miriam is his mate. He announced it to his teacher this morning. Apparently, she makes his heart feel"—I lift my fingers into air quotes—"fluttery."

Shepherd stops and plants one big hand on my shoulder, his expression more serious than I've ever seen it. "Alo. Your child loves Miriam. You have the hots for Miriam. Miriam is head over heels infatuated with you. When are you going to realize that having her solves a lot of your problems?"

I want that; I do. I've wanted it for years. But duty holds me back. And if I'm honest, I've had my heart broken once, and I don't want to go through that again.

Scowling, I shake his hand off. "Iggy's my focus, Shep. I don't ever want him to feel like he's not my number one."

Shepherd rolls his eyes. "I swear to gods, you'd better come to your senses before someone new moves to town and swoops her right out from under your nose. She's not gonna wait around forever, Alo."

I bristle at that, battle spines slipping up out of my skin along my shoulders and forearms.

He gestures at my battle form, one black brow curled upward. "If the mere fucking mention of another male around Miriam sends you into a tizzy like this, then maybe you should consider asking her out, you big idiot. I don't remember you being so grumpy when we were kids."

No, I want to shout. I was a happy person until the moment my mate looked at her rapidly swelling belly and told me she didn't want a child. We were never on the same page about it. I know that now, since hindsight is 20-20.

My thoughts go to Miriam and Iggy's mention of his heart fluttering when he's near her. My own heart is still as a stone these days. But I know how fucking good it feels for it to start beating. I know how horribly soul-splitting it was when mine stopped beating for Keira.

And I don't ever want that again.

CHAPTER THREE

MIRIAM

The following morning, I rub the sleep from my eyes as I leave the sweets shop and lock up. My assistant won't be here to open the store for hours yet. My feet drag as I pass Scoops Ice Cream and cross Sycamore, heading for Higher Grounds. The beloved coffee shop isn't super busy yet. I glance down at my comm watch as I open the door. Six thirty a.m. Ugh.

I mutter under my breath as I enter, the scent of perfectly roasted coffee beans filling my nostrils. I'm desperate for the jolt of caffeine to my system. When I place my order, Alessandro, one of the two vampire owners, shoots me a sympathetic look.

"Long night partying, Miriam?"

I snort. "I wish." I'm too tired to expand, and Alessandro doesn't question me, but he does lay a hand on my shoulder and rub it gently.

"Your work is very much appreciated, Miriam." With his accent, he rolls the *r* in the middle of my name. It sounds nice. He's flirted with me plenty. I'm just not interested.

I make some appropriate comment or another and then

slump against the counter to wait for my latte. When Alessandro calls out my name, I jolt upright. Shit, I fell asleep standing there! Gods, that's embarrassing. The handsome vampire hands me my latte with an understanding smile.

I thank him and take it, trudging for the front door. Yanking it open, I step out into the sunlight, closing my eyes as warmth spreads across my cheeks.

A big body crashes into mine, knocking into my hand. The coffee spills down my shirt, burning like shit. I yip and jump back, but a thick arm slides around my waist and hauls me upright.

Eyelashes fluttering in surprise, I look up to see Alo. He's covered in coffee too, his wet shirt clinging to every fucking ab.

"Mir, I'm so sorry. I was distracted and didn't see you step out of the door."

I glance down between us. Fuck. My shirt is see-through, and my tits are too small to need a bra. My very hard nipples are pressed to the front of it.

Horrified, I peer up at him. His dark eyes are planted firmly on my chest, but he drags them up when I clear my throat. A dark gray blush spreads across his angular cheeks.

I try not to read anything into this. We're just friends. But tits are tits, and dudes like tits, so it's not weird that he'd look at them.

And, shit, I still haven't said anything.

Alo saves us both any further embarrassment by grabbing my coffee cup and holding the door open for me. "Let's get you another coffee, and you can tell me why you came out of there with your eyes closed."

I smile and follow him dutifully back into Higher Grounds.

Alessandro's dark eyes flash, but he takes one look at our

wet shirts and laughs. "Another latte coming right up, Miriam." There goes that rolling *r* again.

Alo puts the empty cup on the counter. "Put it on my tab, friend. I ran into her."

Alessandro tries and fails to hold back a smirk, but nods. "As you wish, Aloitious."

Alo grabs a bunch of napkins off the counter and dabs carefully at my chest, avoiding my boobs and sticking to the middle. And I watch, because, like always, I'm entranced by him and half tempted to suddenly shift to one side so he touches my boob. But that would be terrible, because he knows how I feel about him. And I know he knows how I feel.

He's never encouraged me, and that hasn't stopped me from pining, but it does make me careful not to add weirdness to a fantastic friendship.

He purses his lips and shakes his head. "Sorry, Mir. That's gonna stain for sure." Pitch-black eyes flick to mine.

"Mhm," I agree. "It's fine. I'm headed to work anyway. I had my head in the clouds as usual."

Alo crosses his arms, which draws my gaze to his bulging biceps and miles of dark gray skin. Veins trail over the backs of his hands and up his forearms. My favorite one carves a path along the inside of his left biceps. Gods above, he's beautiful.

"Mir?" His resonant, lilting tone breaks me out of my reverie.

"Yeah?" I glance up to see him trying not to laugh.

"You're more distracted than usual. And you never get an extra-large latte. What's going on?"

I run one hand through my green pixie cut, blowing air from between my lips. He's not gonna like what I have to say. "I was up all night stirring the dust, and then I had to run some supplies to the sweets shop. I'm on duty this morning too." I look up to find him scowling like somebody pissed in his breakfast cereal. I shrug. "Hence the super huge coffee."

Alo's perfectly arched brows form an angry vee in the middle, brilliant white fangs flashing from behind dark, plump lips. "Mir, that's—"

"How's Iggy?" I cut in. "Is he doing okay after that biotch from the Hearth mentioned Keira?"

Alo's scowl deepens, but he shrugs. "He's moody one minute and his usual self the next." Dark eyes meet mine. "He asked about you yesterday."

My heart nearly bursts in my chest, and it's hard to resist the urge to run to the elementary school, pixie my way through his classroom window, and wrap him up in the biggest of hugs. I don't have wings big enough to cocoon him like Alo does, but Iggy gives the best damn hugs.

"Can I bring you both dinner? I'd love to see him!" The exuberant offer is out of my mouth before I can remind myself not to push too hard into their lives. It stings that Alo didn't rely on me at all this past week, but I'm not his mate, and I'm not Iggy's mother.

It doesn't hurt that delivering food and caring for one's mate are standard gargoyle mating rituals. We just watched his brother Shepherd mate one of the Hector triplets. I've never seen a girl so inundated with snacks.

I'm jealous as hell.

Alo shakes his head, and like every time he doesn't let me in, my heart squeezes tight in my chest before deflating.

"Let me cook. I'm meeting the Keeper about the hunter team HQ wants to send, but I'm free after that. Plenty of time to cook up something. You can come over and rest your wings for a while." He gives me a soft smile. "Iggy will be thrilled."

I'm grinning like an idiot. I know I am. I'm not reading anything into Alo cooking for me, but I can't wait.

I shrug, trying to find my chill so I can put it back in place. "Sounds good, friend."

Alo's smile falters a little bit, the light from his eyes dulling.

I don't want to read into his reaction to the word "friend" either. It doesn't matter how much I wish things were different—if he was ready and wanted us to happen, he'd do something about it.

Still, a small and very hopeful piece of my heart wonders if him offering to cook is him finally getting out of his own way and seeing that I'm right in front of him.

CHAPTER FOUR

ALO

Gods, I'm a dummy. Because I can't stop thinking about Miriam's tits in that shirt. And I didn't mean to mention cooking for her. Excited butterflies zip around my stomach. The very idea of Miriam in my house gets me hard, and every damn time she comes over, I have to sneak away and adjust my cock in my jeans—it fucking throbs with need when she's around. And when she leaves, her scent is everywhere. The whole cottage smells like spun sugar and cotton candy. I've lost track of the number of times I've jacked off to that scent once she's gone.

I've seen Miriam naked—we've swum in the mermaid's grotto plenty of times. But there's something about the tease of her body underneath a wet shirt that has heat curling deep and insistent between my legs. Gods, I want her.

Frustration claws at me. Shoving my desire down hard, I climb through the sky and head to the Keeper's castle for the second time this week. Apparently, Hearth HQ has "news," and they need to speak with us urgently.

Fifteen minutes later, the Keeper, Ohken, Richard, and I

stand in the Keeper's communications room staring at a hologram that rises up from a disk on the floor.

"As I mentioned," the dark-haired woman in front of us
says, "now that Wesley has attacked Ever no less than four
times under your watch, I'll be sending a second Keeper,
along with a hunter team."

A tick starts in the Keeper's jaw, a swatch of blond hair
falling over the scar trailing down the left side of his face.

"That's really not necessary, Evenia. I—"

"Of course it's necessary," she hisses, leveling her son with
an angry sneer. "If one haven falls, they all could, and everything we worked for in creating the haven system would be
for nothing. The only reason anyone is safe is because we
have safe places to hide."

Richard, the shifter pack alpha, steps forward and cuts her
a shitty look. "We don't need a primer on haven history,
Evenia. We're all well aware of how life was before Catherine
built the haven system. Each of us here"—he gestures around
the room—"is confident in our ability to keep Ever safe. Most
especially, we're confident in our Keeper." His gaze goes
narrow and fierce. "I've been to Hearth HQ, and I've met
every other Keeper in the system. There's no one as good as
ours."

Evenia sputters, dark red eyes flashing with apparent
anger.

I stay silent because I have a tendency to make things
worse in meetings like this. It's probably good I didn't go with
Keira to Hearth HQ to work. I'd report to Evenia, and she's a
fucking nightmare.

Her hologram crosses her arms and scowls. "I'll discuss it
with the rest of leadership, of course. But there's no way
you're getting out of a hunter team. We need to locate
Wesley."

"Of course," the Keeper purrs in the evil tone he reserves

for his mother. "My job is to protect Ever and my residents. *Your* job is to hunt for Wesley. Do what you have to."

She purses her lips and signs off without another word, the hologram disappearing back into the flat comm disk.

The Keeper sighs, then uncrosses his long arms and turns toward the rest of us. "I wouldn't put it past my mother to send a second Keeper and a hunter team. We should be ready for that. I'll pull files on the candidates I think she'd send. We can revisit this tomorrow."

I growl as frustration mounts. "We'll run them off if she sends someone. We don't need another Keeper."

His fingers twitch against his leg. "I appreciate the show of solidarity, Aloitious. But if she sends another Keeper, I'll have to work with that monster, whoever it may be. I can't give Evenia any reason to fault me. She talks a big talk about me embarrassing our house, but if she thought the haven system would benefit from me being removed from my post, she'd do it."

"We won't allow it," Ohken assures him. "Everyone in this room is committed to keeping you at your post."

The Keeper smiles, the corners of his pale lips tilting up into a half smile. "I don't say this often enough, but I appreciate your efforts. I couldn't ask for a better leadership team."

Pride swirls through me as I nudge his side with my elbow. "Are you going soft on us? Sweet nothings? I don't think I've ever heard you say thank you since I moved here." I huff out a laugh that he matches.

He runs both hands through his slicked-back blond hair. "I don't know, I just felt like I should say something."

"The Morgan effect," Richard murmurs. "Perhaps her presence softens you a bit."

The Keeper's body goes tense, and a neutral mask slips down over his features. "Miss Hector's presence here is noted, but we have very little interaction."

Richard shifts forward, staring the Keeper in the face. "And maybe it's time for that to change, old friend. You're doing nobody any favors keeping her at arm's length, most especially her."

The Keeper grits his jaw. "I'll take it under advisement."

Richard smiles, and having said his piece, he claps the Keeper on the back and strides out of the cramped, screen-filled room.

The Keeper's jaw clenches and unclenches rhythmically. He stares at Ohken and me. "I suppose you two have an opinion on the topic as well? Or can we get on with our jobs?"

Ohken shrugs his big shoulders. "You know my opinion on it."

The moment grows long and tense, but when the Keeper says nothing, the bridge troll leaves.

Ruby-red eyes snap to me as the Keeper crosses his arms.

Throwing my palms up, I give him an understanding look. "You'll never hear it from me, friend. I have no leg to stand on when it comes to dating advice."

He plants both hands on his hips, a wry laugh escaping him. "I suppose I'll refrain from offering you the same, then."

My own smile falls. "Yeah, man. I—" But words don't come to me. There's so much unsaid between us. Despite his austere and brusque exterior, the Keeper sees every-fucking-thing about Ever's residents. Of everyone here, he's probably most aware of my true feelings about Miriam, and the reasons why I've never pursued her despite my interest.

When I can't think up a response, I nod awkwardly. As I turn to leave, my comm watch pings. I glance down at the name and groan.

Noctis Raven Rygold.

I bite back a growl, shooting the Keeper an exasperated look. "Duty calls."

He laughs, but just like me, it's bitter-sounding.

I direct the comm watch to answer as I make my way through the dark castle halls toward the front entryway. Most comm watches don't allow for inter-haven communications. Mine does only because I'm a haven protector. But right now, I wish I didn't have the extra access.

"Aloitious," my father's voice booms in greeting. It's as deep as always, like boulders tumbling down a rocky slope. "How are you, son?"

And so it begins. He'll ask about me first, and then we'll move on to the topic of my child.

I exit the castle and push off the ground, climbing into the sky. "Good," I answer. "Taking off to patrol." It's better to keep things short and sweet. My parents are both legendary protectors—the minute I share any detail about my life, he'll nitpick my choices. Attention to detail is why Shepherd and I are so good at our jobs, and we get that from our parents, but it's infuriating to be on the receiving end of Father's scrutiny.

He gets right to the point. "I heard Ever was once again attacked."

"We've got a plan," I respond, my tone direct. "We just got off the comm with Evenia, in fact."

"Good," he states. "Come home to Vizelle, Aloitious. Your mother would be thrilled, and—"

This again. Gods, I hate arguing with him about where I chose to live.

"I'm not interested in returning to Switzerland, Father," I remind him for the millionth time. I swoop out of the sky and land on the top of a tall pine, settling on my haunches with a wing claw gripping the trunk and my tail wrapped around a sturdy branch. "We're happy here, and Shepherd's here. Ever is exactly where I want to be."

"What about Iggy?" Father's voice sounds bitter and disappointed.

"What *about* Iggy?" I prod. "He loves Ever. He's got friends and Shepherd, and now Shepherd's mate Thea, not to mention *my* friends. Iggy's happy here."

Father's not done, of course. "Ignatius is my only grand-child, Alo. I'd like to see him grow up. Your mother and I—"

"Can come visit," I cut in. "But I've got to go. We've got a friend coming for dinner, and I need to finish my patrol so I can grab Ig and get ready."

The moment I mention a friend, I wish I hadn't.

Father's voice goes deep and cutting. "What sort of friend, Aloitious?"

I bristle, my battle spines slipping up out of my shoulders and shredding my shirt. "A *good* friend," I purr cruelly into my watch.

He's quiet for a long moment, then growls. "I'm certain I don't need to remind you how poorly your last relationship ended. You need to focus on Ignatius at all costs. He is the only one around to carry on the Rygold name."

That's a little dramatic. No doubt Shep and Thea will have children one day, but my father loves to fucking remind me how I need to put Iggy first at the expense of everything else.

"This conversation grows tiresome, Noctis," I droll, exam-ining the dark nails on my left hand. "I'd love for you and Mother to visit if you're up for it. If not, well, that's fine too."

"Alo," Father warns.

I hang up, silencing whatever fresh "advice" he planned on giving. Closing my eyes, I lift my face to the sky. Ever's weather is always the same—sixty-five degrees and pleasant. The sun's warmth shines down, soaking into my skin. I smile despite the repetitive conversation with my father.

And I come to a determination then. He and Mother helped me with Iggy when he was first born, and I am eter-nally grateful for that. But it doesn't mean they get or need to have a say in every parenting decision I make.

Screw Noctis Raven Rygold and his infernal meddling.

Iggy's my son, and I know what's best for him.

And for me, for that matter.

Leaping into the sky, I flare my wings wide and climb closer to the ceiling of Ever's wards, grabbing a balmy current. I catch it and swoop toward home.

I've got dinner to cook.

The rest of my day passes in a blur, because all I can focus on is Miriam coming to the cottage. She's been to dinner at my place hundreds of times, but this is different somehow. Maybe it's the conversation with my father or my decision to let his opinion hold less sway over me.

Iggy barrels through the door at three forty-five and flies through the house like a madman. I'm stirring Miriam's favorite chicken noodle soup at the vintage stove in my small kitchen when he zips past, whipping at me with his tail spade. I duck and grab for it, missing purposefully. I let out a fake-angry roar, holding back a laugh when my son shouts triumphantly and darts into the next room.

The cottage has been quiet all afternoon, but the cabinet to the right of the stove opens, and the shelf pops out and wiggles. A box of salt falls off it and onto the countertop. I roll my eyes. My lack of salt consumption is a constant source of disagreement between us, although the cottage always wins. The countertop ripples and rolls, shoving the salt toward the pot of soup.

"Alright, alright. I get it," I mutter. I grab the box and pour a smidge of the white grains into my palm, trickling it into the soup as I stir. The cottage vibrates a little, her version of preening. Like Iggy, she loves it when Miriam comes over.

Everybody loves it when Miriam comes over.

I cock my head to the side and twitch an ear to listen for Iggy's imminent attack. This is a game we've started playing every day, and although it's play now, one day he'll go to the Protector Academy, and he'll have to use these hunting skills.

Heavy breaths echo softly from the living room. He leaps through the arched entry and lands on my shoulder, wrapping himself around my head and neck as he stabs at me with his sharp tail spade.

"Die, evil scum!" he shrieks between a fit of giggles.

With a pained grunt, I fall carefully backward into the wall, sliding down with my wings askance. My head lolls back, and Iggy unwraps himself, poking at my cheek with his tail.

"Got you, Dad. Admit it, I'm getting big and strong enough to ask Miriam to be my girlfriend."

I sit up with a smile, resting a forearm on my knee. "Is that what this is all about, this warrior training you seem to be doing?"

Iggy crosses his chubby arms and shrugs with a smug, imperious look on his round face. "Yep." He pops the *p*, his long tail lashing from side to side.

"Well"—I reach for him—"help me up, protector."

He places his three tiny fingers in my much larger ones, wrapping them together and pulling. I shove off the ground and grab him under his arms, placing him on my shoulder.

Iggy's tail winds around my neck the way it has since he was a baby. The spade slips into my shirt to rest above my heart. If I were still mated, it would comfort him because he'd feel it beating. But it's silent as a stone now that his mother and I have split.

He grasps one of my horns and leans forward, peering into the bubbling pot. "Miriam's favorite! Is she coming over? Oh my gosh, please say she is!"

I grin. "She's coming over."

Pounding footsteps tell me his friend Kevin is headed for our back door. A second later, there's a loud rap, and the small pixie lets himself into the kitchen.

His black wings flutter behind him as he sniffs the air. "Ooo! Miriam's soup! Is she coming over?"

I laugh. "Yes, she's coming over. But she's working, so it'll be a few hours yet. If you boys want to go play, you can. I'll battle cry when she arrives."

Iggy hops off my shoulder and slaps Kevin on his pudgy tummy. "Noted, Commander. I await your instruction!" He salutes me like human soldiers do—it's something Thea taught Shepherd, and Shepherd taught Iggy—then he and Kevin dash out the back door.

Two hours later, the soup is on low heat, and I'm kneading biscuits to go along with it, my hands covered in flour. There's a knock at the front door. That'll be Miriam.

Stony butterflies bash around my insides. It's always like that when I see her. My desire for her is dark and primal, and if I were childless, I'd have pursued her long ago. Having Miriam in my home is the greatest of teases.

I clap my hands to get some of the powder off, then head for the door. When I open it, she's standing there. Like every other time I see Miriam, she takes my godsdamned breath away.

Her green ombre hair is almost iridescent in the late afternoon sun. Irises the most shocking, stunning shade of hot pink crinkle in the corners as she smiles. They're the same color as some of the wacky candies she makes in her shop.

But then I notice the puffiness under her eyes and the droop of her beautiful, bright wings.

She must sense me looking, because her broad grin falls a little. "I bet I look like hells, huh? Ezazel has really become a pixie dust taskmaster since the thralls ripped the vine down."

I hold back a sharp comment. I've heard Ezazel berate her

a time or two, and it takes everything in me not to rip him a new one. Opening the door wide, I usher her in.

Miriam grabs one of my hands and looks at the dust. "You making biscuits, Alo?"

Leaning against the doorframe, I smile. "I made your favorite soup." I don't pull my hand from hers. My breath hitches in my throat as her thumb trails along the back of my hand. Bright eyes move up to mine, a guarded expression on her face.

Don't stop touching me, I silently beg.

Somewhere outside, a car horn honks, breaking the moment. Miriam yanks her hand away and slides them both into her back pockets. It's like she has to do that to control herself.

For a moment, I wonder what would happen if I just tossed her against my front door and devoured her. I'd like to. Scratch that, my mouth *waters* when I think about touching her that way. But my job as protector is time-consuming, and Iggy deserves as much attention as I can lavish on him—it's not common for gargoyles to unmate.

Plus, I'll never forget what my father told me when I broke the news that Keira and I were splitting.

"You'll be both parents, then, Aloitious. Never let anything take time from your child. Ignatius deserves only the best."

My father's words have always squashed any thoughts I had about a second chance at finding a mate. While I don't want his opinions to hold total sway over my decisions, he's right about one thing—Iggy will always come first for me, and that means I can't give Miriam the attention and focus she deserves. Still, it takes everything I have not to pull her to me and bury my nose in the crook of her neck.

Shit, I haven't said a word, and I'm staring at her like an idiot. I reach up to run my hands through my hair, but she hops into the air, wings fluttering wildly behind her.

She grabs my arms with a chuckle. "Don't! You're full of flour!"

I guide my arms back down. She's still holding on to my wrists, and I can't resist the urge to lean forward, my gaze falling to her pink lips.

Screw my father and his godsdamn interference.

She wants me.

I want her.

What if it's really just that simple?

"Did I get any in my hair?" My voice goes low as gravel, my dick throbbing between my thighs. Gods, I need to take my frustrations out on one of my toys tonight, because I'm flirting with a woman I really, really should not play with.

The truth is, if I start playing with Miriam, I don't think I'll be able to stop.

She cocks her head to the side, putting a finger to her chin as she examines my hair for errant flour. When she reaches up and brushes something off my hairline, I grin. Then her deft fingers move along my scalp. She brushes away flour I'm sure isn't even there, her touch igniting sparks along my skin. I'm *starved* for touch like this—gentle, tender, sensual.

I don't even realize I've closed my eyes, my head falling forward as Miriam strokes my scalp with long, languid motions. Gods, if she'd just go to one side or the other, she'd touch my horns. I pray she does, and pray she doesn't. Because if those delicate fingers rub the sensitive surface, I'll come in my fucking jeans.

Miriam's still fluttering in the air in front of me, and our size difference is enough that her chest is right at face level. I ball my fists to stop from slinging an arm around her waist and pulling her to me. I haven't hugged anyone I wasn't related to in five years.

I don't mean to let out a pleased sigh, but when I do, she chuckles.

"You sound ready for a nap, Alo. Iggy running you ragged?"

"Always," I grumble.

One of her hands comes to my jawline, and she strokes it with her thumb. I open my eyes to find her looking at me with a serious expression.

"Let me help you, Alo. Please?"

I swallow hard. I didn't ask her here for this. I want to be a safe haven for her, not the other way around.

It takes all my willpower to step away and gesture her toward the kitchen, changing the subject. "He's thrilled you're coming to dinner. Come talk to me while I finish cooking?"

Miriam wraps her long arms around her torso and nods, trailing me into the kitchen where she alights gracefully on one of my three barstools.

I've noticed her wrapping herself up a lot lately. It was never something she did before. But after Wesley's thralls attacked the moonflower vines and set pixie dust production behind, she's seemed more...nervous isn't the right word. Maybe on edge? And I hate that, because it's my job to keep this town safe, and it doesn't sit well with me that she doesn't feel perfectly at peace here.

I return to my biscuits, kneading and punching. Miriam leans forward with her forearms on the black countertop and a devilish glint in her eyes.

"I had the best idea today."

I love it when she says that—her ideas are always wild and crazy; it's one of the things I adore most about her. I think it's one of the reasons Iggy loves her so much. Her brain is a fantastical wonderland.

I laugh and move around the island to open the back door. I let out Iggy's special battle cry to call him home, and then return, grinning at Miriam. "Tell me everything, Mir."

She cackles and slaps both palms down on the countertop. "Okay, do you know anything about human Halloween?"

I shake my head.

"Oh my gods!" Miriam laughs, and it's bright and joyous. "Humans are so nuts! Apparently, Halloween began as an end-of-harvest celebration for humans hundreds of years ago. But now it's morphed into this whole thing where people give out candy to kids, and they put pumpkins and creepy decorations everywhere, and they dress up like monsters, because we're"— she does air quotes—"frightening."

I snort. "That's fucking weird."

"Right?" Miriam puts both hands on her cheeks like she just can't believe how odd the humans are. But I already hear a lot about human sayings and beliefs from Shepherd and Thea.

"Is that in the welcome packet?" I muse aloud.

Miriam shakes her head. "I definitely don't remember hearing anything about that when we got our new human resident packets. I would have remembered a holiday based on candy." She giggles, and it's fucking adorable.

Just then, the back door swings open, slamming hard against the wall. Iggy darts in and barrels across the kitchen to throw himself into Miriam's arms, peppering her face with light kisses.

She laughs and wraps her arms around his tiny body, careful not to squash his wings. She squeezes him hard, and when they part, she looks overjoyed.

"I missed you this last week," she murmurs, pressing her forehead to his.

Iggy cocks his head to the side and rubs his horns along her cheek. "I missed you too, but Dad and I played a lot. And we talked. And I want you to be my girlfriend."

Miriam's mouth pops open, eyes wide with faux shock. "Girlfriend? My goodness, that's unexpected! What nice things will you do for me if I agree? 'Snack up, shack up' is the motto, right?"

Iggy laughs and points at the dough I'm still kneading. "I'll cook for you like Dad does."

Miriam stiffens, some of the light fading from her happy gaze. But she puts a smile right back on and ruffles Iggy's dark hair. "I think I'm a little old for the girlfriend title, but you know what's cooler?" She leans in close like she's telling him a secret. Iggy reaches out and places a hand on either side of her face as he turns to the side, presenting his ear.

"Besties," Miriam whispers. She reaches into her pocket and withdraws a tiny beaded bracelet. The beads are chunky, and each one has a letter that spells out the word "best." She grabs one of Iggy's hands and brings it down, sliding the bracelet up over his claw-tipped fingers. She tightens it by pulling on a tiny piece of string, and then pats Iggy on the back of his hand.

"Best friends forever, Ig. I've got one too." She holds up her own wrist, and a matching bracelet sits there with the word "friends" spelled in beads.

Gods, I'm dying. I swallow hard around a lump in my throat. Could she be any more perfect?

Iggy hops up onto her shoulder, his long tail snaking around her neck. When he slides the spade-tip into her shirt, she doesn't bat an eye as it flattens between her small breasts. They both grin at me, and I'm so fucking overwhelmed by her thoughtfulness, all I want to do is take a moment and hide in a room by myself to pick through a mountain of emotions.

Instead, I clear my throat and put the biscuits on a baking sheet, then into the oven. When I turn back around, Miriam pinches Iggy's haunch playfully, and he giggles, trying not to fall off her shoulder by hanging on to one of her ears.

"I've got a good idea," he shrieks. "Biscuits take a long time to cook, so let's play hide and seek!"

It's on the tip of my tongue to tell him Miriam needs to rest because she had a long day, but she claps her hands together and stands.

"You hide first?"

"Duh!" Iggy shouts, pushing off her shoulder and out of the kitchen.

Miriam winks at me and counts loudly to ten.

"I'll do the upstairs," I whisper conspiratorially.

"I've got the down!" She trots out of the kitchen and down the hall that goes along the back of the house. At the very end are the stairs to our second floor. There are a few rooms leading off the hall that Iggy loves to hide in. I follow behind her, staring at the beautiful, smooth skin of her back. Because of her wings, she nearly always wears backless shirts.

I'm entranced watching her walk gracefully in front of me. Her skin is like silk, long dragonfly-esque wings sprouting elegantly from between her shoulder blades. My gaze falls even lower to her waist. Matching dimples above her ass have my mouth watering, fangs aching with the need to sink into her.

I'm so lost staring at her that when she stops and cocks her head to the side, listening, I crash into her.

She lurches forward with a giggle. I wrap my arm around her waist to pull her upright. My breathing goes slow and deep, my protector focus lasered on Miriam. She clears her throat.

I rip my hand from her waist. "Sorry," I mutter, shoving them both in my pockets lest I try to touch her again. My fingers itch with the need to know if her skin is as soft as it looks underneath her clothing.

"It's okay, Alo," she says, but it feels like she's talking about a whole lot more than me accidentally touching her. My stony heart cracks under the weight of all the things I want to say to her but never have.

She disappears into the closest room, playfully calling for Iggy as she searches. I trudge up the stairs and look around, but it's too quiet up here for him to be hiding on the second floor.

There's a shriek downstairs, followed by the sounds of a small scuffle. Miriam and Iggy laugh hysterically.

Jogging back down, I see them once again wrapped in each other's arms. They're happy together, so fucking happy. My mouth dries up as I watch them. Every instinct in my body, mind, and heart tells me to pursue her, despite my father's words ringing in my head.

Iggy points at me. "Okay, you guys hide, and I'll try to find you!"

Miriam tosses him gently into the air and darts back toward the kitchen. I follow but dive into the living room as Iggy counts. He misses a few of the numbers and skips up to thirty before going back down to fourteen. He'll probably end at twenty. I can't hear Miriam, she's probably in small form somewhere. She's way better at hide-and-seek than I am.

I quietly open the storage closet inside the foyer and shove my way to the back behind extra hanging clothes someone gifted me for when Iggy gets bigger. He won't be able to see me unless he really comes in and looks.

"Come out, come out, wherever you are!" Iggy cackles from the depths of the house, and the cottage shimmies a little around us. She loves his laugh.

The closet door rips open, and Miriam shoves her way inside, closing it quietly behind her. She hasn't noticed me. My predatory nature rears its fucking head, seeing her distracted.

She looks around frantically. "Shit, shit!" Her voice is a hissed whisper. There's nowhere for her to hide right inside the door.

Iggy clomps toward us from somewhere up the hall.

Without thinking, I reach for Miriam's hand and pull her behind the clothes with me, her back to my front. She squeaks, her body tense, her heartbeat racing. Her natural candy-coated scent laced with the smell of surprise.

That intoxicating sound she just made brings out a deeply instinctual need I have to chase. My breathing goes heavy and slow as I slide my left arm fully around her. I bring the right one up and cover her mouth. Her breathing goes faster, her body trembling against me.

Miriam. Miriam. Miriam.

You're perfect.

That's what I want to tell her. But instead, I admire how beautiful her wings are, crushed between us. The larger veins are a brilliant pink and the shimmery veil between them an iridescent aqua green. I want to touch and taste every inch. Would her wings be as sensitive as mine are? I think so, from the research I've done on pixies' sexual habits.

My hard cock is nestled firmly between her ass cheeks. I should be embarrassed. I know she can probably feel it.

But instead, her head falls against my chest. My hand slips, my fingers brushing her lips. My dick leaps in my pants. Heat streaks down the back of my neck, and I have to fight to keep from flaring my wings wide. I want to show them off, to show her how strong they are. How strong I am. How right we are.

I'm touching Miriam's mouth. Gods.

Her lips are soft as velvet, with a similar texture. I rub my fingertips along her lower lip, tightening my grip on her waist.

With my left hand, I play with the hem of her shirt. I could resist my need for Miriam when I wasn't touching her. But this? I stand no chance.

She pants softly, her chest rising and falling under my forearm.

I'm wound so tight, I might snap under the pressure if she

makes any sort of move. If that pink tongue snakes out to taste my fingers, I'm gonna explode right here.

I growl into her ear, relishing how her body stiffens against mine, her head falling to one side. Slipping a hand beneath her tee, I stroke her firm stomach. Then I slide my fingertips between her lips. Her godsdamned tongue is so wet, so hot. I choke back a desperately needy noise. Miriam freezes.

The door flies open, and Iggy stands there, gleeful joy in his eyes. "Got you! Got you both! Suckers! It was a dumb idea to hide together!" He flies in a circle.

Miriam steps out of my arms, and I nearly reel from the loss of her. She and Iggy dart down the hallway, starting all over, and I hide in the closet, rubbing at my dick with the heel of my hand. I touched her. I touched her in an entirely we're-not-just-friends way.

I need more, and I need it now.

Frustration has me grinding my teeth. I can't have it now. I love being a father more than anything I've ever done, but sometimes I feel constricted by what I can and can't do.

The oven timer dings, and the cottage kindly opens the closet door wider for me, the extra clothes sliding to one side.

I breathe in deeply, willing my cock to lie flat as I pat the planked wooden walls. "Thank you, friend." Plastering a smile on my face, I leave the closet and rejoin Miriam and Iggy in the kitchen.

She looks up at me, her expression guarded and uncertain. Still, the pink blush dusting her cheeks tells me she's not unaffected. I need to say something about what just happened, but I can't do that with Ig right here. I bite my tongue and smile carefully, hoping it's not too awkward for her.

Two hours later, we've finished dinner, and Iggy's asleep in Miriam's arms on the sofa. Her eyelids are fluttering too, and

I'm sitting at the opposite end, thinking about how beautiful they are together.

I touched her. And I wanted to do a lot more.

When Miriam yawns, I shift forward onto my knees and grab Iggy with one hand. He flutters sleepily over to me and nuzzles into my neck.

"Let me put him to bed. I'll be right back, okay?"

Miriam nods and pulls her legs tight to her chest, her head resting on the side of the sofa.

I take Ig upstairs and deposit him into his nest. He burrows under a blanket, immediately snoring.

Nerves jangle in my stomach as I head back downstairs. I'm going to ask Miriam to stay for a drink. I'd like to talk about what happened in the closet, and I'm not ready for her to go home. But when I get back downstairs, she's softly snoring against the sofa cushions. When I cross the room, she wakes up.

With a yawn, she stands and stretches her long arms over her head. "I'd better go."

"Miriam," I start.

But she yawns again, rubbing at her eyes. "What's up, friend?"

Friend.

I'm starting to fucking hate that word, even though it's always been me who insisted on us remaining friends.

Bitter disappointment crashes through me, drowning my hopes and desires. "Never mind," I say. "Get some rest, alright?"

She shoots me a sleepy smile and thumbs-up, but it feels wrong. I want her sinking into my arms so I can carry her to our nest and kiss that beautiful back until she falls asleep beneath me.

Disgruntled, I cross the living room and open the front door.

She pats me on the chest before leaving. "I had fun, Alo. Thanks for letting me see him. And you, of course." Her eyes shine bright under my porch lights.

"Always," I murmur, wishing it felt like the right time to talk to her.

For a long moment, she says nothing. Then she rubs at the back of her arm with one hand. "Okay, I'm going now. See you later?"

"Definitely," I purr.

Her expression remains neutral, giving away nothing about what she might be thinking. When she turns to leave, I watch her go as a familiar sensation snakes down my spine.

Need. Desire. Domination.

I watch as she crosses Sycamore and disappears into the garden, popping into small form to enter her gourd home.

Then I go quietly upstairs and pull a box out from under my bed. I lift the cardboard top off and look at the dozens of handwritten riddles she's sent me over the last year. That's when she started making her interest in me more obvious. She does for me what a female gargoyle might—presenting me with gifts and snacks. She's trying to say she can care for me, that she can stimulate my body and mind.

She hasn't sent me one for weeks, though. Has she given up on trying to make her attraction clear?

Mir's riddles are all silly and easy to figure out. It's more that most of them paint a picture I'm desperate to make come true. I open one of the riddles and read it.

What do you call a friend who goes down on you?

I flip the page over to see the answer in her bubbly, disheveled handwriting.

M-oral support.

Groaning, I fall into my nest and drop the riddle, shoving my pants down my hips. My cock bobs free, dripping precum.

Remembering her lips under my fingers, I imagine sliding my thumb into her mouth. I fantasize about what it might feel like for her to suck on the pad, swirling her pretty pink tongue over it.

My hips roll rhythmically. It never takes me long to come when I daydream about Miriam. Gripping my cock, I give it a rough quick stroke.

Having her body pressed to mine in the closet felt so right, the way my cock nestled perfectly between her ass cheeks. Would she like being mounted from behind? I know just how I'd do it to get her off. My brain plays the scene out like a human movie reel. A few hard strokes later, I explode, back arching as I shoot cum all over my hips.

The stars behind my eyes disappear as bliss fades. But instead of feeling satiated, I'm more frustrated than ever. I don't want my whole future to be filled with lonely nights and masturbating to visions of the woman I'm crazy about.

As I stare at the glass ceiling of my nest, I decide that the entire world can fuck off with their opinions on how I'm raising Iggy and what Iggy needs. The biggest of fuck-offs goes to my father, who loves to remind me that I should put my own needs aside in favor of ensuring Iggy has everything.

I'm not playing that game any longer. I'm going to start a new one instead—pursuing Miriam Saihem.

I'm going to ask her out. I'll do it tomorrow.

CHAPTER FIVE

MIRIAM

I wake up refreshed and rested, despite being at Alo's until late. It was so nice to see him and Iggy for the first time in a week. My heart is full this morning. Humming, I slip out of bed and into the shower, feeling thankful.

I play my evening with Alo over and over, trying to sort out exactly what happened. He touched me when we hid in the closet, and it wasn't the touch of two buddies. Shaking my head, I guard myself not to read into it. He didn't seek me out. I stumbled into the place he happened to be hiding. If I hadn't, we'd never have touched.

That's a sobering thought, so I cast it aside and muse over Halloween instead. I don't have to be at the dust factory until this afternoon, so I've got a little time. I decide I'll go to my office at the sweets shop and sketch out my Halloween plan. I'm going to need a little help to pull it off, but I really want to do something for the Hectors. Discovering that a secret monster town existed was a big shock for them, and even though two of the three are now mated to monsters, their decision to remain in Ever is a big deal.

I slip into fresh clothes, then flit out my front door. The A-frame where the pixie gourd homes hang is quiet this early, but that's just as well. I always dread seeing Ezazel and getting some dumbass reminder about being timely. I've never been timely. My father used to always say I had my head in the clouds.

I leave the garden and walk up Sycamore Street, resisting the urge to knock on Iggy and Alo's door to see if they're up. Instead, I cross over Main Street and hook a right toward my store. I go small form to enter the pixie door, inhaling the smell of candy with a smile. Nobody's here this early; my opener won't be in for an hour. Plenty of time to work on my plan for Halloween and get back to the garden on time for my shift.

Popping into large form, I pace through the storage room and open my office door. My office is simple, just four walls and a tiny window at the very back. But in the center sits a cherry-red, high-gloss desk. It was a custom order from a troll in another haven. I sent him pics of a few desks I liked with the caveat that I wanted mine to be the color of a candy apple. This desk is where I get my best thinking done. I cross the room and drop into the black glossy swivel chair, laying Wren's Halloween book open on the desktop.

As I flip through the pages, themes begin to merge into ideas. We definitely need pumpkins, but I don't love the idea of them simply sitting on porches. I grab a pencil and paper and start sketching, outlining potential designs. Main Street itself needs a spooky vibe, maybe even something to actually scare folks. And then, of course, we need streamers and flags across Main, and decorations for the stores that want to participate. I need to think through how to make that happen without alerting the Hectors to my sneaky plan.

Oh, and the candy. I can't forget the candy!

There should absolutely be some hair-color-changing

candy, maybe even some candy to make monsters' voices go creepy and scary. Perhaps I'll even wrangle up some candies that disappear when you reach for them; that would be cool.

I can't forget that there's more to Halloween than candy though. There should be other food as well—creepy finger foods and spooky snacks.

I bet I can even get the Scoops folks to do black, purple, and orange ice cream with skull-shaped sprinkles. Ooh! If I ask really nicely, I can probably convince Ohken to do a pumpkin brew or maybe a pop-up bar with seasonal cock-tails. Wren's book has a recipe for something called a "Grim and Tonic," featuring gin and apples. Sketching out skulls, I decide they'd make great "skullipop" lollipops. Gods, there's so much I can do with this holiday!

I lose myself in the planning, sketching out Halloween-themed candies and ideating on a few surprises for the Hectors. I don't think I'll be able to have Halloween in general be a surprise, because I'm garbage at surprises, and at the very least I'll need Wren's help. But on the actual evening of the main event, I'll have a few tricks up my sleeve.

Between now and then I'll teach candy-making classes and we can make candy skulls or...something. Iggy would probably love that.

Maybe I should check with the Keeper before I put too much of this plan into place. Lifting my wrist, I speak into my comm watch, "Call the Keeper."

His deep voice rumbles out of his name hologram moments later. "Miriam, everything alright?"

"Oh, yeah!" I chirp. I launch into a whole explanation about Halloween and what it is, but he stops me.

"Mir, I lived in the human world for a while, remember? I've seen them do Halloween."

"My gods!" I shriek. "That's right! Can you help me make sure it's accurate-ish?"

There's an awkward pause. The Keeper is low on emotion and high on protective instinct. Taking part in Ever Halloween probably isn't top of his priority list.

"You know," I say, "this event would be for your mate too. It might behoove you to do something nice for her."

The uncomfy silence stretches long until he clears his throat. "Happy to help, Miriam. We'll need to re-glamour downtown, so as detailed of a plan as you can draw me would be helpful, if you're insistent on this being a surprise."

I clap my hands together with a squeal. "I'm insistent! I just need you to look at the plans and tell me if they make sense. But also, I need a clever name. Have you got any ideas?"

He clears his throat again. "Miriam, it's twelve thirty. Aren't you supposed to be in the garden?"

I look down at my watch, alarm sending a dreadful panicky sensation into my guts. "Oh, shit! Gotta go!"

I don't wait for him to say anything. I poof into small form and zip through the store, out the door, and toward Sycamore Street.

My heart sinks into my stomach when Ezazel stands in large form at the entrance to the garden. He holds his black wings stiffly at his back, his thin arms crossed over his narrow chest. Dark brows are furrowed to a harsh vee. He looks mad as all get-out.

I pop into large form and throw my hands in the air.

He holds up a palm to stop me. "I've had it up to here with your excuses, Miriam."

Shit, shit, shit!

CHAPTER SIX
ALO

I woke up at four and started baking. Kevin showed up early to get Iggy—they wanted to fly to school together without me "hovering," as Kevin bluntly put it. So, I've been baking ever since. I've got a tray of blueberry lemon scones and two plates of cookies, the sprinkle-covered ones Miriam and Iggy both love.

I untie my apron, which was a gift from her when we first moved to Ever, and toss it over the countertop. My stomach rumbles, blood rushing through my body. I'm surprisingly unsettled about asking her out. When I look at the plates of cookies and snacks and realize I've gone totally fucking overboard, I almost throw them all away.

The cottage shimmies a little, the floral-painted walls laughing at me.

"It's not too much?"

The house shudders around me. Grinning, I grab a baking sheet, ready to bake another batch, but the front door swings open, voices carrying in from the garden. Angry shouts ring out, followed by Miriam pleading in low tones. Urgency has me out the door as fast as my wings can take me.

Across the street, Ezazel and Miriam stand in large form. Ezazel waves his hands around, his face purple as he shouts at her. I'm so angry at seeing him direct the verbal assault at Miriam I can't even focus on his words. She cowers in front of him, both arms wrapped around her torso.

I jog across Sycamore and stop next to Mir, who looks up at me with an absolutely distraught expression on her face. Her pale cheeks are flushed pink, unshed tears filling her eyes.

I turn my head slowly to the angry pixie, crossing my arms to match his stance. "What's going on here? I heard you shouting from inside my cottage, Ezazel."

Miriam flinches next to me.

Ezazel balls his fists, then raises an arm to point at Miriam. "She's late. Again. And not a little late. Half-a-gods-damned-hour late. We're behind on pixie dust production, and it's all hands on deck, except, when Miriam doesn't bother to show up, we're down two hands. We're behind, Alo!"

Miriam steps forward, raising her hands to plead with him. "And I'm sorry, Ezazel. I know I'm not the best with timeliness, but—"

He cuts her off with the wave of a hand. "It's not just that, Miriam." His voice drops low and cruel. "You're twitterpated all the damn time. Your head is constantly in the clouds, and your work suffers as a result. Which means we all suffer."

"Stop it," I snap. "I know for a godsdamned fact that Miriam churns out more dust than most of the rest of your team combined. You're just mad because you can't work her to the damned bone. Listen here, you overgrown—"

Ezazel's nostrils flare. "I blame you, too, if we're being honest."

I step back, shocked. "What the hells are you talking about?"

Miriam reaches for Ezazel, but he swats her hand away, frowning at me.

"Break her godsdamned heart already, would you? We all know she's in love with you, and you don't return the sentiment. Cut her loose, and maybe I have a chance to get us back on track."

Miriam squeaks and raises both balled fists to her mouth as if she's holding back a scream.

I'm too surprised by what he said to even respond. But before I get a chance to, Miriam poofs into small form and flees to her gourd, zipping inside and slamming the door shut.

I watch her go, fury building to a rage in my chest at Ezazel's casually cruel treatment. Taking a step forward, I relish the way he stumbles backward and away from me.

"That was uncalled for," I manage, my voice ragged with emotion. "You don't know what the hells you're talking about, and it's none of your godsdamned business anyway."

Ezazel lifts his chin and recrosses his arms. "It is when I can't do my part to protect our home because she can't be bothered to show up on time. Every pixie works at the factory no matter what our other hobbies and interests might be. You know that, Alo. We all put the dust factory first. And it takes all of us to produce enough dust for the Keeper. Even at full capacity, we're behind."

I flare my wings out wide, casting a dark shadow over Ezazel, but all he does is lift his chin higher. I'd love nothing better than to kick his ass for hurting her feelings. So what if she's late now and again? She's the hardest worker I know, and the kindest person in this entire town.

"Hurt her again, and you'll answer to me," I demand. "Are we clear?"

Ezazel shrugs. "And you'll what, Aloitious...beat me up?"

"Maybe," I snap, even though I'd never do that, and he

knows it. My job is to protect the Evertons, not to hurt anyone.

He shakes his head, his harsh expression softening a little. "I mean what I said, Alo. Let her down so she can move on." Without waiting for me to respond, he pops into small form and disappears into the garden's singular tree.

I jog to the A-frame, stooping inside to look for Miriam. Her gourd, expanded to twice its size thanks to Wren's green power, swings softly in the breeze. Reaching out, I thrum my fingers against her front door.

"Mir, it's me, open up." I keep my voice soft. Most of the pixies probably aren't home right now, or, if they are, they're sleeping. They work at the dust factory in shifts.

I twitch my ear, listening for any sound. Faint snuffling is all I hear. Grabbing her gourd, I turn it around so I can see into her bedroom. It's a breach of protocol to invade her privacy like that, but the need to comfort her is strong, and I'm dying to hold her.

"Mir, I made you cookies. Open up, please."

The sounds of crying intensify, and a curtain snaps shut over her bedroom window.

For once in my life, I wish I carried pixie dust around like the Keeper does. I could dust myself and get small enough to go into her gourd and ensure we talk about this.

"Miriam, please, sweetheart." I keep my voice gentle, hoping it'll encourage her out. Five minutes and a dozen pleas later, it's obvious she's not planning to open up. My heart splinters in my chest, knowing she's probably embarrassed and mad and upset. I don't want her to feel any of those things, not for a single minute.

Eventually, I give up on getting her to come out, but the beginnings of a plan form in my mind.

Ezazel was a dick for throwing her under the bus and calling out her interest in me. She and I have been dancing around that tension for easily a year or more. I planned to ask her out today anyway, but suddenly asking her out doesn't feel like enough. I don't want her to think I did it just because of Ezazel's horseshit.

What Miriam needs is a grand gesture, and I know exactly how to do it.

I leave the garden and stalk back to the cottage. Up in my nest, I drag out her box of sexy riddles and get to work. She loves a game, so I'm going to make this fun. For two hours, I craft riddles, sketching them out on scratch paper.

Then I leave the cottage and go to the historical society, hiding my riddles in a half dozen different books. I make my way back along Main, dropping a riddle off at Fleur, where Ohken agrees to help me. Another one goes to Scoops.

Finally, I go to Miriam's Sweets and announce that I need to put something on her desk. Her assistant gives me a knowing look as I stride through the store toward the back hall. I drop the last riddle on top of her cherry-red desk. I can't wait for her to find it.

By the time I get home, Iggy's arriving. He and Kevin wrestle as they drop out of the sky together, slapping one another and shouting. They love to play fight. Kevin has designs on being a protector when he grows up, although pixies don't usually fill that role in most havens. That doesn't mean it can't happen. If he really wants it, it's not impossible.

Iggy shoves Kevin away, giggling, and looks at me. "How come you smell like cookies?"

I slip my hands into my pockets, watching as Kevin sneaks up on Iggy while Ig focuses on me.

"I was baking for Miriam; she had a bad day."

"Awww," Iggy's voice is sad. "What happened? Should we go over?"

"You can try," I encourage him. "She didn't want to talk to

me about it, but she might talk to you. Want to take some cookies to her?"

Kevin pounces on Iggy, yanking Iggy's hair. They fall to the ground in a fit of screeches. Iggy slaps his friend, wrapping his tail around the pixie's waist and yanking him away. "Listen here, you troglodyte, our friend needs our help!"

Kevin scrunches his nose. "What's a troglodyte?"

Both boys look up at me.

Iggy shrugs. "Dad, what's a troglodyte?"

I groan and wave them inside. "Come on in; you can take cookies to Miriam."

And then I need to comm Ohken and ask what the hells a troglodyte is.

CHAPTER SEVEN

MIRIAM

Well, that's it. I'm officially done pining over Aloitious Rygold. Ezazel's commentary ripped a hole in my heart, and I don't think anything will ever fix that. I know I'm forgetful and always late. But I'd hoped being a great employee otherwise would be enough for Ezazel to overlook my imperfections.

Apparently not.

And what's worse is him telling Alo to go ahead and break my heart. Gods, I don't think I've ever been so mortified in my life.

So, I'm done. I'm giving up on Alo. No more fun riddles, no more dinners at his house. I have to distance myself. We can be casual acquaintances, and that's fine. Our roles don't overlap since he's patrolling and monitoring the wards, and I'm either at the candy store or making dust. I don't have to see him all the time.

Ezazel's a jackass but he's right about one thing—I have important responsibilities, and those need to come first.

But then Iggy shows up with cookies, and I can't resist the hopeful look on his face when he asks to come inside. I dust him and Kevin so they can hang out for a while. Iggy grills me, but I die a second death when he tells me Alo mentioned I had a hard day.

Gods, I don't know how I'll ever look Alo in the face again!

I hang out with the boys for an hour, but eventually they leave to tackle their homework.

I spend the rest of the evening thinking about my life and exactly where I went wrong. I think about my long-gone parents and wonder what advice they'd give me. And I try desperately to come up with a solution. When anguish spears through me for the hundredth time I give up and go to bed.

By the next morning, I've gone from being distraught to downright livid. Ezazel had no right to mention my feelings for Alo, none at all. I've got an early morning shift, and then I'm working at the sweets shop in the afternoon.

I'll prove Ezazel wrong, that asshat.

Zipping out of my gourd at a quarter to eight, I head for the community garden's one and only tree, flying up through the branches to the large platform that holds the dust factory. It's not visible from outside the tree, and only pixies are allowed here. Our magic is what makes the dust ingredients, well, magical.

I stare at the underside of the factory's platform. It's mirrored and painted to reflect the leaves and branches beneath, so that even from below, nobody sees it.

Zipping through one of a dozen pixie-sized doors, I fly through the domed factory entryway and into my assigned changing room. Gritting my teeth, I open my locker and take out my overalls, slipping them over my front and knotting them underneath my wings. Ezazel's working this morning, and I'm going to let him have it when I see him.

Grabbing my dust gloves, I slide them over my hands and zip out of the changing room, down the long hall to the largest of the factory's domes. The round glass ceiling overhead lets in enough light for the dust to cook in the sun's warmth.

Smaller domes on all sides of this larger main one hold the dust ingredients. Ohken crushes them for us, and then we work them through a series of machines until the dust gets to the main room. At that point it's stirred for twelve nights and imbued with pixie magic. Once it's done, we deliver it to the Keeper to reinforce the wards.

I grit my teeth tightly as I head onto the production floor. I'm the first one there with the exception of the shift manager, Tenzel.

She looks up from a book and smiles at me, tapered ears twitching. "Morning, Mir! How are ya?"

I frown. "Irritated as shit. You?"

Her friendly smile falls, and she pushes thick glasses up her button nose. "I heard Ezazel was quite rude yesterday. I'm sorry. He shouldn't have brought your personal business into *business* business."

I cross my arms, fuming. I swear steam is probably coming out of my head. "He told you? Or you heard us arguing?"

Tenzel's cheeks turn pink. "Well, he might have made a few comments when he arrived back here, so we picked up the gist. Plus, you didn't do your shift, not that we blame you," she tacks on at the last minute.

That does it. As soon as I see Ezazel, I'm going to rip him a new one for being incredibly unprofessional. And then I'm never going to be late again, so help me. I could always quit, but it would be highly frowned upon by the rest of the pixie community. I kinda have to do this job.

The hours pass slowly. Stirring pixie dust and muttering spells is not my favorite work. It's what all pixies do in all havens that protect themselves with wards, but it's not my heart's work. That's Miriam's Sweets. But after yesterday's altercation, I'll have to let the store suffer to get back on track with my main role. Ever's safety is more important than candies that'll turn your hair purple.

Fifteen minutes before the end of my shift, someone taps me on the shoulder. I turn to see Ezazel, my cheeks heating at being faced with him.

He clears his throat and checks his clipboard. I know exactly what he's looking at, so I cross my arms and start tapping my foot. He clears his throat a second time.

"It seems we've caught up during your shift, Miriam. We're only a few days behind now."

"And…" I encourage, waving my hand for him to continue. We all know I work faster and harder than anyone else when I'm here.

He runs a hand through his thinning hair. "Now listen, this is still your job, Miriam, and I shouldn't have to apologize for trying to keep you on track."

I throw my palm up between us. "I'm gonna stop you right there," I snap. "I'm not the timeliest of employees. We all know that. But I do my level best to make up for the odd delay here and there by busting my butt from the moment I clock in until the moment I leave."

He opens his mouth to say something, but I barrel on.

"My personal life is none of your business. What I do or don't do isn't a topic of discussion, and it should *never* be used the way you did. This is my one warning to you, Ezazel. Keep your mouth shut about my life choices. Are we clear?" I slap both hands on my hips.

For a moment, it looks like he'll say something, but he closes his mouth and nods curtly.

"Good," I say, my muscles beginning to tremble slightly. I don't argue and fight. I hate confrontation. I hate that I even have to address this with him. But I just can't let it go.

I thump the top of his clipboard. "You're welcome for catching us up by another day." I urge softness into my voice.

"If you want me to work extra to keep eating away at the gap, I can. Just let me know."

He shakes his head, casting a look around the bustling factory. When he turns to face me, his expression is resolute. "We're in this together, Miriam. You've done your part. Thank you. And noted"—he waves a hand around—"about your personal life. I shouldn't have done it."

I uncross my arms and play with the hem of my tee, swallowing the lump in my throat. "Erm, that's fine then. I'll see you when I see you."

"Okay, Miriam."

Now that the dam of anger inside me has broken, I'm eager to get far away from Ezazel and the awkwardness.

The next shift of pixies arrives as I flit to the changing room. I switch out my work clothes for clean ones and head for the sweets shop. I'm working an afternoon shift, and that, at least, will improve my mood.

Hours later, I'm still a little out of sorts, burning the candies and tossing my tools around. By five p.m., one of my assistants taps me on the shoulder with a kind smile.

"Miriam, honey. Why don't you handle the office work today? Celset and I can finish restocking."

I know what she's doing—trying to get me and my funk out of here. I can't even blame her, so I place both hands together in a prayer position and incline my head—an elvish apology for my dark elf employee.

She nods her acceptance of my apology, and I disappear into my office. When I see the stack of papers on my desk, I decide I'll focus on the Halloween party for the Hector triplets. A smile tugs my lips upward.

I am a great friend. Which is why I'm going to make this party for the Hectors absolutely amazing.

As if I summoned her by thinking about her, Wren sails through the door to my office with a smile on her round face.

"I heard you were hiding in here." Her green eyes slide down to my desk, where stacks of papers have drawings of pumpkins and all the things I've ideated for the party. I rise, round the desk, and sit on top of the papers, hoping I'm not too obvious. I'll admit it's awkward, my butt isn't big enough to cover all the doodles.

"What's going on, Miriam?" She crosses her arms and grins at me. "I saw jack-o'-lanterns, bitch. What are you up to?" She's practically preening.

I shrug. "Nothing to see here, soulfriend."

"Bullshit." She laughs and darts around the side of the table, grabbing a stack of papers. I hop off and chase her, smashing her into the wall to grab for them.

"It's supposed to be a surprise!" I shriek and yank at them, and, when I do, a folded page falls out of her hand and onto the floor.

Wren drops to the ground and grabs it, handing it to me. "That's got your name on it, Mir." She waggles her dark chocolate brows at me. "Who's it from?"

I roll my eyes. "I dunno. I'm just now seeing it." I cock my head to the side and give her a look. "You know, one of my new candies will match your hair to your eye color. Ever wondered what you'd look like with green hair?"

She rolls her eyes back and slaps my hip. "Stop changing the subject. What are you cooking up in here besides candy?"

I toss the note onto my desk and cross my arms. "Listen. I'm going to let you in on what I'm planning for two reasons. First, I can't keep a secret to save my life when it's something fun. It was pretty much a foregone conclusion that you'd find out. And second, you could probably help me make it extra amazing with your green-witch skills."

Wren claps her hands together. "Hit me, girl. I love a good secret."

I flutter around her and pull out the empty chair in front

of my desk. Then I round it and drop into my own, putting my boots up onto the glossy red surface. I spread my arms wide and smile. "You ready for this?"

"Hell yes," Wren chirps, leaning forward.

Half an hour later, I've explained the whole idea to Wren, and we're drawing additions to all my noodlings. She's helping me figure out what makes sense to humans, and how we can monsterfy some of the usual Halloween treats and traditions.

The note with my name on it slips to the edge of the desk and onto the floor. I reach over and grab it, having forgotten about it. When I open it, the blood drains from my face. It's Alo's intricately scrolled, heavy handwriting.

"Miriam, you okay?" Wren's voice breaks through my thoughts.

My eyelashes flutter as I try to understand why there's a freaking note from Alo in my office. Oh gods, he probably wanted to tell me it's not a big deal what Ezazel said.

I set the note down, hands trembling, and then I tell Wren the entire story.

By the end of it, she's livid for me, tapping her foot against the desk with her arms crossed. She glares down at the note. "Want me to read it so you don't have to?"

I look at the note and at her. I don't know if I can bear any more embarrassment today, but in the short time she's lived in Ever, she's become one of my very best friends.

"Read it." I cover my mouth with one hand and lean back in my chair.

She reaches for the note and unfolds it. Her eyes scan the page and furrow, then she hands it to me with a confused look.

"I don't get it. It's a riddle or something."

A riddle?

I grab the note and scan it, confused.

*Go to the building with the most stories. Five.
Sixteen. Forty-Five.
Alo*

I grin and look up at Wren. "It's a riddle."

"Right," Wren deadpans. "Like I mentioned."

I laugh. "I mean I used to send Alo riddles, and now he's sending me one."

She leans forward. "For what purpose?"

My heart sinks a little at that because I don't know why he sent this to me. I refused to even speak with him yesterday after the Ezazel fiasco. But my interest is piqued.

Wren stands with a sigh. "I can already tell you're trying to figure out what it means, so I'm gonna leave you to it. But let's get together tomorrow to start planning the party stuff?"

I wave my agreement, and she heads back out into the store, the scent of fresh candies wafting in after her.

The most stories.

Hmm.

Town Hall is the tallest building in Ever at three stories, but literally nothing happens at Town Hall. Still, it's a place to start.

I pop into my small form and zip out of the store, heading for the town gathering place. But when I get there, the doors are locked. I grab the handle and twist, but the building lets out an angry noise, and the doors snap tighter in their frames.

Throwing my hands up, I sigh. "I get it! But I'm supposed to go to the building with the most stories. Is that not you? I'm following a riddle trail."

The black iron railing leading up to the front door breaks apart and reforms into an arrow that points across the street to the historical society.

Of course! Snapping my fingers, I thank Town Hall and

zip over to the historical society. It's full of books, and books are stories. I should have gotten that. Iggy would have gotten that.

Slapping my forehead, I open the door and stride inside. The historical society is usually empty unless there's a specific event going on, and there's nothing going on today.

Pulling Alo's note out, I look at the numbers.

Five. Sixteen. Forty-five.

Perhaps it references book rows. I'm guessing I'm here for a book.

I head for aisle five, and a sign for topic sixteen, "monster lore," catches my eye. Each book under each topic is numbered, and, my gosh, there's a book forty-five! Grabbing it, I flip through the pages to find another note.

Grinning, I flip it open. A note leads me to another book, then another, and finally back to Fleur, the florist shop on Main. By the time I get there, I'm grinning from ear to ear. I'm nervous that Alo wants to have a conversation about what happened yesterday. I'm equal parts horrified and thrilled, but I love that he did this.

When I get to Fleur and swing the glass door wide, the scent of hundreds of flowers fills my nostrils. I suck in a deep breath, pulling the sweet aroma deep into my lungs. Everything about Fleur is so natural and peaceful—I love this store.

Ohken's resonant laughter echoes from a room in the back. He appears from the darkness of the checkout area with both thumbs slung through his belt loops. "Miriam, you figured it out. Well done, friend."

I beam at my troll friend and cross the gorgeous shop to the checkout station. "I'm not sure what to do here."

Ohken reaches behind the counter and hands me a small bouquet of flowers, russet eyes crinkling in the corners as he smiles. "I am under specific instruction to hand you this and to say nothing else other than to go to the place where your favorite five-year-old lives."

I laugh. That's not even a riddle. But butterflies sprint around in my stomach because I have no doubt Alo wants to talk. My smile falls.

Ohken comes around the counter. "What's wrong?"

I rub at the back of my elbow, staring at the bouquet in my other hand. "An awkward thing happened between Alo and me yesterday. I suspect this is his really nice way of saying he wants to talk about it."

Ohken slips his hands into his pockets. "Good, Miriam."

I look up, confused. "Good?"

"Good. Because it means he finds it important to communicate with you. It means he went to great lengths to do so in a way you'd appreciate. He's trying to do things in a way he knows will delight you. This is *good*, Miriam."

I don't want to read too much into his statement, but my heart flutters wildly in my chest.

I point to the door. "I'm gonna go now."

Ohken grins. "Good luck."

Good luck, indeed.

Bouquet in hand, I sprint out the door and up Main Street, only slowing when Alo's house comes into view. My heart hammers so loudly in my chest, I barely hear anything else. My entire body is flushed and tight and hot. I have no idea what I'm going to find when I see Alo, but I hope it's not some horrible conversation I'll have to relive for the rest of my days.

My footsteps are loud on the cottage's front steps. She waves her pretty shutters at me. Then the front door opens. A folded page is taped to the door itself. I grab it and open it.

Come to the porch.

Sucking in a deep, steadying breath, I head into Alo's cottage.

CHAPTER EIGHT

ALO

I don't have a heart to pound in my chest. But once upon a time it did, and I have phantom sensations of that right now. Miriam's light footsteps echo through the cottage. Glancing around, I run both hands through my hair. The back porch is covered in snacks and food. A few candles sit on the table, lit and glowing faintly. The shades are down so nobody can see in. It's private and cozy, and I'm somewhere between nervous and shocked.

Am I really doing this?

When Ohken comm'd me to let me know Miriam made it to Fleur, I nearly lost my nerve.

But then she appears in the doorway with a beautiful blue and purple bouquet in her hand. Pink lips part, and she places one hand on the doorway, stepping through and looking around the room. Shock splashes across her face.

"This is beautiful Alo. You did this for me?" She looks up. When I nod, she shakes her head, pink stealing across her cheeks. "You didn't have to do all this. I'm sorry about yesterday. I should have just talked to—"

Reaching out, I wrap my wing around her and pull her to

me, placing my thumb over her mouth. Her eyes go wide, her heartbeat a steady whomping sound.

"This isn't about that, Mir," I murmur, stroking her plump lower lip. Gods, she's so soft. "At least, it's not about that in the way you probably think."

I pull her tighter to me until every possible inch of her body is pressed to mine. Her pupils overtake the dark rose of her iris, the blush across her cheeks growing deeper. The vein throbbing in her neck fills me with joy. She's so vibrant, so amazing.

So perfect.

I've got to get this out before I chicken out and think about my father's advice.

Reaching up with my left hand, I grip the back of her neck gently, stroking her skin. "I want to take you on a date, Miriam. Will you go with me?"

She gasps, stepping backward and pushing against my chest. "Don't do this because of Ezazel." Her tone sounds frustrated.

I slide my hand down her back, stroking her wings softly. A pleased growl rips out of my throat. Her wings are firm but soft, just like I always imagined.

"Ezazel has nothing to do with this," I murmur. "I had already planned on doing it yesterday before that happened. I got up early and baked all of this for you. I'm sorry it's taken me this long to ask you out, Mir. It's not for lack of interest. Not at all."

She looks around, her expression still disbelieving. "You did all of this before Ezazel?"

I tip her chin back toward me. "Mhm."

"You swear?"

I grab both her wrists and pull them behind her back, looping the fingers of one hand around them both. Cocking my head to the side, I hover my mouth over hers.

"I swear to you, Miriam. Do you believe me?"

Her breath mingles with mine, her chest rising and falling against me. Her frustrated look smooths out, her lips parting into a soft, sweet smile. "Yes."

I slide my free hand along the back of her waist. "And you'll allow me to take you out?"

A look of pure joy takes over, and she grins. "Yes, Alo."

Relief floods through me. So much relief. I didn't realize how big a part of me was worried she wouldn't agree.

For a long moment, she beams, and it's then I'm sure I'm doing the right thing. Because Miriam's smile is my new favorite thing to look at. I want this smile, and the next, and the one after that. I want every single one directed at me. I want to be the male who puts them on her face.

Leaning forward, I press my forehead to hers. "I hate what Ezazel said. Please don't think that had anything to do with this."

Her happy look falls, but she turns wide fuchsia eyes on me. "I believe you."

She believes me, just like that.

Smiling, I take her hand and pull her to the center of the room where I've laid out a blanket and picnic. I take a seat, offering her a spot next to me.

I gesture at the snacks. "I know snacks aren't really a pixie ritual, but I couldn't help myself. I hope you like them."

Miriam grins, reaching for a scone. She bites into it with a soft, happy moan. "Perfect," she murmurs.

I rest a forearm on my knee, leaning against the porch wall. It gives me so much joy to watch her eat something I made for her.

"I'd like to take you to Herschel's." I hand her another plate of treats. "Shepherd offered to watch Iggy, but I can't promise he won't escape once he hears I'm taking you out. He's convinced you're meant to be his girlfriend."

Miriam laughs. "I don't care if Iggy comes with us, do you?"

Do I care if Iggy comes with us?

I run a hand through my hair with a huff. "A little, yeah. I want time alone with you."

Miriam's cheeks flush pink, but her broad smile gets bigger. "I'm not opposed to that. What are you planning to do with this alone time?"

I shift forward, backing her against the nearest chair. My chest brushes against hers. Gods, she's beautiful.

Slanting my mouth over hers, I chuckle. "There are plenty of ways for me to occupy time with you, Miriam. Ways I've been thinking about ever since you sent me that first riddle."

Pink spreads down her neck.

Gods, I'm enjoying this.

I wondered if I had forgotten how to flirt. I'm years out of practice. But it comes back easily with Miriam caged between my arms.

Her head falls back against the cushion, baring her neck to me. Growling, I drag my fangs up the slim column, the very tip of my tongue poking out to taste her.

"I've wanted you for years," I admit.

She whines softly. "Alo, I—"

"Everything about you entices me," I say. "I love your smile and your bubbly personality." I plant a tender kiss in the hollow at the base of her throat before moving up. "I love how hardworking you are, and how much joy you bring to our town." I brush my lips under her chin. "I love the way your shirts accentuate your fucking beautiful wings. I want to touch you everywhere, Miriam," I breathe out.

Her hands come to my chest, her touch careful, as if she's not sure I'll invite it.

"Touch me," I command. "I need it, Mir."

She lets out a needy whine, and the front door of the cottage slams open.

I hear Iggy before I see him, but Miriam shifts out of my arms and sits cross-legged facing the door. It's like we just got caught red-handed doing something naughty.

Which we did. Almost.

I'm frustrated I didn't get to tease her for longer, but Iggy barrels through the kitchen and out the back door into her arms. He nearly knocks her over, but she wraps her long arms around him and squeezes him tight.

"Cookies, yes!" Iggy hops down into her lap, pressing his back to her chest and grabbing two fistfuls of cookies. As he shoves them in his mouth, she looks up at me and smiles, and I'm fucking gone.

The following evening, I'm dressing for our date when Shepherd comms me, his name popping up above the blue band around my wrist.

"What's up?" I know I sound terse, but I'm surprisingly nervous for my date. It's been a long time since I courted someone, and it hurt like hell when she left.

"You ready for your date?"

"No," I grumble. "I'm out of practice, and I don't know what to do."

"Oh, that's easy." Shepherd laughs. "Kiss her, touch her, open the door, give her snacks. Dote on her the way Father dotes on Mother. Make her feel like the center of your world."

His words stop me in my tracks.

"That's the problem," I whisper. "That's why I never asked her out to begin with, Shep. I can't make her the center of my world because I need to focus on Iggy. And Miriam deserves to be the center of someone's world."

Fuck. Am I doing the right thing?

Shepherd sighs. "Brother, I love you, but you're making Miriam pay for Keira's sins. You being happily mated would be good for you and Iggy, and Iggy already adores Miriam. If you don't snack up, shack up, your son might beat you to the punch."

"He's already mentioned something to that effect." I shake my head even as my father's words continue to ring in my mind.

"Just have fun, dude."

"You're using more humanisms," I grumble.

"They're really the best. Just overwhelm Miriam with snacks and your tongue, and it'll all work out."

"That's enough," I bark. "I get it." It's been years since I did anything fun with my tongue, but now that I'm thinking about it, I feel awkward talking to my brother about it.

Shepherd laughs and clicks off, and I'm left staring at my reflection in the mirror, wondering where the confident young protector I used to be has gone. It's not that I lack confidence in any area of my life except this one.

I remind myself that Iggy adores Miriam, and I've secretly adored Miriam since the day I met her. It's going to be fine.

Heading downstairs, I grab the box of blueberry scones I made this afternoon and check my hair one final time before leaving the cottage. She whacks me playfully on the back with the front door for good luck.

I laugh, and then I look across the street. Miriam stands there in tight jeans and a shimmery spaghetti-strap top. The fabric is ruched over her breasts, dipping in the middle to give me an intoxicating view of barely there cleavage.

Fuck.

My libido roars to life, and I'm down the steps toward her with all my worries forgotten. When I get to Miriam, I grab her hand and give her a spin, whistling while I check her out.

Tight jeans accentuate her firm, muscular legs. The dimples at her lower back tempt me. The shirt hides nothing. She's all exposed skin and those beautiful fucking wings.

She laughs and blushes, playing with her hair.

"You look gorgeous," I murmur. "I've been looking forward to this all day."

"And I've had this outfit planned for a while," she teases.

"Oof, I probably owe you an explanation on that." I laugh. "Over dinner? Does Herschel's sound good to you?"

Miriam looks up at me. "You've been my best friend since the day you arrived in town, Alo. Whatever you want to do is perfect."

I don't mean to, but, like a dummy, I fucking choke up and have to clear my throat. Keira was never overly affectionate, especially once we got pregnant with Iggy. To hear someone value time spent with me is new, and I didn't realize until just now how nice it would be.

I don't let go of Miriam's hand. Instead, I thread my fingers through hers and pull her to my side. Miriam rests her head on my shoulder, and we walk like that all the way to Main, hooking a right to go to Herschel's.

Herschel himself greets us at the door, chubby arms thrown wide. "Aloitious! Miriam! What a pleasure to see you both here. I have something quite special planned for you this evening. Come, come!"

Miriam laughs at the elderly elf's exuberance, but she tugs me to follow him, winding our way through the busy front room and toward a small table tucked in a quiet back corner.

Herschel shoots me a wink when I hold Miriam's chair out for her.

Two hours later, we've eaten dinner and dessert, and Miriam's still not done. She wants ice cream, so I pay the bill, and we go across the street to Scoops.

I've never taken Miriam anywhere and just hung out with

her. I've also never laughed so hard in my life as I have the last two hours. Everything she does is full of joy. She tells me all about her Halloween idea for the Hectors. It sounds like a lot of work, but I offer to help, because, now that I asked her out, I don't think I can deny Miriam a single thing. The gargoyle instinct to protect and provide is strong, riding me, demanding I help her.

Miriam licks her ice cream cone and looks over my shoulder before returning her pretty fuchsia eyes to me. "Your adorable son is barreling up the street with Shepherd right behind him. He must have escaped."

I let out an irritated rumble, but she reaches across the table and rubs the back of my hand. Iggy rockets into me, wrapping his body around my head and squeezing me tight. His tail comes around my neck and chokes me.

Miriam laughs when Shepherd drops out of the sky beside us, both hands on his hips as I try to unwrap Iggy.

"Don't make me go!" Iggy shrieks as he bursts into laughter.

Shepherd gives me a baleful look, then grabs Iggy's tail spade and unwraps him from my neck. Iggy hops onto Shepherd's outstretched hand and crawls his way up to my brother's shoulder, giving me a sad look.

Shepherd glances over at Iggy. "Ignatius Zion, what were you supposed to be doing?"

"Hanging out with you so Dad can hang out with Miriam. But—"

"No buts," Shepherd says in a stern voice.

Iggy gives Miriam and me a sad look. "I just wanted to hang out if they're hanging out! Why would they need to have fun without me?"

Miriam stands and opens her arms, and Iggy leaps off Shepherd's shoulder and onto hers. She reaches up and pats his chubby haunch as he yawns. She gives me a look. "Shall we take him home and get him to bed?"

Iggy leans over and rubs her head with his horns, humming happily under his breath. His eyes are already closing.

Shepherd groans and gives me a look. "Sorry, man. He slipped out when we were playing hide-and-seek."

I laugh and clap him on the shoulder. "No worries, brother. Kids are unpredictable on the best of days."

Shepherd gives us a quick salute, then pushes off the ground and takes to the sky.

Miriam reaches for my hand. "You ready to go?"

Looking at her, I see a glimmer of how things could be with her in our lives. My choice doesn't have to be between Miriam and my son. I can have them both.

I take her hand. "Ready, Miriam."

She smiles and leads me home.

CHAPTER NINE

MIRIAM

I'm having the best time of my life. Alo looks a little grumpy that Iggy busted in on our date, but I wasn't joking when I gave Ig the BFFs bracelet. I adore him. He slumps against my head, his tail wrapped around my neck and his spade down the front of my shirt. As we cross Main and head up Sycamore toward their cottage, Alo scoops him off me and lays him over his shoulder, one big hand on Iggy's back.

I've always known I loved Alo. But watching him rub his son's back gently as Iggy starts snoring...it does things to my heart. I scoot around his other side and wrap my arms around one of his. He's rock-hard muscle, but when he threads his fingers through mine, I can't help but wonder if there's a soft side to him that even I never fully saw.

We make it to their cottage, and I'm not sure if he'll want me to come in, but Alo doesn't let go of my hand. I trail him upstairs to Iggy's nest, watching as he lays his son gently in the middle, pulling a thin blanket over him.

Iggy mumbles something, but he's already passed out.

Alo watches him for a moment, but then takes my hand and leads me out of Iggy's room. We head back down to the kitchen, and he pulls a barstool out for me.

He crosses the room and opens a cabinet full of wine and liquor, throwing me a cheeky look over his shoulder. "Nightcap, Miriam?"

"Hells yes!"

"Wine? Or something stronger? I have tonic."

"Ooh," I murmur. "Pixie tonic? Where'd you get it?"

Alo grins, and it's intoxicating the way a smile lights up his face. His job is so serious, and he's such a devoted father, but he wears stress like a mask. That falls away when he smiles.

Big, strong wings are folded neatly at his back. Long, thick horns swoop up and away from his elegant forehead. I can't stop staring at him as he pours the tonic into a glass and smirks over the island at me.

"Ohken delivered it earlier today. I do believe he and Wren are committed to making our date the best it can possibly be."

My grin matches his, I'm sure. Points to Wren, my soul-friend who made sure things were perfect for tonight. I'll thank her later.

Alo's gaze drops to my mouth as he leans over the small bar. "I had a wonderful time tonight." Near-black eyes flick up to mine. "Can we do it again?"

My heart flutters around in my chest, trying to beat right out of my body. I lean forward, reaching around my glass to put a hand over one of his. "I'd love that."

He sets his glass down and rounds the island, never looking away. I resist the urge to scoot back in my chair. The look in his eyes is possessive and hungry. I've wanted Alo to look at me like that for years.

He reaches for me, pulling me out of the chair and lifting me onto the countertop. He shoves his way between my thighs and plants a hand on either side of me, leaning into my space.

Glittering eyes fall to my lips, and he grins. "I'm going to kiss you, Miriam."

"Gods, yes," I mutter.

He laughs, a low-pitched noise that sends heat flaring between my thighs. "We might have been a slow burn, Mir, but we'll burn all the hotter for it now."

My mouth falls open. Somehow in all my daydreams of Alo, I didn't picture him as much of a dirty talker. I'm not sure why.

He slides a hand up my spine and grips the back of my neck, using leverage to arch my body against his chest. "Mmm," he murmurs. "Your body feels good against me."

I'm too lost to Alo in seduction mode to come up with an appropriate response. I need his mouth on mine. I need that kiss like I need air.

He chuckles again. "You're squirming, Miriam. Are you in a hurry?"

I groan. "You're not gonna make me say it, are you?"

Alo pushes forward, brushing his lips over mine. "Fuck yes, I'm going to make you say it."

"Kiss me, Alo," I whisper as I wrap my arms around his neck, pressing my forehead to his.

He reaches down and rubs his horns from side to side along my collarbone, then up the side of my neck before nipping just below my ear.

"Kiss you where, Miriam? Be specific."

Oh gods.

"Lips," I decide. "Alo, please!"

A deep, rumbly growl reverberates out of his chest, sending sparks down my thighs. He presses forward, slanting his mouth over mine, his tongue carefully tasting me. His lips brush against mine; they're so soft, so fucking confident. He groans and cocks his head the other way, devouring me as he pulls me to the edge of the countertop and against his waist.

All I can do is hang on as his lips grow more frenzied and wild. My hands are everywhere, in his hair, stroking his horns. I can't get him close enough to me.

A sudden slamming door jolts us both out of our reverie.

"Dad!" Iggy's tear-filled voice echoes down the hall and into the kitchen.

Alo lets out a disappointed groan before pressing his lips tenderly to mine. "Be right back," he murmurs, shifting me back onto the countertop. He gives me a heated, sorrowful look before disappearing down the hall and up the stairs.

The countertop jiggles, and the cottage sends a tray of cookies my direction. I take one and bite into it. So fucking delicious.

"I'm gonna be here a while, huh?"

The kitchen windows jiggle up and down.

Half an hour later, Alo still isn't back, and I hear the occasional whimper from upstairs. The cottage opens a drawer to show me pen and paper. I scribble Alo a quick note that I'll see him later, and I head home.

I wasn't anxious for that date—or that kiss—to be over. But gods, at least I've got something to go home and dream about.

The following morning, there's a spring in my step as I head for the sweets shop. I've got a bit of work to do there, and then I'm working the midday shift at the dust factory. I've already set a few alarms to make sure I'm not late. Screw Ezazel. Although he's right about one thing— it's not fair of me to be late.

I lose myself in candy and Halloween planning, sketching out my final ideas for not only the town's Halloween decorations, but also a few surprises for the Hectors. I've got a whole list for the Keeper to review of decorations, food, candy, fancy drinks—the works.

A knock at the door pulls me out of my thoughts. When I look up, the breath wheezes from my lungs.

Alo stands in the doorway, beautiful wings tucked tightly at his back and a tray of brownies in his big hands. Like always, he's wearing a tee that barely contains his huge muscles. Jeans barely contain his thick, muscular thighs.

He smirks as if he can see my thoughts. I'm probably being pretty obvious about what those thoughts are.

"May I come in?"

I nod.

He enters and sets the plate of brownies down on my desk. "I made these for you, Mir. They're filled with those little fizzy candies you like."

My eyes go wide, and I grab one, shoving it in my mouth.

Alo laughs when my eyes roll back in my head. A popping sensation explodes across my tongue every time I chew.

"These are...mmph...favorite." I struggle to speak around a mouthful of the sweet treat, but Alo looks pleased as hells.

"Thank you," I manage once I get the brownie down. "But I know you're busy; you don't have to do the whole cooking for me thing. I don't want to add more to your pl—"

Alo silences me with a sharp look. He rounds the desk and spins my chair, caging my legs with his thick thighs. "It's my privilege," he growls. "And my pleasure to cook for you, Miriam. You are not an inconvenience to me."

"Okay."

"I'm serious."

"Okay."

"You need more brownie. Come here."

I rise and prop myself on top of my desk, carefully scooting my designs to the side. Alo breaks off a piece of brownie and brings it to my lips.

"Eat."

Dutifully, I open my mouth. He places the small bite on my tongue, but his finger doesn't leave my mouth. I close my lips around it, swallowing the bite and sucking on the tip of his finger.

Alo's nostrils flare, and his wings open wide, gripping the walls on either side of my small office. They're so big and dark, they blot out the faint light from above.

"Again," he demands, removing his finger and grabbing another bite of brownie. He places it in my mouth again, and again I suck on his finger, watching the way his breathing goes stilted and heavy.

"Miriam," he chokes out. "I had every intention of coming downstairs last night and ravaging these sweet lips. I'm sorry it took so long to get Iggy back down."

"I understand. Timing isn't always in our favor."

He growls and collars my throat, bringing my mouth close to his. "You don't have to be anywhere for a while, and neither do I. I'm gonna lock your office door and ravage you now. How do you feel about that?"

He doesn't wait for an answer before letting me go and crossing the office to the door. He closes it and turns the lock, eye fucking me from the doorway. My heart pounds so loudly in my ears, I can barely focus around the sound of it.

Alo stalks over and pushes me backward onto the desk with his big body. One arm wraps around to support me from behind, and he plants the other on my stack of drawings.

His black eyes fall to my mouth. "You've got the most kissable lips I've ever seen, Miriam. I've never told you that. But I've thought it every fucking day since we met."

I groan. Gods, all those times I touched myself thinking about him. Maybe he was doing the same thing all alone in his nest.

His smile goes feral. I'm drunk on how good he looks, happy like this. Alo reaches up with one big hand and undoes the buttons along his shoulder. The front panel of his tee falls away, and he undoes the other side, tossing the fabric to the ground.

My mouth goes dry as a desert at seeing Alo shirtless. I scramble mentally, trying to recall the last time I saw him without his shirt on. But it's been a while since we swam in the grotto. Even still, I was fucking unprepared for Alo in half-nude glory.

His shoulders are huge and round, his pecs gigantic slabs of muscle. They're coated in a dusting of black hair, dark gray nipples forming hard tips. I drag my eyes down to his core, where every muscle is outlined and clear. Even his abs are perfectly formed, a vee directing my gaze down into his pants. The outline of his cock is clearly visible against the front of his jeans.

I try to swallow and almost choke on my spit. "Gods, Alo," I mutter. "You're fucking beautiful."

He laughs, grabbing one of my hands and sliding it up and down his abs. "You like what you see, Mir?" He's teasing me.

Well, two can play that game. I reach up and unclip my shirt at the back of my neck. It falls down my torso, revealing my whole upper body to him. I have tiny boobs, so I never wear a bra.

Alo sucks in a harsh breath, his eyes falling to my chest.

I lean back on the desk, planting my palms on the glossy surface. "Like what *you* see, Alo?" If he can tease, I can do it twice as well.

His long tail lashes side to side, his muscles quivering with tension. He looks ready to pounce, and, gods help me, I hope he does.

Instead, he surges forward, closing his mouth over one of my hard nipples. I'm so fucking shocked he went right for the goods, it's all I can do to reach up and hold on to one of his horns as he sucks.

Fireworks go off between my thighs as he alternates between a gentle nibble and a hard suck, swirling his tongue over my bud. I roll my hips against him, desperate for enough friction to get off. He feels good, so good, but I need more.

Alo snarls and moves to my other breast, cupping the first with his big hands. He pinches my nipple, pulling until I squeak, then bites me. I jolt in his arms, the varied sensations confusing my body even as I flood my panties with slick wetness.

He rubs his horns over both breasts then angles his mouth over mine. Dark eyes sear me with intensity as he pauses. I don't know what I read there. Possession, surprise, desperate need. But they close when he takes my mouth. This kiss is unlike the first. There's no slow buildup. Alo is all wild energy, sucking and licking at my lips, his hands running all over my body. He pinches, scratches, growls until I'm nearly sobbing with the need to come.

In all my fantasies, I never knew he'd be this good. "Fuck, Alo!"

He lets out a wild growl and collars my throat, guiding me onto my back on the desk. Both hands come to my waist. He pulls what remains of my shirt down over my hips. My jeans get the same treatment. He tosses my clothing to the side and puts a hand on either knee, spreading me wide.

"Miriam," he growls, one hand sliding up my inner thigh to stroke my pussy. I arch on the desktop, desperate for more. His fingers are confident and slow in their perusal, his touch sending feathers of heat tickling through me.

When I gasp aloud, he growls his approval. The chair in front of my desk creaks and groans as he gracefully drops down onto it. He places one of my legs over his shoulder, leaning in to lick a slow stripe up my pussy.

We let out matching groans, and he looks up from between my thighs. "You taste like candy, Miriam. I wanna play with you and candy one day."

I sob and lie back on the desk, just imagining him sliding a sticky sweet candy inside me and eating it out.

I shudder when he nibbles along my folds. That cry turns into a literal wail when he retracts a claw and slides a thick finger slowly inside me, rubbing at the rough patch inside my pussy that makes me wild. It's the sweet spot for pixies, and he found it on the first fucking try.

"Godsdam—ahhh!" I scream, arching up off my desk when orgasm hits me so hard, I can't even see for the blackness that overtakes me. Sound muffles, my sight disappears, and there's only Alo's frenzied sucking and licking, and the pressure he's putting on that place inside.

Orgasm crashes over me like a tidal wave. I don't know if I'm screaming or fully silent. All I know is he continues until the waves subside, and then he starts back up again.

And my fucking alarm goes off.

"Gah!" I jolt upright, dislodging his face from between my thighs.

Heat flares across my cheeks and down my chest. I rub at the back of my arm.

"Gods, sorry, Alo," I mutter. "It's my alarm to make sure I'm not late."

He sits back in my chair, big legs spread wide and a satisfied look on his face. "I won't let you be late. Come here, Miriam." He crooks one finger at me.

And I obey, because I am helpless against Alo like this.

Please don't break my heart, I think with sudden desperation. *I won't survive it if you decide you don't want this.*

I slide off the desk, and he reaches for me, pulling me into his lap with a thigh on either side of his waist. He points to his lap, where the front of his jeans is wet.

Oh gods, he's horny from what we just did. And I don't have the time to do anything about it.

"Look what touching you does to me, Mir." He reaches out and slides his fingers gently along the outer edge of my wing, a confident smirk on his face.

I cry out and arch my back, my head falling to one side. "Sensitive," I grit out.

"Same." He laughs and plucks at the bottom tip of my wing, sending a jolt of electricity through my pussy.

He curls a wing around us, dragging the sharp tips along the topmost bone of my right wing. I hold back a scream at the sensation. Every inch of my body is tense and tight again.

Alo's satisfied chuckle has me panting.

"We're gonna have a lot of fun with these wings, pixie girl. I can't wait to have you in my nest. You need to leave in precisely three minutes to get to work on time, and I'm patrolling tonight. Come with me?"

I gasp around the steady stroke of his claw against my wing bones. "You want me to patrol with you? Will you even be able to concentrate?"

He laughs. "I'm an excellent multitasker, Miriam."

"I'm aware," I mutter, crossing my arms. "I don't want to go to work."

Alo's happy smile falls. He pinches my chin gently between his fingers. "If Ezazel gives you a single second of shit, tell me. I'm not one to get violent, but I won't stand for his treatment of you."

"Okay," I agree. "But he's already gotten an earful from me."

"Good, my saucy, sweet girl." He looks down at his comm watch and frowns. "Time to go, Mir."

I absolutely refuse to be late another time and give Ezazel a reason to come down hard on me, but I don't want to go either. Because being like this with Alo reminds me that he's always been my favorite part of any day.

CHAPTER TEN

ALO

I trail Miriam through the sweets shop, ignoring snide looks from her two helpers. They must have heard the screams, not that I care. Mir seems oblivious, checking in with them before flitting out the front door. She looks back over her shoulder for me. Like always, a pink blush covers her cheeks and the tips of her ears. I don't think I'll ever get enough of seeing how her body responds to mine.

We walk hand in hand to the garden. When I drop her off, she pops up onto her tiptoes to plant a kiss on my lips. "I have candy-making class later, but I can patrol with you after?"

"Perfect," I murmur, slicking my mouth over hers. I need more than a peck; I need tongue. I need to taste every inch of her sweet mouth. Groaning into the kiss, I slide one hand up the back of her head to hold her tight to me.

When we part, we're both breathless, and I'm nowhere near done with her. But I have to be, because I don't want her to be late.

Tucking a lock of green hair behind her ear, I grumble, "I'll bring Iggy to candy class, then I can drop him off at Shepherd's."

"Okay," she whispers. She kisses me again, and this time it's frantic and needy until a cleared throat from somewhere in the garden stops us.

Miriam's cheeks go bright red, and she pecks me on the cheek once before popping into small form and disappearing into the garden. I watch her zip into the tree where the dust factory is, and then I head home. I've got a few hours before Iggy gets back. Normally I'd nap, but I'm not in the mood for that today.

No.

I'm in the mood for something far filthier.

I think back to having my face buried between Miriam's thighs, choking down a groan. Jogging to my cottage, I bypass the kitchen even though the cottage opens the oven door for me. I've been cooking a lot this week.

"Not now," I mutter, taking the stairs to my nest two at a time. I fall backward into it and reach into a hidden drawer on the far side. I had to build it when Iggy stumbled across my sex toy stash and started asking questions. I withdraw a long tube and set it on the bed next to me before yanking my jeans off.

My cock bobs up against my stomach, leaking a sticky stream of precum onto my abs. I reach for it, stroking my length and rubbing the small rectangular plate that sticks out over my shaft. Pleasure streaks up my spine, my brain supplying images of Mir spread wide on her cherry-red desk, showing me that soft candy-sweet pussy.

She tasted so fucking good.

Groaning, I coat my cock in precum, then grab the tube and slip it over my rigid length. The ruffles on the inside mimic pixie pussy. I bought it after I met her.

Gods, I was a fool to think I could deny my feelings for Miriam. And now that we've opened the floodgates, my instincts are kicking in fast. I want her all over me, and then I want to bring her snacks in our nest and fill her with my seed. The only reason I'd get so possessive over her this fast is because she's mine, my mate, and my soul knows it.

And that means my mate isn't with me now, and I want her to be. Scratch that, I'm desperate for her to be here. So desperate that I'm going to fuck my toy and imagine it's her pussy sinking onto my length. Her pussy squeezing me tight as I tug my balls. Her beautiful pussy clenching around me.

Growling, I rock my hips, driving my cock into the tube as the ruffled interior strokes me. It's not nearly as warm or perfect as she would be, but I fantasize about touching Miriam, holding her, teasing her, loving her, and I explode into the toy. Her name falls from my lips like a prayer, and I scream it until I'm hoarse and the pleasure subsides.

Gasping for breath, I slide the tube off my soaked cock as I stare out the glass ceiling of my nest. The room is painfully empty without her. She's never even been in here.

It's high fucking time to change that.

~

Hours later, I'm in the kitchen baking spaghetti when Iggy arrives home from school. He lands on the island countertop and lovingly stares at the baking dish. "Aww, Miriam's other favorite. Are you cooking for her again?"

I smile at my son. "I am. What do you think about that? Want to help?"

Iggy hops around the mess on the island's surface, whooping victoriously. I push a tray of shredded cheese toward him, pointing at the dish.

"Okay, Ig. We're gonna do a layer of cheese, then a layer of noodles and sauce, then a layer of meatballs, alright?"

He grins at me, blue eyes sparkling with joy. "Think Miriam will agree to be my girlfriend if I help you?"

It's the perfect opening to talk to him about my pursuit of her. The reality is that gargoyles mate quickly. I've danced around physical and emotional attraction for a long time, unsure if I wanted to open myself up to a female again. But... Miriam's different. And Shepherd is right—I can't make Miriam pay for Keira's choices.

Reaching out, I ruffle my son's hair. "Bud, I want to talk to you about something important."

Iggy grabs a handful of cheese and places it evenly across the spaghetti's surface. "Are you mating Miriam? Is she gonna be my mom?"

I'm so shocked, I grip the countertop to avoid stumbling backward. Did he put that together when he saw us at Scoops?

I clear my throat and cross my arms, stepping back to lean against one of the cabinets. "What makes you say that?"

Iggy grins. "Kevin says his dad told him that one of the centaurs saw you holding her hand."

Shit. I had hoped to have a conversation with him before he heard something like this.

I nip at my lip as I consider how to answer, but my son beats me to the punch.

"It's okay, Dad. I was gonna ask her to be my girlfriend, but I think you're right—she's better as my best friend." He lifts his wrist, her bracelet still around his tiny arm. "When she gave me this, I think she was trying to tell me we're just friends."

"I—she loves you a whole lot," I counter.

Iggy gives me a curious look. "Do you like her in a different way from friends?"

I gulp. Hells, this is harder than I thought.

"Yeah," I finally admit. "I like Miriam in a mates sort of

way. I wanted to talk to you about it because I'd like to formally date her, but I figured you and I should talk about it, man to man."

Iggy gives me a knowing look. "Snack up, shack up? That's what Uncle Shepherd says."

"Pretty much, buddy." When he's silent, I decide to probe him for more information. Surely it can't be this easy...can it? "How would you feel about Miriam being a bigger part of our lives? Maybe even living here in the cottage one day?"

He grabs another handful of cheese and lets out a beleaguered sigh. "If it was up to me, Miriam would have lived with us, like, a really long time ago, Dad. She's my best friend. I always want her here." He holds up his wrist again, shaking his arm so the bracelet jangles.

"Hey," I continue, "she's teaching a candy-making class at the sweets shop tonight. You wanna go?"

Iggy hops up and down on the counter, his tail lashing from side to side before he remembers to wrap it around his leg. "Yeah! Can we go now?! Do we have to finish the spaghetti?"

Laughing, I reach for him and pull him up onto my shoulder. Warmth fills my chest when his tail slips into the neckline of my tee and stops above my heart.

"Make you a deal, bud. Let's get this in the oven, head to candy class, and I'll run back here to take it out when it's time."

"Yes!" Iggy lets out a war whoop and then tugs on my hair. "Dad, if you're going to court Miriam, you really need to do something with your hair. It's looking a little wild, and girls don't like that."

I snort. "Girls don't like that, huh?"

He hops off my shoulder and flies down the back hallway and up the stairs. A minute later, he returns with his hair brush, landing on my shoulder and combing my hair for me.

He yanks and pulls on it, but I hold still because I can scarcely believe my luck.

After a torturous few minutes, he hops back onto the countertop and waves the brush at me. "Looks good, Dad!"

"Thank you," I murmur, pulling him in for a hug. "Love you, kiddo."

CHAPTER ELEVEN
ALO

Iggy hops onto my shoulder, wrapping his tail around my neck. The cottage shakes her front windows at us when we go. Iggy waves back at her, blowing a kiss. We head for Main, crossing to the opposite side before hooking a right to Miriam's Sweets. The glossy red front door that matches her desk—the desk I ate her pussy on—is thrown wide open, the sugary scent of candy saturating the air.

When we enter, the small store is filled with monsters. Iggy lets out a happy squeak and leaps off my shoulder, zooming into the crowd. A few people call out greetings asWren and Ohken enter behind me.

The big bridge troll claps me on the back. "Good to see you here, friend."

A hot blush travels up my neck.

Wren shoots me a wink. "I know all about the big Halloween plan, so you don't have to keep it a secret from me."

I return the happy look. "Your sisters don't know, though, right?"

She shrugs. "Thea's a former detective, honey. She can tell

something's up. But for now, I think she's just letting it all happen."

I frown and cross my arms. I don't want Miriam's big surprise to be spoiled.

Just then, her voice echoes from the back of the shop, "Okay, everyone, if you'll please follow me to the classroom, it's time to make some candy!"

I look over the crowd and get a glimpse of her. Iggy's perched on her shoulder, his tail wrapped around her neck and one chubby arm around her head. They're grinning at one another, and, somehow, that brings my father's words to mind.

Focus on Ignatius, Alo. He is the only thing that matters.

But my father was wrong about that. Iggy might be the center of my world, but I think Miriam is the center of his. I watch them until the room has cleared, and it's just Mir and Iggy standing there, staring at me.

She places her hands on her hips, cocking her head to the side. Her friendship bracelets jangle loudly. "Cat got your tongue, Alo?" She beams at me, iridescent wings fluttering gently at her back.

I open my mouth with a quick retort, something like I know how she feels about my tongue, but I can't say that in front of Iggy.

He beats me to the punch, speaking first. "Dad made you a spaghetti casserole. He has to leave class to make sure it doesn't burn. He wants you to be his mate."

Oh gods. Blood rushes to my cheeks, but Miriam grins at Iggy. "And how do you feel about that, bestie?"

Iggy lays his head against hers and sighs. "I wanted you to be my girlfriend for a little while, but you're probably better for Dad, so it's okay with me. Plus, if this means we can have sleepovers, that would be awesome!"

She turns that gorgeous smile on me again. "Sleepovers,

huh?" Her voice is a low murmur, and it sends the wheels in my head spinning. "Sleepovers do sound pretty amazing."

"Yeah," I say breathlessly. "We need to do that soon."

Mir reaches for my hand. "Agreed. But tonight is about candy. You ready to make skullipops, Alo?"

I don't know what the hells a skullipop is, but if I get to stare at her while we make them, I'm down.

"Hells yes," I say, taking her hand and following her through her office and down a short hall into the classroom. It's a big, cheerful room painted in turquoise, red, and white, with long tables and stations at each spot. This is where Miriam makes her candy, and her scent is all over the room.

She drops my hand and points to a table up front, indicating I should go there. Iggy leans over her shoulder. "Can I be your assistant?"

She snorts. "Duh. I assumed you would be."

Iggy laughs, and a few monsters from the crowd join in.

For the next fifteen minutes, Miriam—with commentary from my five-year-old—walks us through making spicy pumpkin lollipops and black lollipops shaped like skulls. Iggy gets a huge kick out of explaining to the gathered crowd why they're called "skullipops."

Apparently, it's Mir's twist on something the humans do for Halloween. Except these lollipops will change the color of your hair or eyes for a few hours.

Wren and Ohken joke back and forth at the table next to me. Ohken can't seem to keep his hands off his new mate. For the first time, seeing them so openly affectionate doesn't make me jealous. No. If anything, it just cements what I know to be true—Pursuing Miriam is the right choice.

Partway through the class, Wren joins me to correct my stirring method. "Sooo, Alo. Now that you and Mir are a thing, wanna do a double date?"

I shouldn't be surprised she's asking. It's not as if I've been quiet in about Miriam, but it's still new. I glance over at Wren, watching how she stirs the liquid candy, and take my spoon back. "What do you have in mind?"

She gives me a devilish look and clasps her hands together. "Shifter Hollow. Ohken has been telling me all about it."

He leans over. "I'm thinking we should take the girls to Bad Axe for drinks and dinner. Thoughts?"

I look to the front of the classroom, where Miriam and Iggy are tickling one another while she stirs her own bowl. Father's words fade into the recesses of my brain, and in their place, a memory of my solo sexy time rears its head.

I want a night with her and our friends. I want to touch and tease her like Wren and Ohken are doing right now. Grinning at a beaming Wren, I nod. "Let's do it."

Eventually, I slip away to take the spaghetti out of the oven. By the time I return, the class is ending. Miriam threw my lollipops into the oven for me. They're perfect, and Iggy is thrilled. They cool off fast, and he crunches into one, his hair sticking straight up and turning purple. His eyes go brilliant amethyst too.

"Aww"—I snort—"you look adorable, Ig."

He flits to the nearest window, which has just enough of a reflection for him to see his now-purple hair and eyes. "So cool," he whispers.

Miriam tries another of my lollipops, giving it a quick lick with her eyes locked on mine.

Fucking tease.

"Tastes good," she murmurs. "I like your lollipop, Alo."

I growl and lean into her ear. "You're gonna like it later, too, pixie girl."

Miriam laughs, and Wren joins us, opening her arms for Iggy.

"C'mon, kiddo. Dad's patrolling tonight, and Miriam has stuff to do. Catherine wants us to hang with her for a bit."

I had already arranged for Catherine to watch Iggy tonight, but I shoot Wren a grateful look.

I wasn't the nicest monster when the Hector triplets arrived in town. I don't think I was all that nice to anyone, in general. I was in a state of permanent grump, but it's lifting off me like a fog. I let myself grow bitter and distant when Keira left, but I don't want to be that male anymore.

Miriam helps everyone get their goodies packed up. While she does that, I clean the classroom, trashing burnt candies and wiping sticky syrup off the work tables. Once she manages to get her patrons out the door, she comes back, hands clasped together.

"Alo, you didn't have to clean. But thank you!"

Her eyes and hair have turned a brilliant pink from the lollipop. But it's how surprised and pleased she seems that warms my heart.

Tossing my rag down, I reach for her with my wing, pulling her into my arms. "I want to take care of you, Miriam. That smile on your face? I want to be the male who puts it there, every damn day."

She places both hands on my chest. "You always have, Alo. It's always been you for me, since the day you arrived in Ever."

I stroke the tip of one pointed ear, trailing my fingers down her neck. Goose bumps follow my touch. "I'm sorry it took me so long," I mutter.

"Better late than never." She laughs.

"You're far too understanding. Shouldn't I be groveling?"

Miriam snorts and presses away from me, her expression serious. "Listen to me, because this is important. It might have taken a while for our love story to start, Alo, but I was your friend first. My goal is to never make your life harder. I want to make it easier, and you're hard enough on yourself already."

I choke back my surprise, but she's not done.

"I see you, Alo, the real you. The monster behind hours

99

spent protecting this town and putting your son before everything else. I see a monster who's had to do all of that alone,
and I know it's a fucking lot. So no, I don't plan to make you
grovel or do a single damn thing to make your life harder. I
want to be the one who makes it better, because that's what
you are for me."

She scoffs, crossing her arms in seeming irritation.
"Grovel. That's a terrible idea. Unless…" She brings her
fuchsia gaze back to mine. "Unless you wanted to get on your
knees in the bedroom and beg for sexual favors. I could get
into that sort of groveling."

I growl, hauling her close to me again. Wrapping my wings
around us, I form a pitch-black cocoon that blocks out everything but the sound of our heavy breathing.

"You want me on my knees, Miriam? Like earlier today?
Or something else?"

"Technically you were seated in my chair," she corrects
with a laugh. "But, yeah, that was nice."

"Nice?" I scoff. "I need to try a little harder if that's what
you have to say about it." I lean down and grip her throat,
using my thumb to push her chin back. Her head falls against
my wing, a breathy sigh leaving her lips.

"You screamed my name over and over, Miriam.
Remember that, pretty girl? You screamed my name until you
were godsdamned hoarse. Tell me that wasn't more than
nice."

"Very nice," she sasses. "It was very fucking nice."

I slip one hand up her back, stroking along the base of one
of her wings. When she shudders, heat surges through me. My
fingers make their way up along the hard bone and back
down the delicate skin between each segment. Miriam's chest
rises and falls fast against mine, a soft whine falling from her
lips.

"Tell me how you want me to beg," I growl, licking a stripe

up her neck to bite on the pointed tip of her ear.

Miriam shudders. "Alo, I—"

"Do you want me to get on both knees, part those pretty thighs, and show you with my tongue how long I dreamed of touching you?"

She lets out a desperate little cry.

I piston my hips against hers, rubbing my rock-hard length against her waist. "Maybe you need me to pull you into my nest and show you how I fuck my pixie pussy sex toy, wishing like hells it was your sweet depths I was plundering."

"Fuck," she cries out.

I can't stop teasing her, not now, not with how her hips jerk hard against mine, her throat bobbing under my grip.

"Or maybe the best way to make up for my delinquency would be to flip you onto all fours and fuck you until you're boneless, Mir. And when you're sated, I'll play with your wings until you can't wait to have me again, and then I'll hang us from the ceiling and help you ride me until that pretty pussy comes all over my big fat cock." I bite a perfect spot along her shoulder. "What do you think?"

"Yes," she cries out. "Can we do it now?"

I let out a groan. "I'm patrolling tonight." I pinch the tip of her wing. She jolts in my arms, both hands going to my forearm where she holds me like I'm her lifeline. "You said you'd come with me, Mir. Still want to?"

"Gods, yes," she blurts out. "Tell me you're not done teasing me, though. This is the most fun I've had in a while."

There's a skylight in the classroom. Grabbing her tight, I push off the ground and fly for it with her caged in my arms. When we reach the skylight, I pop the lock and open it, setting her down on the roof. I carefully shut the skylight, then turn Miriam so her back is to my front. I wrap my tail around her waist, slipping the spade into the front of her pants. My left arm comes around her waist, my hand resting over her heart, which thumps wildly beneath my palm.

I lean over her to nip at the shell of her right ear. "Let's patrol, pretty girl. And I'm going to tease you the entire time."

"Count me in." Miriam laughs, and I press hard off the gravel-covered roof, bulleting up into the sky.

Flying with her in my arms is the best feeling, her body warm against my cooler skin. She laughs when I catch a current and fly along the faintly glowing green wards toward Shepherd's gas station. He only has to man it if new people are coming to Ever, and at the moment, we're only expecting one visitor—the Hector triplets' Aunt Lou. It'll be days until she arrives, so the gas station sits empty, but I often start my patrol there.

Thralls—the evil, soulless monsters who try to destroy monster havens—are often drawn to the gas station. They're attracted to haven protective power, and it's strongest here where new residents enter town.

My comm watch pings. I grip Miriam tighter with my left arm as I bring my right up. The Keeper's name pops up.

When I answer, his voice resonates through the device. "Alo, I see you've started your patrol. Let me know if anything is abnormal about the wards. They should be in good shape— I dusted them earlier today—but let me know what you find."

Without another word, he clicks off.

Miriam giggles. "Nice to see he's just as brusque with everyone as I thought."

I snort and hold her tighter, working my way along the wards and past Hel Motel. The wards there are always strong, but thralls seem repelled by the wraiths that own the motel, for whatever reason.

"The Keeper's so focused. Although, I wish he'd try to spend time with Morgan."

"Well"—Miriam laughs—"maybe you should talk to him,

one reformed bachelor to another."

I match her laugh, sliding my hand down her chest to cup her breast. Pinching her nipple, I growl into her ear, "Entirely reformed, pretty girl. I was a fool to hold out for so long."

Mir falls silent as we fly past the mermaids' grotto. I swoop up and over the northwestern section of the haven—I don't patrol there. Richard and the shifter pack have full responsibility for that section of Ever. I catch a current and bypass their forest, dipping behind the now-empty skyball stadium.

When she doesn't say anything for another quarter hour, I wonder if it was stupid to referencing my holding out. We casually mentioned it after her class, but she's been silent for so long, and that's not Miriam's way.

By the time we make it back to the gas station, Miriam still hasn't said a word. I land us in front of the station and uncurl my tail from her waist, spinning her to face me.

She's nipping at her lip, her usual easy smile gone.

"Mir, what's wrong? Is it what I said about waiting so long? That was stupid of me."

She waves my concern away.

I catch her wrist and pull it to my mouth, gently nipping the inside. "Talk to me."

Fuchsia eyes flick up to mine, her expression tense. "It's just, I said it wasn't a big deal that you waited so long. I mean, I said I didn't expect a grovel or anything, but…"

My nostrils flare. "You need a grovel, pretty girl?" I'll drop to my fucking knees right now and beg.

"No." She smiles. "I don't need a grovel, Alo."

I've known Miriam for almost five years, ever since Iggy was a baby. And we've been amazing friends that long. I think I know exactly what she wants to ask. But Miriam always putting others first means she doesn't want to ask me what she thinks is a hard question.

I cup her chin in one hand. "Mir, you deserve answers as to why it took me so long to ask you out. I had intended on talking to you about it, and this is the perfect time." I grab her hand and pull her toward the forest behind Shepherd's station. "Finish the last little bit of patrol with me, and I'll tell you everything."

Dark eyelashes flutter over fuchsia irises. Her eyes are intoxicating.

"It's two things, really," I admit. My voice trails off as I think about how to explain my resistance for five damn years.

Miriam rubs my chest with both hands. "We don't have to talk about this, Alo; it's not—"

I silence her with my thumb over her mouth, rubbing at her soft lower lip. "Don't say it's not important," I murmur. "You and Iggy are the center of my world, Miriam. You deserve answers. I just…I'll just start at the beginning."

She nods, looking relieved.

Clearing my throat, I barrel right into the context I've never shared with her. And I never shared it because it was so damn painful to talk about. But if we're going to continue on this path, Miriam needs to know my whole sordid history. I grab both of her hands, rubbing the backs with my thumbs.

"When Keira and I got together, we were the stars of the Protector Academy. Top students in our class, great protector partners—everyone expected us to mate. And I thought she was mine. We got assigned to Hearth HQ, and my parents were so proud of that. We served there for a few decades, but then we got pregnant. Iggy wasn't planned, but the moment we found out, everything I'd centered my world around shifted."

Miriam is silent as stone, pulling my hand to her chest. Her wildly chaotic heartbeat comforts me. And now that the floodgates are open, I want her to know everything.

Still, the memory I'm reliving sends stabbing, crushing sensations to my heart.

"When we found out Keira was pregnant, she didn't want Iggy. She didn't want to be a mother. Mostly, she didn't want her career to be derailed. We were so foolish to never have talked about that, because I didn't know what her desires were, and I never asked. She had every right to those choices, but I *did* want him, so we decided to mate formally, move in together, and I'd raise him while she worked." I stop for a moment, thinking back to asking Keira to become mine. She said yes, but it was never right.

I huff out a breath before I'm able to continue. "I never told anyone this, but I had to take a potion to help my heart start beating after we mated. It didn't happen naturally like it should have, but my father guided me when we had that issue."

I look at Miriam, who's got one hand over her mouth and unshed tears in her eyes. This story is horrible. But I want her to know it all.

"We thought being formally mated would help us deal with an unplanned pregnancy, but it didn't. Our relationship fell apart quickly after that. I knew I wanted to be a father, and she knew she didn't want to be a mother. We had never even discussed it, so being confronted with a child was something we weren't prepared to deal with. We decided that when she had Iggy, we'd formally unmate, and I'd leave Hearth HQ. I didn't want to raise a child in that environment, and once I knew Iggy existed, he was all I wanted."

"Alo," Miriam murmurs, stopping and turning me to face her. "I'm so sorry."

"It's not just that, Mir. I—" I look down at our joined hands, and I pull her close to me because I need to comfort her, and she looks so distressed.

My voice is a mere whisper as I share the rest of my story.

"My parents were furious at the situation. There's never been an unmated gargoyle in the Rygold family tree. But they wanted a grandchild, and they agreed with my desire to raise him, even if it was by myself. When Iggy was born, they came to the hospital with me. We signed the unmating docs in front of Evenia right in the birthing room. My heart stopped beating as soon as I signed the paper."

I don't realize tears are streaming down my cheeks retelling the story about that horrible day. All I can think of is how I clutched a wailing Iggy to my silent chest and left the hospital with my parents in tow.

"I spent a month at my folks' place in Vizelle, learning how to care for a baby. Shepherd came to help too, and he couldn't stop talking about the small, remote haven of Ever and how much he loved it. Against my parents' wishes, I followed Shepherd here. He said Ever had more of a small-town homey feel, and that's what I wanted for Ig. I haven't seen or talked to Keira since."

Miriam sobs in my arms, throwing hers around my neck. "I'm so sorry, I'm so fucking sorry," she whispers on repeat.

"Mir," I murmur, "I'm not trying to let myself off the hook for taking so long to ask you out. I just—I just needed you to know what was going on behind the scenes. Because the reality is that that first day I bumped into you in Higher Grounds, and you smiled at me? I wanted you, even then. And it terrified me because I knew what it felt like to lose my heartbeat, to lose what I thought my future was. And my father loves to remind me how Iggy comes first. I let that be my excuse for a long time."

Her sobs get louder, and all I can do is stroke her back, her wings, her shoulder, desperate to tell her with my touch how much I care for her.

"It took me a long time because I was afraid," I admit. "Afraid to love you and get my heart broken again. Afraid to love you and it not work out and crush Iggy. I was afraid of my father's wrath if I did anything but focus on my child twenty-four hours a day. But after seeing you with Iggy last week, after realizing how much my son adores you, I couldn't deny it any longer. I don't want to be afraid, Miriam. I was never that male until everything happened with Keira. That broke me. But you've been putting me back together, piece by piece, for five years."

And there it is, the truth. I was a chicken shit because I'd been burned. I'm not proud of that, especially as a gargoyle male. But the reality is that Keira not wanting a family gutted me. And feeling my heartbeat stop? There's no worse thing for a gargoyle.

Miriam sobs into my neck, her thin arms wrapped tightly around me. Reaching down, I pull her up into my arms, wrapping her legs around my waist. I grip the back of her neck and bring her tear-stained face up. And then I slant my mouth over hers and devour her, licking and sucking the tears away.

I dart my tongue into her mouth, tasting her, needing her close. I want her with me always. I'm fucking obsessed.

And it was never like this with Keira. I know she wasn't meant to be mine; otherwise, I wouldn't have had to get a potion to help things along.

Miriam kisses me back like it's the last time she'll ever have me, her hands running over my cheeks and face and horns, up into my hair to grip it tightly.

"Need you," I gasp between bites.

"Alo," she cries out, throwing her head back, presenting that slim column of neck to me.

It's everything I can do not to bite her and claim her right now.

Miriam is mine, my mate, and it's my job to prove to her that I'm a mate worth having.

CHAPTER TWELVE
MIRIAM

Oh gods, I'm destroyed. My emotions are a tattered, frayed mess at hearing all of Alo's story. I knew some of it from comments he'd made over the years. My poor broken male.

I kiss him like I can banish all that hurt away with my touch, ravaging his lips as his kiss grows hungrier and hungrier. He lurches across the forest floor, pushing me against a broad tree. His wings come around us, cocooning us so all I hear is his lips on mine, his hands running up and down my body.

"Mir," Alo growls. "I don't deserve you, but I want you with all of my heart. Allow me to prove I can be the male you think I am?"

I press my hand to his lips, quieting his declarations. "Take me," I whisper into the darkness between us. His hands go tight around my waist. "Please, Alo."

His breathing turns rough and ragged, his hands moving from my body. A zipper rips open and his jeans hit the forest floor. Then he drops to his knees in front of me, shoving his face between my thighs and licking at my core. One big hand comes to my thigh, and he tosses it over his shoulder, feasting on me like he's never tasted anything quite so good. The way he moans as he eats sends my pleasure skyrocketing.

When he slips one thick finger inside me, rubbing gentle circles on that sensitive spot in my channel, I detonate, shrieking his name as I flood his hands and face with my release. Waves of ecstasy blur my senses. There's only a deep sense of satisfaction.

I grip his horns and drag his attention up to me. He parts his wings, letting the early evening light in. Dark eyes glitter possessively as his lips work over my core, but those beautiful eyes flutter closed as he groans.

"Alo," I whine. "Please, let me touch you."

He pulls away just long enough to growl. "I'm making up for years of not touching you, Mir. Let me. Please."

I stroke his horns a little harder, loving how they flatten against his scalp. "Aloitious," I say a little more sternly, eyes rolling back into my head as the finger in my pussy starts stroking again. "I need to watch you fall apart. I'm very insistent."

He laughs, and that chuckle reverberates against my skin, causing me to jolt in his arms. But he doesn't stop his sweet torture. In fact, he doesn't stop until I flutter my wings and try to escape his grasp.

"I don't think so." He laughs, dragging me back down when I dart up into the air. "And don't you dare—"

I pop into small form and zip around his head, reappearing behind him. Placing both hands on my hips, I shoot him a look.

Alo turns slowly in place, tail lashing from side to side like an overgrown, angry cat. He scowls, and sharp spines shoot up out of his shoulders, all the way down his forearms and outer thighs. Spikes emerge along the top of his tail, the spade lengthening to form a deadly-looking dagger.

"You want me to chase you, Miriam?" he utters in a low, predatory tone, chocolate eyes utterly focused on me.

"I want to touch you." I laugh and cross my arms. "But I wouldn't be opposed to making you work for it. Good as you are at protecting Ever, I don't know how you'd hold up against me in small form."

He launches forward, but I'm expecting it. When he swipes out with one big hand to snatch me out of thin air, I dive underneath and land on the tip of his nose. He roars and reaches for me, but I'm there and gone in a second, diving through the forest. I reappear in large form in a tree branch above his head, waving as he glares up at me from down below.

"Get down here, pixie girl," he snaps, pointing to the ground at his feet. "Don't make me come up there and retrieve you."

I shrug, crossing my arms. Before I can say another word, he presses off the ground, and this time, he's so fast, I barely track the movements. Big arms snatch me up, his tail wrapping tightly around my waist. There's no time to shriek before we're back on the soft, crushed-pine needle ground. It's a rough carpet under my back as Alo straddles me, naked as the day he was born.

His cock is long and thick, the plate that sticks out above it rigid and quivering. If I let him, he'll push that whole thing inside me. I've heard whispers of the pleasure gargoyle males can dispense with that extra appendage.

"Flip over, Mir," he commands. When I don't move fast enough, he grips my waist and flips me onto my knees, shoving me forward so my cheek presses to the soft earth. He grips my hips and drags me backward, nestling his cock between my ass cheeks.

"I'm going to fuck you, Miriam," he states simply. "And then I'm going to eat your ass and fuck you again. After that,

I'll consider slowing down, only because I haven't fed you yet, and the spaghetti's probably cold."

I laugh and wiggle my ass. I'm wholly unprepared for his big hand to lay a slap on my fucking thigh, and I shout at the pain that blooms along my sensitive skin. But pleasure follows it, soaking my core as Alo groans.

"I never thought you'd be a brat. I godsdamn love it, Miriam."

I surge forward like I'm going to escape, but Alo grabs my hip and drags me back and onto his cock all in one go. He impales me, filling me so fucking full I can't breathe around how godsdamned thick he is. The move is so hard, his plate slips inside, rubbing against my most sensitive places.

It starts godsdamned vibrating, sending fireworks through my pussy as I arch my back against the onslaught of pleasure.

Alo laughs, a low and devious noise that pulls goose bumps to the surface of my skin. "You're gonna come so hard and fast, pixie girl."

"Ungh." It's the only sound I'm capable of making as I struggle to adjust to how fucking big Alo is, how completely he fills me. But then my breath leaves me in a whoosh when he slips out slowly, his thickness taunting me. He yanks me back onto him, muscular hips snapping against my ass.

And that's when I learn Alo isn't the gentle, kind lover I always imagined he'd be. I thought he'd be all tender kisses and sweet nothings.

But this male fucks me like he's going to war. A string of expletives leaves his mouth, his voice going lower and deeper. His tail snakes between my legs and up my stomach, between my breasts, to rub against my lips.

I open my mouth to pant. He feels so damn good, every jerk of his body drives me higher, higher, higher.

When he pops my mouth with the tip of his tail, I jerk and

cry out. My pussy clenches around him. A satisfied-sounding growl is my reward.

"Suck, Mir," he commands, his voice like boulders tumbling off a rocky cliff.

And suck I do, licking and nipping at the rough edges. Alo's insistent growls morph into high, keening cries that have me clenching rhythmically as I try not to fall too damn fast. There's nothing sexier than making a man moan. Absolutely nothing.

The harder he grinds, the wilder it drives me until I'm biting the shit out of his tail and he's yanking me onto his cock over and over. When his fingers slip between my ass cheeks to play with my back hole, I detonate, my lips curling back as I claw at the ground beneath me.

Alo falls right after I do, roaring so loud, a flock of birds bursts from a nearby tree and takes to the sky. The pump of his hips grows sloppy and jerky as hot cum lashes me from the inside out, dripping out of my pussy and up my stomach because of the angle. His big thighs quiver against my ass. Shifting forward, he grips my throat and pulls me upright, my back to his chest. It heaves with exertion.

This angle hits deeper, and I cry out as he continues a slow, steady drumbeat in and out of me.

Soft lips come to my neck, nibbling their way up to my ear, which gets the same treatment. I cry out something, his name maybe. I don't even know what I'm asking for. For it to never stop. Because nothing has ever felt this pleasurable.

He growls seductively in my ear. "You took me so beautifully, Mir. I'm not done though, pretty girl. Can you handle more?"

Oh gods. It's well-known in monster circles that gargoyles are prodigious lovers. I just never thought he'd be so...dominant. I don't know why, because he dominates everything he does. But I just, I'm shocked and blissed-out and struggling against rolling waves that still haven't stopped. I'm a tiny ship, battered on a shore of ecstasy. There's no fighting this.

Taking my silence in stride, Alo growls and pulls out of me, flipping me carefully over and laying me on the forest floor. His nostrils flare, his upper lip curled into a feral sneer. Like this, he looks like some sort of gorgeous dark demon, all sensual promise and predatory intention.

I shift up onto my elbows, eyes locked with his. They crinkle in the corners as his grin grows bigger, revealing sharp fangs.

He jerks his head between us. "I'm gonna fuck you again, pixie girl, and I want you to watch us." He pushes my thigh until the front hits my stomach. "Hold on, Miriam."

And then he surges back inside me.

My back arches, hands grabbing at the earth beneath me, but Alo's insistent snarl drags my focus back to him.

"Watch how good you look taking this big dick, Mir. I always knew you would."

I pant at his words, struggling up onto my elbows to watch. And he's right, the scene is so damn delicious. The big round tip of his cock nudges my folds open and then disappears inside me, sending heat and ecstasy blistering through me. I cry out as he withdraws slowly, then rolls his hips again, thick abs clenching with every powerful move.

This round is slower but harder. Every snap of Alo's hips sends me across the forest floor. And he feels so damn incredible that I lose focus a dozen times.

Finally, he growls and hauls me into his arms. My back arches as his plate hits that sensitive spot, and I come again, shattering and soaking us both. Alo's panting rises in intensity, his brows furrowing into a vee, then every vein pops in his neck, and his mouth falls open.

He unloads deep inside me with an ear-splitting roar, pressing his forehead to mine. I hover my mouth over his, swallowing his screams as his release sends me over the edge a third time.

Time slows, the world fading around us until all that's left is me and Alo—his touch, his trust, his love. He huffs against my lips as we come down. When his dark eyes reopen, they're softer than I've ever seen them. He rocks onto his heels and lays me against his chest, stroking the back of my neck.

"You're more than I ever imagined, Miriam."

In my post-sex haze, all I can do is laugh and give him a thumbs-up. Alo chuckles, clutching me to his chest. He carefully slips out of me but doesn't let go. Standing with me wrapped around him, he gathers our shredded clothes and bullets up into the sky.

Cool air rushes over our bodies as I snuggle into his neck. By the time we get back to his cottage, I'm biting and kissing his jaw, and he's nearly fallen out of the sky three times.

We land in his backyard and sneak into the house like teenagers. Then we stay naked in the kitchen, and he feeds me baked spaghetti until it's time to retrieve Iggy for bed.

That's my cue to go home, and when I get there, I fall into the sheets for the deepest, soundest sleep of my life.

CHAPTER THIRTEEN

ALO

Gods know why I ever thought I could resist Miriam. Tonight was…it was *everything* to me, having her in my arms. She was the perfect fit, just like I always thought she would be. I was beyond reluctant to let her leave the cottage to return home, but I don't know if Iggy is ready for her to be in my nest. I haven't spoken to him about that specifically. He mentioned sleepovers, but I need to bring it up again to prepare him. The reality is that I want her there. I want her there now. I want to fill my nest with Miriam's scent, her release, her everything. I want to bring all the snacks into the bedroom and eat them off her body.

Now that I've had Miriam, I know I'll never be able to let her go. There's no lingering doubt, no worry about what my father will think when he finds out. I don't give a fuck. What's best for Iggy and me is Miriam, and I'm what's best for her. I hate that she's sleeping in her gourd tonight.

Jogging next door to the Annabelle Inn, I laugh when the stately pink bed-and-breakfast opens her front double doors wide. My neighbor Catherine comes out of the kitchen with a woozy-looking Iggy over her shoulder.

She gives me a soft smile. "He was full tilt until about five minutes ago. Wren just left. We ran him pretty ragged. How was the patrol?"

My cheeks heat. "Good. Nothing to report."

Catherine nods but looks lost in thought. "I'm certain, now, that Wesley is trying to get at me, which leads me to wonder if Evenia was right. Perhaps it's best I go stay at Hearth HQ rather than remaining in Ever. He'll keep attacking, Alo."

I lift Iggy carefully and tuck him against my neck, shaking my head. "Only go if you want to, Cath, which I know you don't. Don't leave because Wesley is an asshole. We'll protect you."

She looks torn though, biting her lip and not meeting my gaze. "Something has been bothering me," she murmurs, glancing out the Annabelle's open front doors. She looks back at me with a frown. "His last few attacks were so close together, where his prior one was almost forty years ago. If time passes faster here in Ever than outside the wards, how did he manage that?"

I cock my head to the side. "I hadn't considered that, but you're right. That would mean, in the human world, he needed to launch the attacks mere hours apart. I suppose it's possible, but..."

She shrugs. "Hours apart is doable. I just can't shake the feeling there's something we're missing."

I reach out and rub her shoulder. "I'll speak with the Keeper about it. He might have other ideas."

She huffs out a frustrated-sounding breath but forces a smile. "How are things going with Miriam? You're the talk of the town, you know."

I groan and rub Iggy's back. He lets out a cute little snore in my ear.

Still, I can't help the grin that splits my face.

"It's great, Cath. My only regret is not asking her out a long time ago."

She smiles and places her hand over mine on Iggy's back. "You deserve all the happiness, Alo. You went through a lot with Keira, and you weren't ready until now. Things happen when they're meant to; I'm a firm believer in that."

"We lost years," I say regretfully.

"And you've got centuries ahead of you," she reminds me. "Centuries to cherish and adore her. Centuries to raise your child together. And a whole community here to support you both."

I wrap my wing around my beautiful friend, pulling her in close for a hug. Of all the monsters in Ever, I'm closest to Catherine.

"Thank you," I whisper.

She squeezes my waist with a little sigh. "Love her hard, Alo. You both deserve it."

She's right. We really do. Screw anyone who feels otherwise about it.

When we part, I give Catherine a final smile before heading home with Iggy over my shoulder. I resist the urge to go into the garden and say goodnight to Miriam, but the A-frame is dark. Everyone's asleep.

The cottage opens the doors for me, closing them softly behind us as I trail through our darkened home and up to Iggy's nest. Star lights along his ceiling blink softly as I lay my son in the cocoon and cover him with his favorite blanket. He automatically curls into a ball, tucking his tail up around his pillow.

He mumbles something but doesn't wake up.

Transfer successful, I sneak out of his room and to my nest, falling into it. My muscles are sore from tonight's… activities. It's a delicious sensation. With a sated smile on my face, I stretch out long in my nest.

Tomorrow, Mir and I have a double date with Wren and Ohken.

I can't godsdamn wait.

~

I patrol again in the morning. After Catherine's comment about Wesley, I examine the wards more closely. I don't know what I'm looking for, but she's right about one thing—the sudden frequency of Wesley's attacks is odd.

I comm Shepherd as I finish up. Nothing looked out of place, but nothing looked out of place prior to Wesley's last infiltration either.

"Hey, bro," Shepherd's voice rings out of my comm watch.

"Catherine brought up an interesting point last night." I launch into the whole story as I glide past the gas station and back along the highway toward town. By the time I'm done, Shepherd hasn't said a word.

Silence stretches for a long moment, then he sighs. "She's right. That's odd. It's possible, given there were a few weeks between attacks, that he could have coordinated that from the human world. But it does seem unlikely. He would have to know one attack wouldn't work, then he'd have mere hours to plan another at the right time? That's a lot, even for a warlock who's that powerful. I'm on my way to the Keeper's; I'll tell him."

"Need me to come?"

"Nah, I've got it, brother. Don't you have a date to get ready for?"

I bristle at that. "Is everybody talking about my love life?"

Shep laughs. "Fuck yeah, Alo. The entire godsdamned town has been waiting for you to make this move. Now we've all got our metaphorical popcorn, and we're watching to see what happens."

I grumble, landing in front of my cottage.

"Aww, don't be grumpy." My brother laughs. "I thought Miriam would sex the grump right out of you."

"Shepherd," I bark. "Enough."

"Guess not." He snorts. "Wait, did you have sex with her yet?"

"Shepherd!"

"What?!"

"I'm...not talking about it."

He laughs again. "So you did! Knew it! I won a bet with Thea, then. And how was it? Was it everything you hoped for?"

Growling, I hang up on him. I hate being the center of attention, and I don't like the idea of everybody talking about Miriam and me. I've never considered myself a grumpy person until Keira. Our breakup was enough to put anyone in a rough mood. But maybe that grumpy streak runs deeper than I thought.

Catherine's planning to pick Iggy up from school so I can get ready. Guilt eats at me over that. Spending alone time with Miriam means I don't spend that time with Iggy, and I don't want him to feel left out. I resolve that our next date will be something we can do with him, because it's important to me that he's included.

I shower and change. At exactly five p.m. there's a knock on the door. The cottage opens the front door. Miriam steps in, a huge smile splitting her face. Her fuchsia eyes fall to my chest and travel lower.

"I like the vest," she murmurs. "And the pants."

I laugh and reach down to adjust my cock. I'm hard for her already, aching to sink back inside her heat.

Reaching for her hand, I pull her close and twirl her. She's wearing a fitted dress that snaps at the back of her neck and dips low, exposing the two divots above her ass. The front covers her completely, but it's tight enough I can see the outline of her small breasts and hard nipples. The dress cuts off at mid-thigh, so I get an eyeful of long, fit legs.

"Come here, Miriam," I demand, pulling her toward the sofa. I flop down on it and adjust her in my lap, straddling my waist. "I dreamed about you last night and woke up covered in cum, pretty girl. You're fucking perfect."

The cottage helpfully shuts the blinds, and Miriam giggles. "Aren't we supposed to meet Wren and Ohken in twenty minutes?"

I growl, shifting forward to unclip her dress at her neck. It slips down her skin, exposing her breasts to me. I press between her shoulder blades, drawing her body to mine. We're wearing too many fucking clothes.

"I need you to fall apart at least once before we leave, Mir." Dipping my head, I pull one taut pink nipple into my mouth and suck.

Miriam arches her back and lets out a soft cry, grabbing my horns and stroking. They flatten against my head as her thin hips work against mine.

Reaching my other hand around her back, I caress the base of her wings, then up the inside of the delicate patchwork skin between each wing bone. She pants, then flutters her wings and leaps off me.

"No," I growl. "Get back here and let me taste you, Miriam." I scowl, but she only laughs. When she drops to her knees in front of me, I hiss in a breath. Is she...?

"You've tasted plenty, Alo," she murmurs, reaching for my zipper. "Let me. I've dreamed of this for so long."

My vision narrows in on her, nostrils flaring. The scent of spun sugar fills the air, along with a heaping dose of her arousal. I flick my tongue out to taste it, licking the air as I huff out a soft breath.

"I don't think I can say no to that," I admit, shifting backward against the cushions with my wings resting to the sides. I grip my waistband. Her slim hands join mine in pulling my jeans down over my big thighs. The moment my cock is free, it bobs up toward my stomach, already dripping sticky precum.

Miriam makes a soft, pleased noise and drags my pants to my ankles and off before tossing them away. Her gaze never leaves my bobbing cock, her lips curled into a mischievous smirk.

Pride and pleasure surge through me. Miriam stares at me like I'm the answer to every question, and I can't get enough of it.

She shifts forward, her breasts rubbing my legs, and strokes both hands teasingly up my length. A flash of heat sears through my gut at her warm grip. My balls draw tight up against my body. But when she leans down and licks precum from my slit, all the breath leaves me in a whoosh.

That pinpoint of pleasure radiates through me, my hips rolling of their own accord. More. I have to have more of her.

I draw one foot up onto the edge of the sofa and let my knee fall out wide to give her space. She leans onto my thighs and opens wide, taking me into her mouth for the first time. I'm ashamed of the sounds that leave my lips as I watch her suck me further and godsdamned further, until I hit the back of her fucking throat.

And keep going.

Soft, hard heat encloses my cock. It's all I can do to even breathe as she takes every godsdamn inch of me between those pretty lips. She takes me until her nose touches my stomach, and then she sucks and licks her way back off while I pant and try not to hump her face.

Mir pops off my dick and gives me a saucy look. "Not having a gag reflex comes in handy when your boyfriend's got a huge dick. I suppose I never mentioned that though. Or did I?"

I groan. "I think I would have remembered." Gods, I was not expecting that. I thought she'd be all sweet innocence for some reason. But my wonder at that disappears when she does it again, and again, until I'm barely hanging on by a thread, one hand fisted on my thigh and the other slung over my head.

She sucks on my cock head, nibbling gently, testing to see what makes me feel good. But it all feels good. Better than good. I'm barely holding back from exploding all over.

Just watching my best friend on her knees between my thighs does things to my heart. Heat sears me from the inside out as I claw at the sofa to avoid dragging her on top of me.

I bring a hand to the back of her head, not pushing, just reveling in the feel of her dipping down onto me and sucking back off again. My thighs start to quiver, and she goes wild with deep pulls and teasing bites. When her left hand comes to my sack and gently pulls, I detonate, back arching as I shoot my seed all the way down her throat, bellowing her name as the veins in my neck pop to the surface.

Black stars pool together until I can't see a godsdamned thing. There's only the sensation of Miriam's soft mouth as she swallows my cum and licks me clean.

By the time orgasm fades to hazy relief, I'm fucking destroyed.

"Miriam," I pant. I can't seem to catch my breath, my chest heaving. She stares at me from between my thighs, still play-fully licking my cock.

The words "I love you" are on the tip of my tongue. Gargoyles mate fast and rough. It was only a matter of time once I decided to pursue her. But I don't want to say those special words with her on her knees in front of me. I want to make a big damn deal the first time I say it, because we've been pining for one another for years.

Mir might not have expected or wanted a grovel from me, but she deserves every godsdamned ounce of effort I have to give.

She stands and reaches for her dress straps. "We're gonna be late, Alo, and I've sworn never to be late again."

"Fuck that," I snap, pulling her to me as I lie down on the sofa. I drag her on top of my chest as she laughs.

"There's no time, Alo!"

"I'll make time," I bark back, hauling her on my mouth to suck on that sweet pussy. Her sweet candy scent covers me. She's soaked, honey dripping from her slick folds to tease me. I grip her hips hard, digging my fingers in to help her fuck my face. I snake my tail between her thighs, wetting it with her heat, and then I curl my spade into a cone and slip it inside her.

Miriam grunts and falls forward, hands on the arm of the sofa. Her channel clenches around my spade, and it sends a fresh wave of heat shooting down my spine.

She's so close already. I could come again from touching her.

I growl, slipping my spade all the way in to rub at that sensitive spot along the bottom of her pussy. She throws her head back and grabs one of my horns, using it for leverage as she rocks on and off my tail, fucking herself.

Snarling, I bring both hands to her ass and trail my fingers down the cleft. I want her here soon, but that takes time and prep, and we certainly will be late if we start that right now.

Miriam comes on a scream, my name falling from her lips as wetness floods my neck and chin. I play with that sweet pussy as she flutters and falls apart around me. Her bliss makes me rock hard.

I'll never have enough of this. It'll never be enough to make up for the time we lost, but I'll godsdamn try my best.

A quarter hour later, we drop out of the sky in front of Bad Axe, the axe-throwing bar in Shifter Hollow in the northwest corner of Ever. Wren and Ohken stand there. Ohken looks stoic as ever with one big arm wrapped around his mate. He's showing off his glowy new mating tattoo. Wren barely represses a grin.

When we land and I let Miriam out of my arms, Wren rushes forward to fold her into a big hug. Ohken gives me a knowing look.

I try my best not to look sheepish—we're at least fifteen minutes late. Instead, I lift my chin and watch my woman, loving how at ease she seems. But Miriam's always at ease. Always happy. Always helping others and being a joy in our community. I don't know how she manages to personify a ray of fucking sunshine, but she does it effortlessly.

Wren pulls out of Miriam's embrace and smiles at both of us. "I hope you two don't mind, but I invited Morgan. She's feeling a little..." She waves a hand around as if it'll help her find the word. "Lost," she finishes.

"Of course!" Miriam chirps. "Your sisters are always welcome." She gives Ohken and me a look. "Just remember Morgan doesn't know about my Howl-O-Ween plan, so we can't talk about it while we're here. That's what I decided to call it."

"How original," Wren deadpans.

Miriam slaps her arm. "Hey! Don't laugh! I was gonna call it Human-Ween, but that sounds dirty."

Wren snorts. Then they fall into a fit of giggles together while Ohken and I watch.

Just then, a beat-up Honda pulls into the parking lot on one side of Bad Axe. Morgan hops out, slipping the keys into her back pocket. She glances around the hollow in wonder before joining us, gray eyes wide. "This is fucking incredible! I knew the shifters and centaurs mostly lived away from downtown, but I didn't realize there was *another* downtown here."

Miriam takes Morgan's hand and pulls her across the gravel road. "We'll give you a quick tour before we go in." Wren follows, and Ohken and I trail the girls.

For half an hour, Miriam leads Wren and Morgan along the hollow's main thoroughfare, talking about how the businesses and homes fan out in a spiral away from the hollow's "downtown." The vibe here is far different from the retro vibe of Main Street and downtown Ever. The businesses and homes are all built into giant redwood trees. Everything gives off an earthy, natural feel, and it's all oversized to account for the centaurs and pegasi that live in this part of our haven. Not to mention the shifters when they're in half-shift or full-shift form. They're fucking big.

When the girls stop to peer in the window of a potions shop, Ohken turns to me. "You look happy, friend. Everything good?"

I can't help but grin as Miriam excitedly explains something to the Hectors, her arms waving around in the air.

Turning to Ohken, I nod. "Really good. Pretty much perfect."

He claps me on the shoulder, careful to avoid touching my wings. "I'm glad, Alo. You and Iggy deserve all the happiness."

I sigh. "I feel guilty as hells spending time here and not with him."

Ohken stops and turns, his russet gaze serious. "Alo, it's good for Iggy to spend time away from you. I know Catherine has him tonight, and he adores her. They have a blast playing with the Annabelle. It's not selfish to spend time tending to your happiness."

"Logically I know that," I admit. "But my emotions aren't always in line."

He smiles. "You're hard on yourself; you always have been. It's part of what makes you such an excellent protector—you're wired to go hard and be vigilant. But I hope you recognize that your happiness is fucking important too, and Iggy thrives when you're happy."

I scratch at my chin awkwardly. Ohken and I don't discuss matters of the heart. I feel...squirrelly, like his emotions are infecting me with something dreadfully close to understanding. I'd prefer to grab Mir and shoot up into the sky to be alone with her again. I don't even really talk about feelings with my brother. Ohken seems to read the room, though, and leaves me to join the girls, reminding them we have a reservation for an axe-throwing lane.

Mir jogs back and loops her arm through mine, hanging on to my biceps. She looks up and beams, and I'm lost in her beautiful gaze. "Morgan's very competitive, and I might have talked a little shit just now, so I need you to help me kick her axe." She winks.

I laugh out loud, pulling the back of her hand to lie flat on my chest. "Got it. Team Miriam and Alo for the win."

"I like the sound of that," she chirps, rubbing my forearm with her free hand.

Stepping to the front door of Bad Axe, I grab the giant branch that forms the door handle and pull it open. She glides inside, pulling me along with her.

"I can't stop touching you," she admits. "I didn't even want to let you go to walk through the door."

I pull her to me while Ohken gets us checked in with the hostess, bringing my lips to Miriam's ear. My hand goes to her lower back to play with the dimples there. "I don't want you to ever stop touching me, Mir. Once our triple date is done, I need to take you home and fuck you, pixie girl."

She presses close to me, rubbing her cheek against my mouth. Predatory anticipation coils in my chest, every shred of my focus on the gorgeous pixie leaning against me.

Mir turns with a glint in her eye. "I'm holding you to that, Aloitious." She reaches down and cups my cock through my pants, and it's everything I can do to hold back a groan. Bad Axe is dark inside, and where we're standing, nobody can see her hand on me.

I brush the pad of my thumb across her glossy pink lips. "Naughty girl," I whisper. Mir bites my finger playfully, sending sparks down the backs of my thighs. I resist the urge to cocoon her with my wings and have my way with her right here. There's something seductive about the slow, deep throbbing music playing from somewhere. This place is boisterous and busy, and I don't think a single soul would care if I fucked her right here in front of the hostess stand.

"Table's ready!" barks a muscular shifter hostess to our right.

Mir and I part and laugh, caught like misbehaving teens. The hostess holds back a grin, but Ohken and Wren smirk at us like fools. Normally I'd snark at him not to look at me like that, but I'm too damn happy to be here.

We follow the hostess from the small entryway into a cavernous room. Dozens of round wood tables hold giant flagons of beer and trays of nachos and fries. Rustic chandeliers above our heads swing softly, casting a pale source of light onto the patrons.

A bar to our left is full of clamoring monsters—shifters, centaurs, and pegasi. There's even a miniature-sized section for gnomes. Dozens of the pointy-hatted males crawl over one another to get their drink orders in.

The Hectors stare around in obvious fascination.

"This is so fucking cool," Morgan murmurs, turning to look at Ohken and me. "If I'd known this existed, I would have been here, like, all the time. This vibe is my absolute jam."

"The shifters are welcoming but private," I share. "Info about Shifter Hollow never makes its way into the welcome packet on order of the shifter king."

"Richard?" she asks.

I shake my head. "Richard is the pack alpha here, but their king lives in South America. Technically, he's the alpha of alphas."

She nods and grins. "Well, I love him already. Secret axe-throwing bar? Treehouse village? This place is great!"

Ten minutes later, we're firmly ensconced in our lane. Morgan tosses an axe and hits the damn bullseye.

Wren goes next and misses by a mile, but talks shit to her triplet anyhow.

When it's Miriam's turn, I give her a grin. "Want a quick lesson, pixie girl?"

She nods and pulls me up out of my chair. Someone behind us snickers, but I can't be bothered to turn around and see who's giggling. I grab an axe, feeling its heft in my palm before I hand it to Mir.

She takes it with a tentative look, her grip unsure. I pull her to the yellow line at our end of the lane, guiding her feet into a wider stance. After wrapping one arm around her axe wrist, I lift it and show her the motion.

"When you let go, it should feel a little awkward because you're letting go during the forward motion, not downward. Otherwise, your axe will end up on the floor or in your leg."

Miriam leans into me, glancing up over her shoulder. "I have to confess that the idea of you swinging weapons around makes me horny, Alo."

I groan softly, my cock nestled firmly against her ass. The hand around her waist tightens, my fingers dipping into her jeans. "I've got a weapon for you to handle, Mir. As soon as we get home. Are ready to kick Morgan's ass?"

She snorts out a laugh and shimmies, rubbing her ass against my hips. It's all I can do not to toss the axe away and throw her against the cage walls to have my way with her. Deciding to pursue Miriam is the best thing I've done for myself in years. Satisfaction at being with her warms my belly like Ohken's famous mead.

"Go on," I encourage, stepping out of the way. Miriam's wings flutter carefully down her spine and out of the way of her arm. She leans back, raising the axe, and hurls it with a mighty roar that makes my balls go swollen and heavy. The axe flies down the lane and sinks deep into the bullseye.

She turns with a happy shriek, throwing both hands up in the air as she dances around. I swoop toward her and pull her into my arms, covering her mouth with mine.

I. Can't. Stop. Touching her.

Her plump lips are so soft, so pliable. Her tongue slides easily against mine as her arms go around my neck.

A happy chorus of cries rises up behind us. Miriam pulls from me and turns to look, eyes sparkling.

"Nachos," she whispers. "I fucking love nachos."

I stroke the edge of her wing once before I'm willing to let her go. When we return to our table, a giant plate of nachos sits in the middle. A waitress sets a round of beers down next to it before asking if we need anything else.

A move at the table to our left catches my eye. Richard, the big shifter alpha, raises a glass of mead and gestures at the nachos.

"Thank you," I mouth. He's an integral part of the protector team, but I've never just hung out at his bar like this. Maybe I should bring Iggy here during the day sometime. He'd get a kick out of it.

Richard goes back to his conversation, his second,

Connall, sitting to his right. They look to be deep in discussion about something.

Miriam slides onto the bench seat next to Morgan and digs in.

For an hour, we laugh and talk, and it's…easy. Fun. I barely remember the last time I had fun without Iggy by my side. He's fun all the time, but this is different. It's really fucking nice to be out with adults.

Mir turns to me, holding a nacho to my lips. I lean forward and take it from her fingers, nipping them playfully in the process.

She shifts close enough to stroke my jaw tenderly, her eyes locked with mine. "I'm having a blast, but I miss Iggy."

My heart damn near explodes in my chest at her words. I never thought I could have someone again. Shit, I didn't think I even *wanted* that. And this woman loves my child just like she loves me. I can scarcely believe my luck.

"Aloitious." The Keeper's voice breaks through the haze of my feelings, calling my attention with his sharp tone. I pull away from Miriam with a scowl to find him standing next to Morgan, Wren, and Ohken, both hands folded behind his back. He's not smiling.

"What's wrong?" I bark. My battle spines slip out along my tail and forearms. When Miriam drops her hold on my neck, spines slip out of my shoulders too.

"Evenia just comm'd me," he says, his tone laced with irritation. "The Hearth HQ hunter team will be arriving momentarily. We're expected to greet them." He glances at Ohken before returning his focus to me. "Shepherd and Thea are meeting us at the portal station."

Disappointment churns in my gut. Date night is over, but Miriam simply threads her fingers through mine, her expression worried but resolute.

"Let's go," she encourages.

Wren and Ohken head for the door. The Keeper looks at Morgan and lifts a pale hand. "After you." For a second, I'd swear she's about to say something, but she crosses her arms and follows her triplet toward the front of the bar.

Bad Axe still rages around us, but a sour taste fills my mouth. When Miriam and I join the Keeper, he gives me a warning look.

"We knew this was probably coming, Alo. We'll be…helpful." He looks disgusted by the word.

"Of course we will," chirps Miriam. "But secretly we'll probably hate them." She rubs my arm in solidarity.

Hunter teams don't have the most positive of histories with the haven system. Historically, they put their quarry first at the expense of whatever haven they're ostensibly there to protect. Whole havens had to rebuild their wards and defenses in the early days because hunter teams were so careless in their pursuit of thralls and wayward monsters.

Needless to say, if we could have gotten out of having a hunter team here, that would have been my preference.

They haven't even stepped out of the portal yet, and I *already* hate them.

CHAPTER FOURTEEN

MIRIAM

O ur group is tense as we leave Bad Axe and head up the hollow's main drag. Alo holds my hand tightly, but when I look up, he's distracted. His focus shifts from side to side as if some threat might appear from behind a tree. His battle spines have sunk back into his skin, but his eyes are narrowed, nostrils flared. He holds his wings slightly aloft, the deadly talons ready to sink into some unseen foe.

He's in full-on protector mode, and I'd find it hot if he didn't seem to dread the hunter team's arrival.

I had hoped Evenia would forget about her threat to send a second Keeper and a Hearth hunter team to our little corner of the monster world, but it seems we're not that lucky. We don't *need* another Keeper because we've already got the best one. And a hunter team just means everybody in town will be uneasy. Hunters mean hellhounds, and there have never been hellhounds in Ever as long as I've lived here, which is my whole adult life.

We follow the street through the black woods, hiking silently for half a mile before we come to a large building in the middle of the forest. It almost looks like a human train station minus the tracks. The Keeper pulls the front door open, and we enter. Inside, a lone attendant sits inside a ticketing booth. Behind him, rows of bench seating fill the tiled floor of the otherwise empty structure. He rises, stepping out of the boxy compartment.

Clip-clopping out of the booth, he joins us with arms crossed, nodding respectfully at the Keeper. "I'm expecting the team momentarily, Keeper." His tail swishes in a lazy arc behind his back legs.

The Keeper dips his head at the elderly centaur, acknowledging what he said. When he turns to cross the expansive room, the rest of us follow. The back wall is a gigantic, shimmery rectangle.

The portal.

Morgan stops beside me, peering up. "What's that thing?"

Wren leaves Ohken's side and joins us, slinging an arm around her sister. They both look at me expectantly.

I point at the shimmery surface. "That's the portal. Each haven is connected to one other through the portal system."

"And there's a secondary backup portal in the event of catastrophic haven failure," Shepherd adds.

Thea joins us, looking up at her mate. "Hel Motel, right? That's what you meant when we met, and you said the motel was a gateway to Hel?"

"Yeah," he agrees. "Hel Motel has its own portal to Hel haven in Singapore."

The Keeper turns to look at us, arms still crossed. "The portal system is how goods make their way between havens, and it's how monsters travel between them as well. This portal is how everyone came for the skyball final, for instance."

"How does it work?" Morgan glances at him, her expression curious.

Footsteps echo across the quiet room as Richard joins us. He gives the Keeper a sharp look, and I know what he's saying. Catherine painted all of this into existence, but very few people know about it. We shouldn't speak of it in front of the attendant.

The Keeper uncrosses his arms, slipping his hands into his pockets. "The portal system is simply part of the haven system itself. Nobody's really sure how it works. It just does."

"God," Morgan snipes. "Does anyone ever disappear along the way?"

Richard joins the Keeper with a toothy grin. "Hasn't happened yet. Might be nice if it happened tonight, though."

Morgan opens her mouth to say something, but the portal's opalescent surface shimmers, sending a wave of energy crackling into the room. It whooshes over us in a stiff, warm wind.

"Here we fucking go," Alo mutters. He leans over and kisses my forehead, then rounds the group to stand with Richard, the Keeper, and Ohken. Shepherd joins them, wings held aloft, the sharp points directed at the portal.

The shimmering portal's surface morphs into big rolling waves that travel from one side of the wall to the other. Pale blue depths begin to reveal the shadow of a group that slowly becomes clearer as they walk toward us. One of the figures is incredibly tall, likely a centaur or pegasus. The other two are big and brawny. But by their side, three smaller shadows slink into view.

My blood freezes to ice, goose bumps prickling painfully to the surface of my skin. All the hair on my nape lifts, and time slows as I attempt to catch my breath.

Three hellhounds come through the portal first, stepping into the room with quiet focus, their wolflike heads swiveling around. I haven't seen one since I was a child.

Seeing one now brings the memory of my last experience crashing down on top of me.

I remember my family fleeing through the forest to escape a pack of thralls. We had been on our way to a newly created haven, but we didn't make it in time. Hellhounds chased the thralls who chased us, but we got caught up in the fight. The thralls ripped my parents apart while fighting the hellhounds.

The three in front of me now split in different directions. One rocks back onto its haunches at the front of its group. The others jog to the side and stand at attention. They're just as horrifying as I remember—cracked black skin with sparse black fur. What looks like rivers of lava travel underneath the openings in their skin. Their eyes glow red, seemingly lit from within by fire. I suppose they sort of look like wolves, but much more horrible.

The Hectors are frozen next to me, until Morgan says, "What in the actual fuck are those?"

I can't find my breath to respond.

The monsters come through the portal next—a stunning female pegasus, a surly-looking rock troll, and lastly, a striking sylph with brilliant blue hair. I blink and try to rip my focus from the hellhounds.

The hounds won't hurt me. They're not here for me. They won't hurt me.

I cling to that mantra in my head, desperately grasping for control of my pounding heartbeat.

The sylph steps forward, jerking his chin at the Keeper. He wears a haughty look, which doesn't surprise me considering who sent him here.

"You must be Evenia's kid, eh?" He's got a strong brogue, so I'd place him from one of the UK-based havens. He's handsome like all sylphs, tall and muscular like Alo but blue everywhere. His skin is the color of the sky, his hair a darker shade. It waves above his scalp like blue flames. Navy lightning seems to flash across his skin as ice-blue eyes narrow.

The Keeper clears his throat. "You may address me as Keeper, just like in every other haven. Leave Evenia out of it."

The male shrugs and casts a dismissive glance over our group, stopping when his eyes land on me. He licks his midnight-blue lips once, slowly grinning before he turns back. "Ah, well, yer mother's involved in basically everything. Hard to remove her from the equation."

The Keeper doesn't address that, but instead gestures at our protector team. "Meet Alo and Shepherd from the team. The bridge troll to my right is Ohken, and you'll know Richard already, of course."

The sylph glances around as he places his hand over a round disk on his chest. "I'm Dirk. Elena's to my right, Grent to the left." His gaze finds me again, his mouth forming a mischievous grin. "And who're you, lovely lass?"

I smile politely, but I'm not playing this flirty game with him. I'm far too on edge watching one of the hellhounds stalk forward to join him.

"Miriam." I wave hello, then gesture at the Hectors to get my mind off the soft pad of the hound's paws as it crosses to the sylph. "Wren, Thea, and Morgan."

"What are you?" Morgan asks, stepping in front of her sisters. She's always the protective one, always the first to guard the other two. It's funny since Thea's the witch with protective power, but she seems to understand Morgan's need to do this, and watches her sister carefully.

"Sylph, darlin'," Dirk croons. He's got knives strapped to both thick thighs and two crisscrossed leather straps over his chest. He slaps the circular disk that holds them together and disappears into thin air. Where he stood, there's only the faint outline of a male. He zips around the room, sending a breeze cascading off the walls to whip our hair up.

The moment he tunnels between me and Wren, wind kisses the sensitive skin between my wings. It causes me to shudder, and Alo appears at my side in a second, looking down at me.

"Mir, you okay?" His dark eyes narrow in concern. He brings one hand to the small of my back and strokes. That move helps me focus on him, and my breathing slows.

The sylph reappears in front of our group, one side of his mouth curled up into a satisfied-looking grin. The pegasus matches his expression, and the rock troll glares like we might be the ones hiding Wesley.

The Keeper shoots the hunters a neutral look. "You'll be staying with Catherine at the Annabelle Inn. Alo's next door if anything comes up. Keep the hounds out of the house; the Inn won't like them inside. I've scheduled a meeting for us to debrief in the morning. I'll show you the monitoring system and share a few of the ideas we've had about what Wesley could be doing."

These monsters are going to be at the Annabelle Inn? I can't imagine the sylph and his hounds living across the street from me. I'm uncomfortable, my skin hot and prickly at the idea of him being right there. If the hellhounds aren't allowed inside the inn, that means they'll sleep *outside,* which puts them right outside my damn door. Ugh.

Dirk gives the Keeper a dismissive look. "I've a map of the haven. We'll find our way to the inn ourselves. I'd like to look around a bit."

"As you wish." The Keeper jerks his head toward the door. "Don't let the hounds in any of the businesses. My people will be uncomfortable."

Alo slides his arm around my waist, his fingers stroking my skin gently.

Dirk stalks toward the Keeper, nearly butting against him with his chest. "We'll go where we must, Keeper. No place is immune from our inspection. The goal is to find Wesley, not worry over yer comfort."

"Wesley is not inside this haven," the Keeper snaps. "And if you upset my people during the course of your"—he makes air quotes with his fingers—"hunting, you'll have me to deal with."

Dirk grins, but it's not friendly in the slightest. It's the sneer of a predator distracting you so his friend can slash your throat. "Evenia said yeh'd be difficult. Do I need to call your mummy, Keeper?"

Our Keeper returns the sneer and bridges the gap between them, cocking his head to the side until his fangs nearly touch the big sylph's mouth. "Call her if you want, hunter. But here, *I* am the law. This is *my* haven. These are *my* people. And I'll do whatever the fuck I have to in order to keep them safe and happy."

For a tense beat, neither male backs down. My heart rate speeds up again because the hellhounds all stand at attention, focused on Dirk and the Keeper. The hair along their backs rises as soft growls fill the air.

Long seconds later, Dirk chuckles and jerks his head to the door, addressing his team. "Spread out; take the hounds. Meet at the inn and report back."

The pegasus snorts and shakes her head, sending a wave of dark red hair cascading down her back. That's when I notice the row of spikes that ring each of her shiny thick hooves. Gods, she's danger personified.

I gulp.

With a quick purse of her lips, she kisses at one of the hounds, slapping her horse shoulder. She says nothing to us as she trots out of the building. The rock troll follows, skirting our group while he examines the building itself.

It's as if they expect to see Wesley pop out of any corner. A second hellhound trails after the rock troll, padding quietly around us. Its flaming eyes land on me, and I have to force myself to look away so I don't relive the horrors of my childhood.

There's a whoosh of wind, and then Dirk stands in front of me with his finger under my chin, tilting my head up. Next to me, Alo snarls, but the sylph ignores it.

I press against Alo and swat Dirk's hand aside.

He chuckles. "Don't let the hounds scare yeh, my pixie sweet." He points at the remaining hellhound, who stands in front of Thea, snuffling her legs. Thea's frozen, staring down at the hound's huge head in obvious concern.

Dirk flicks a finger toward the dog. "That's Minnie. She's preggers, so she's suddenly interested in everyone. She won't hurt yeh, unless she senses yeh're dangerous. Then she'll rip yeh apart starting with your belly."

Nobody says a damn word. We just watch the dog sniff her way up Thea's thigh. Shepherd rounds the group slowly, wings poised to help his mate if she needs it.

Dirk whistles a series of tones at the hound. The sound pulls her attention from Thea. When she trots through our group, the Hectors split in different directions to give the dog a wide berth. She casually glances up at me when she passes, and I see my whole life reflected in those flaming eyes.

Am I even breathing? I can't tell.

The hellhound moves past us and follows Dirk out the door, and then they're gone.

The Keeper lets out an exasperated sigh and crosses the room, addressing the pack alpha. "Richard, keep an eye on them out here. The pegasi and centaurs won't like hellhounds in the forest."

"On it," Richard purrs. "I hate that they're here, but Dirk is renowned in hunter circles. We're lucky it's him and not some of the others."

The Keeper frowns. "I'll consider myself lucky if they locate Wesley and we can put this whole issue to bed."

A muscle twitches in Richard's jaw as he purses his lips.

The Keeper comes over, putting a hand on my shoulder. I'm still frozen in place, still forcing every breath into lungs that feel constricted.

"Miriam, are you alright?" His deep voice breaks me out of my trance, and I look up, eyelashes fluttering.

"Yeah," I chirp on autopilot. "Peachy."

It's a lie. I know it, and he knows it, because he's one of the few people in Ever who knows my whole backstory. He brought me here, after all.

He doesn't call out my obvious fib.

"Find me if you need me," he offers instead. "Anytime, I mean it."

Alo stands quietly next to me, his thumb still stroking a path along my side. He doesn't know about my parents and the hellhounds, and I don't want to talk about it in front of a room full of people.

The Keeper glances over at the Hectors. "Steer clear of the sylph. He'll use his invisibility and command of the air to get under your skin." His ruby-red eyes travel to Morgan, and I'd swear his harsh expression softens slightly. "Watch your back, okay?"

The Hectors nod, and then our group splits up. Date night is over. The good feels are over. All I want to do is go home and hide in my bed to get the vision of those glowing flame eyes out of my mind.

Alo lets go of me to speak with the protector team. I'm still painfully frozen in place, like if I take a single step, I might crack into a million pieces. When he returns, his finger tilting my chin up to face him, the world fades away.

"Mir, you okay?"

"No," I admit, pressing my forehead to his chest. No

steadily thumping heartbeat greets me. His heart is silent. And somehow, today, that hurts. "I don't want to talk about it," I mumble into his shirt.

He runs a hand up my back. "Okay. Want me to take you home? I can grab Iggy while we're out."

I nod, and he scoops me into his arms and carries me outside. I wave to Wren, my soulfriend, who gives me a sad look that says I'll need to clue her in later. I'm sure my behavior looks weird to everyone else. I just...I can't talk about it right now.

I say nothing when Alo pushes off the ground and bullets into the sky. He keeps me tucked to his chest, grabbing a current and zipping toward the community garden. When we alight just outside the entry, he carefully sets me down.

"Mir," he murmurs, sliding his thick fingers up my neck. He pulls me close for a hug. "You ready to talk to me, pixie girl?"

I can't. I can't relive my parents' death right now. I need to sit with it.

"I—I'm not ready," I admit, wrapping my arms around my core like I might be able to protect myself from the horrible memories.

"Okay." He strokes my back with one hand while his other grips the back of my neck and arches me into him. When his mouth comes over mine, the press of his tongue lights me up. His lips are soft and tender. It's the slow kiss of a male learning every inch of me, and I can't resist slipping my hands up his shirt to touch the dips and grooves of his stomach. He feels like home, and I'm in desperate need of that.

I want him to make me forget the last half hour.

He lets out a low moan, but an excited-sounding shriek across the street echoes toward us.

Iggy.

He must have seen us out of the Annabelle's windows.

"Dad! Miriam!" he shouts, zooming out the front of the Annabelle and toward us. He barrels into his father's arms, crawling all over Alo's head and holding his horns like handlebars.

Iggy shoots me a big smile. "Did Dad just kiss you? Are you his girlfriend now?"

That pulls a grin to my face, and I open my arms. "Come here, bestie. I could use a hug."

Iggy leaps off Alo's head and throws his chubby arms around my neck, snuffling against my ear. "You smell weird, Miriam. What's that smell?"

I laugh, some of the pressure dissipating from my lungs. "Probably the axe-throwing bar we went to."

"Awww," Iggy whines and pulls back, giving me a disappointed look. "I wanna do axe-throwing!"

"Definitely when you're older." Alo laughs and rubs his son's back, looking at me over Iggy's shoulder. He still looks concerned.

Iggy yawns and snuggles me, wrapping his tail around my waist. I rock him from side to side as I play with the BFFs bracelet on his wrist. Moments later, soft snores ring in my ear.

Alo holds his arms out, and I transfer Iggy cautiously into them. He places Iggy against his chest, stroking his back, but those dark eyes are focused on me.

"I'm here for you, Miriam. Always. You know that, right? If there's anything you want to tell me about why those hounds bothered you..." He's giving me an opening to share, but I find I just...can't.

"You saw that, huh?" My tone is wry, but I'm too wrung out to care.

"I see everything, pixie girl," he whispers, leaning down to kiss my forehead. "And I don't want you to have a single moment of sadness, so if I can chase that away, tell me."

It's on the tip of my tongue to blurt out everything, but I don't have the energy to go into it tonight.

"Another time," I say, patting his forearm. "See ya later?" I'm deflecting, and we both know it, but I'm eternally grateful when he doesn't push for more info.

"Later," he agrees.

But he waits in the garden entrance until I get to my gourd, and I can feel his eyes on me the entire time.

The following morning, I'm seated at the desk in the corner of my bedroom, looking out into the community garden. The tiny-fied pages on my desk are covered with sketches of jack-o'-lanterns and creepy trees and giant black-and-orange archways. I've just about got everything designed for my Howl-O-Ween surprise. I'm meeting Wren and the Keeper in the morning to talk through how she can use her green magic to help me build some of the glamour in secret.

The scent of freshly baked cookies wafts through the open window.

"Alo," I murmur, my stomach filling with butterflies. I don't know if that sensation will ever fade. I jump up and head for the front door, yanking it open and stepping onto my small platform porch.

He stands outside, one hand raised to rap with a knuckle. In his other, there's a plate of white chocolate macadamia nut cookies. "Heard me, huh?"

"Smelled you coming from a mile away," I tease, crossing my arms and leaning against the doorframe.

Alo dips his head and peeks into my gourd. "Wanna dust me and let me in, pixie girl?"

A chill sweeps through me. Alo's never been inside my

gourd. It's a deeply personal space for a pixie. The only nonpixies who've been in here are Iggy, Kevin and Wren.

I grin and step back inside my door to where I keep a small bowl of pixie dust. Every pixie home has one for situations like this where a guest has no small form. Rejoining Alo outside, I gesture for him to come closer.

"Close your eyes so it doesn't irritate them," I warn. He leans down, and I blow the dust directly in his face.

Chocolate eyes open back up, and he winks devilishly. There's a loud pop, and his body shrinks down to a small form. A fraction of a second later, he swoops onto my porch, still towering over me.

He alights gracefully on the platform and hands me the tray of cookies. "For you, Mir."

I take them and return inside, crossing toward the kitchen. I pause only when I realize he's not right behind me.

But gods, what I see steals the breath from my lungs. Alo leans into the doorway, both hands on the frame above his head. His eyes were down, but they snap back up when I catch him.

"Alo," I snark. "Were you staring at my ass?"

His sexy grin grows bigger until I can see both fangs and all of his teeth. "Ass. Legs. Wings. Back. I'm staring at all of it, Miriam."

I set the cookies down on my pink kitchen counter, then turn to face him, propping my elbows on the countertop.

Alo stalks into the room, crossing it with confident steps until his body presses to mine. His lips hover above my mouth, teasing me. He reaches out to stroke a stray hair from my forehead.

"Talk to me about why the sylph upset you," he whispers. "What happened last night?"

I wrap an arm around his waist. The other comes to his shirt, fiddling with the soft fabric. After a long, quiet moment,

I look up. He looks so sincere. He shared his sorrowful past with me; it's only right I do the same with mine.

One of Alo's hands slides up my back to grip my neck. I anchor on his touch, letting his strength seep into me, reinforcing everything that feels so tender from seeing the hellhounds.

"We don't have to talk about it if you don't want to." The deep bass of his voice slides down my body like the softest of silks, soothing my frayed edges.

"I had planned on discussing this with you eventually," I admit. "But I guess I put it off because I was having fun with you, and I didn't want to bring the mood down."

Alo's hand on my neck tightens, and he arches me backward to look at him. "Your life and past are not an inconvenience, Miriam. Give me the good and bad and everything in between. Don't hold back." There's steel in his voice now, like he's trying to tattoo those words onto my heart. And, damnit, it works.

"It's not the sylph who upset me," I whisper. "It was the hellhounds."

His brows work down into a confused vee as his hand strokes my back. He lifts me onto the countertop and parts my thighs, stepping between them. Big knuckles gently caress my jawline.

"Tell me. I want to know everything about you." His gaze goes soft. "If you're willing to share."

I pick at the soft fabric of his tee but eventually let out a big sigh and look up. He deserves to know. He's told me so much about his life over the last five years.

"When I was a child, my parents and I lived outside a haven. My folks didn't agree with the haven system, and so we lived in a big pixie community about ten miles from the closest one."

I suck in a breath, but Alo wraps both arms around me.

The breath steadies me enough to continue, even as my heart pinches in my chest reliving this for the second time in a twenty-four-hour period.

"Our pixie tree was attacked by thralls, something unheard of in our area, but we knew they had been sniffing around. My father thought they were attracted by the haven itself, because we'd never seen them before. In any case—" Tears clog my throat. It's like I'm there all over again.

My voice breaks. "We, uh...we tried to fight them, but we couldn't. There were simply too many, so my father pushed my mother and me outside, and we flew into the trees."

Alo's arms tighten around me, and he brings his forehead to mine. "Miriam," he murmurs.

But now that I've started telling him the story, I can't stop.

"Mom and I stayed in small form because it was harder for the thralls to track us. The haven had a team of hellhounds who came into the forest to eliminate them. But they didn't see us in small form, and they knocked us apart when they clashed with the thralls. Mother fell to the ground and popped into large form. I watched the thralls circle her, and Father couldn't watch her die so he joined the hellhounds in the fight. There were just so many," I whisper finally. "My parents were in the wrong place at the wrong time."

I look up at Alo. "Father wasn't a fighter and he died trying to protect her." The tears come heavy and hard. Alo's brows furrow.

"They died protecting me," I whisper. "And each other. And when I saw those hellhounds, that's all I could think of."

Alo swipes his lips over mine gently, tenderly. "Mir, I'm so godsdamned sorry. I never knew. I just knew you'd been in Ever a long time, but not how you came to be here."

I nod. "Yeah. The haven took those of us who escaped in, but I couldn't bear to be there. So, when I heard about an upstart Keeper in a diverse haven with a large pixie community, I comm'd him, and we talked for a long time. After that, I knew Ever was what I wanted. I came here and fell in love with this place, just like he said I would."

"Thank you for telling me," he whispers. "I wish I had something to share with you in return, but you already know everything about me."

"Not everything," I whisper. "There's something I want to know, but I've been afraid to ask you."

Nerves jangle and clang in my stomach, both from sharing and from what I'm about to ask.

"Oh?" His brows curl upward, both hands moving to stroke the tops of my thighs. "I'll tell you anything. Ask me whatever you want, pixie girl."

My heart beats like a war drum in my chest. I fidget with my hands before returning them flat to his silent chest. I pat his pec once before looking up. "Do you think this could ever beat for me, Alo?"

You could hear a pin drop in my gourd. One of Alo's big fingers comes underneath my chin, and he holds my gaze firmly locked to his.

"Yes, Miriam." His voice goes low like boulders tumbling from his throat. "It will, because I'm head over heels for you." He slides my hands up around his neck, hovering those beautiful, arrogant lips over mine. "Who feeds you, Miriam?"

"You," I whisper.

"That's right. And who takes care of things you need?"

"You."

"Who's going to be your kick-ass Howl-O-Ween assistant for this enormous party?"

"You?" I question hopefully.

"I'll even dress up," he offers. "Whatever will bring a smile to your face is what I want, Miriam. But on the days you can't smile, I want to be your safe space. Are we in agreement, pixie girl?"

"Yes," I whisper. "Abso-fucking-lutely."

"Speaking of fucking," he murmurs. "Who makes you come, Mir?"

"You." I laugh. "And most definitely not Dirk the sylph."

Alo's eyes go hooded, his lips curling into a sneer. "I hate that he looked at you like he had a chance with you, and if it wasn't my job to protect this place, I'd challenge him for being stupid."

"Sounds hot," I admit. "But all I need is you, Alo."

"Good," he croons. "Because I want to fuck those tears away, Miriam. What do you think?"

What do I think? I think anything Alo wanted to do would be fine with me. But his idea is perfect too.

CHAPTER FIFTEEN

ALO

An hour later, Miriam flops off me with a groan, throwing an arm and leg over my torso.

"Thank you," she mumbles into my chest, her wings fluttering tiredly at her back.

I roll her carefully, adjusting her wings against her spine before I plant a row of kisses between her breasts and down her stomach. My eyes move up to hers as she shifts onto her elbows.

"I love you, Miriam." The words feel perfect, not just for this moment, but for the well of emotions she's dug in my soul.

"I love you too, Alo," she whispers back, her lips pulling into a joyous grin.

My comm watch pings, and we groan together.

I lift it up.

The Keeper.

I direct the watch to answer him.

"Alo." His tone is as brusque as ever. "The hunter team has done an initial assessment, and they'd like to meet the protector team at my place in half an hour. I need you here."

He clicks off without another word.

I slide carefully off Miriam, kissing my way as I go. "Duty calls, pixie girl."

She follows me out of the bed and pulls her clothing back on, her expression shuttered. "I hope it doesn't affect your work, you know, what I told you just now." She nibbles at her thumbnail.

"I already wanted to rip the sylph's head off," I remind her. "But I promise to be a pro. They're here to help, technically." I tack that last bit on at the end. Technically, they *are* here to help us by locating Wesley and neutralizing him.

She gives me a kiss and escorts me to the door, blowing more dust in my face to make me big again. I wave at her and turn to leave, but I feel her eyes on me while I go.

Turning, I give her a seductive look. Gods, I could easily go five more rounds with her just to get that frown off her face.

"I don't like leaving you," I admit, stalking back to her gourd.

She grins and looks around to see if any of her neighbors are out, but the A-frame is silent. "I'd have to kick you out anyhow because I'm working this afternoon, and I refuse to be late. Screw Ezazel."

"Indeed," I deadpan. "And if he says another fucking word to you about that—"

"I've got it, Alo." She laughs. "Go fight bigger fights for us, okay?" She bats her eyes. "My love…"

My love. Those words sound so good from her lips. I shouldn't touch her when she's in small form, which is probably a good thing. Because when I touch Miriam, my plans and schedules go out the window.

Smiling, I leave the garden and nearly stumble over the back of one of the hellhounds—the big female who sniffed Miriam and the Hectors.

My lips curl into a snarl, wings flaring wide with the spines pointed at her.

To my surprise, she doesn't bristle like most hellhounds do. Instead, she plops her ass on the ground, tongue lolling out of her mouth.

Weirdo.

Well, Dirk said she was pregnant, so maybe she's just tired? I can certainly empathize with that.

It's disconcerting.

"Shoo!" I wave my hands at her. She gives me a look of irritation but stands and heads for the garden gateway. "Hells no," I snap, flaring my wings to cover the space.

She jerks her head back and growls at me, but when I shake my head again, she slinks off in the opposite direction, sniffing at the shrubs.

"Asshole," I mutter under my breath. After learning what I did about Miriam just now, I don't want those hounds anywhere near her. Their presence upsets her, and that makes me unbelievably angry.

I watch the hellhound disappear up Sycamore toward Main, and when I'm confident she's not coming back, I press off the ground. Zipping up through a cloud, I grab a current that runs along the town's bubble-shaped ward and bullet toward the Keeper's castle on the far west side of Ever.

By the time I drop out of the sky, Shepherd's already standing out front with his arms crossed. He shuffles his wings in apparent irritation and gestures toward the Keeper's front doors. "*They're* here, and the damn hellhounds went inside too. I hate it; they're so fucking creepy."

'They're not all in the house," I mutter. "I found one of them trying to get into the garden."

"That's ridiculous," Shepherd barks. "Wesley's not hiding in the godsdamned garden."

"Tell her that," I mutter. "I shooed her away, but I suspect she'll be back."

Shepherd's look of irritation fades. "Maybe she scents the thrall that attacked the moonflower vine. What if it, I don't know…left something behind?"

I cock my head to the side, considering that angle. "It's possible, I suppose?" Shaking my head to dispel an army of colliding thoughts, I open one of the front doors for my younger brother.

"How's Miriam, by the way?" he asks while we pace through the darkly gothic halls to the Keeper's comm room.

"Perfect." I say it with a smile, because she is. Abso-fuck-ing-lutely perfect.

"I mean after last night," he prompts. "She seemed pretty distressed when we were leaving."

I glance over. "She doesn't love the hellhounds, but I think it'll be alright. I'll tell you more later." I jerk my head toward the door at the end of the hall, giving him the older brother "not now" look.

He nods and jogs up the hall, swinging the door open and sailing through with his wings tightly tucked. The entire hunter team and the other two hellhounds are gathered with the Keeper, Richard and Ohken.

The sylph, Dirk, turns to me with glacial-blue eyes. He casts a quick glance over us before turning to the Keeper. "This is it, then? Are yeh expectin' anyone else? Perhaps a parade o'gnomes to stuff the room a bit fuller?"

"Nope," the Keeper chirps sarcastically.

Dirk claps his pale blue hands together, then opens his arms wide. "I'll be direct. We've walked every mile of this haven, and Wesley's not here."

"No shit," I bark, unable to hold my tongue.

The Keeper clears his throat, his expression telling me to cool down.

I can't find it in me to give the sylph an apologetic look, though. Instead, I point out the obvious. "We know he's not here; we told you that already. No one in Ever would harbor him."

"Maybe not," Dirk counters, "but we had tae be certain because the alternative is something we'd rather not be the case."

The Keeper shifts forward, intent on the big hunter. "Speak plainly, Dirk."

Dirk's expression grows more serious, blue brows pulling into a vee over those shocking eyes. "Yeh know the haven system was originally painted into existence by yer very own Catherine, but additional havens are now created by Hearth HQ."

"Right." The Keeper rolls his hand in a circular motion, encouraging Dirk to get to the godsdamn point.

The sylph frowns. "We believe Wesley might have developed a spell to create a haven and link it to our system."

"The fuck?!" I blurt it out at the same time my brother flares his wings wide, stepping his feet into a protective stance.

"But," I sputter, "he'd need access to Catherine's original paintings at HQ in order to link anything to our system. That's..." I trail off to run both hands through my hair. Wesley can't have access to the paintings, or he could simply destroy them and the havens. So how's he managing it, if this is truly what's happening?

Dirk looks at us. "Right. Horrifying, I know. We aren't sure, but there have been several odd incidents at HQ, which I'm not at liberty to expand on. Suffice to say, we believe he's figured out how to connect havens, meaning he could be living just outside of Ever, and yeh'd be none the wiser."

"That consideration is horribly disconcerting," Ohken says when the rest of us fall silent.

The Keeper crosses his arms. "If you won't provide details on what happened at HQ, I'll call Evenia. I need to know what's going on in order to help."

Dirk cuts him a sarcastic grin and bows slightly. "Do what yeh will, Keeper. Yer mother might tell yeh, but I don't have the freedom tae do so."

His two partners stand silently.

I turn to Ohken and the Keeper. "How hard would it be to reformat the ward monitoring system to look for any anomalies?"

Richard shifts up off the box he was leaning against, crossing his muscular arms over his chest. "It's a very unique magic that allows havens to portal together. Could the monitoring system be reformatted to look for the same wavelength of magic?"

The castle shudders around us, and the Keeper glances up at the ceiling like he's thinking. Finally, he sighs. "It can be done, but I don't know if it'll be done quickly. Ohken and I built this system long ago, and it's very comprehensive, but this is a big ask of it."

The castle shudders again, and he throws both hands up in the air. "Okay, I get it. I'm just saying this is a lot. But of course we'll try it. Calm down." He rolls his eyes and recrosses his arms, looking over at the beefy bridge troll. "How quickly can you work on this with me?"

Ohken unbuttons his long shirt sleeves and rolls them up to his elbows. "Now, Keeper. This is of the utmost importance. I'll stay until we get a working prototype."

Dirk turns to Shepherd, Richard, and me. "It's possible this isn't what Wesley's doing, that he is simply this well organized. But I think that's unlikely. We need yer help doing visual monitoring. I need—"

"We do this already," I break in. "What would we be looking for that's different?"

Dirk's lip curls up. "A different color tae the wards. An odd sheen. Anything out of the ordinary at all."

"So not necessarily something that looks like the portal in Shifter Hollow?" Richard looks between us. "Could they be using the portal at the motel?"

The Keeper shakes his head. "The wraiths are odd, but their connection to the motel's portal runs deep. I don't think it's even possible for another portal to be close to theirs. They're very"—he casts around for the right word—"protective."

Dirk nods slowly. "As I said, I can't share anything about recent events at Hearth HQ, but it's my opinion we should have caught Wesley before now. This isn't his first attack in recent months."

"You're kidding." The Keeper's red eyes flash in the low light. "Are you saying he actually attacked HQ?"

Dirk glances at his teammates and licks his lips. "I'm saying that perhaps Wesley is still out there because Hearth HQ sits in their glittering towers safe and sound and only gets involved when they need tae save face."

The Keeper scoffs. "Sounds like Evenia."

Dirk nods slowly. "I've no love lost for my employer, clearly. I mention it only because yeh're in a position to ask for details I cannae give yeh. A magic binds all hunter teams to a certain amount of secrecy, but it's my opinion yeh could be more helpful with all the information."

"Fuck," Shepherd murmurs. He looks up at the big sylph. "Thanks, man. We'll dig where we can."

The Keeper stares at the wall as if the weight of the world sits on his shoulders. And I suppose it does, to a degree. He's responsible for this place, although he's obviously not without help.

Two of the three hunters leave the room, but Dirk stops

next to me. "Met yer son today at the school. We were examining the classrooms. Quite a lad yeh've got."

A vicious snarl rises in my throat. I hate the idea of a hunter anywhere close to my child. "Tell me you didn't take hellhounds into the godsdamn school."

Dirk shrugs noncommittally. "Aww, they're not dangerous. Just a little bit misunderstood, I reckon." He cuts me a snide look. "And what about that pretty little pixie from last night? She didn't seem too taken with my hounds. Thought I might pay her a little visit tae check in."

I bristle at that. "You're here for a *job*, hunter."

"Ach." He laughs. "But I can always make friends while I'm here. Evenia's always tellin' me tae do a better job of that."

"Steer clear of Miriam and Iggy," I command, bumping his chest with mine.

Dirk falls back in a fake faint. "Yeh wound me, Aloitious Rygold. If yeh're not mated, and I can steal her, she was never yers to begin with."

I growl, but the big sylph slaps the disk in the middle of his chest armor and disappears into a puff of pale blue smoke.

CHAPTER SIXTEEN

MIRIAM

I'm behind the counter in the sweets shop, having just finished my dust shift at the factory when the door swings open. Iggy zips through, flying across the store and landing on the countertop in front of me. He doesn't bother with a greeting. Instead, he throws both tiny hands flat against his cheeks. "Miriam! I met a sylph today! Can you believe it? And a hellhound! It was kind of nice, even though Dad says they're dangerous, and—"

"Wait a sec," I stop him. "You met the hunter team and the hounds? How? Were they at school?'

I'm horrified. I wonder if Alo knows about this.

When I cross my arms, Iggy matches my stance, tail lashing from side to side. "Aww, Miriam, don't be like that. They seemed nice! And the dog was—"

"Dangerous, honey," I bark more harshly than I mean to. "Hellhounds can be really dangerous, Iggy. They go after their target, and it doesn't matter who gets in the way. If you got between a hellhound and a thrall, you could get hurt. Promise me you won't go near them."

He shrugs and glances at the door, which swings open a second time. A flaming dark head comes through, followed by the rest of a hellhound's lanky but muscular body. It pauses in the doorway, nose lifted to drink in the store's many smells.

It steps gracefully into the shop, and the air leaves my lungs in a whoosh. One of my customers drops a whole plastic jar of color-changing gumballs and edges away from the dog.

I'm too terrified to complain about it scaring my customers away. I pray one of the hunters shows up and gets it. I lift my hand to comm Alo and ask if he can get the hunter team to come retrieve their hound.

"Aww," Iggy gushes, hopping off the counter. I grab for his tail, but he's across the store before I can stop him. I leap over the countertop, but he's already stopped right in front of the damn hellhound's face, reaching out to ruffle her ears.

"Iggy, no!" I shout, but to my surprise, the dog's tongue rolls out of her mouth, and she cocks her head to the side, leaning into his touch.

"She likes me!" he says excitedly. "This is the one I saw earlier at school. She was with Dirk, sniffing around looking for portals or something."

That doesn't make sense. Portals at the school? I make a mental note to ask Alo about it as soon as possible.

I inch toward Iggy and grab his tail, pulling him slowly away from the dog. I don't trust her at all, but she sits on her great big haunches and watches us, flames dancing in her red eyes. Her swollen belly hangs onto the ground. She looks horribly uncomfortable.

Not that I care. Not at all.

Iggy crawls up my arm and settles on my shoulder, wrapping his tail around my neck. "Did you know hellhounds only bond with one person? Dirk found her when she was just a puppy, but I kinda think she likes me too."

"Okay," I hedge. I don't want to burst his bubble, and I don't really know much about hellhounds other than what I learned in my one and only experience with them.

I don't want Iggy anywhere near her.

I round the countertop, trying to put something between the hound and us. Iggy seems nonplussed, hopping off my shoulder and back onto the counter. Behind him, the dog drools, a long string slipping out of its lips to pool on the floor.

Ugh. Gross.

"How do we get it out of here?" I ask Iggy, wondering if he might have gleaned something about the dog from their earlier interaction, even though it horrifies me to think about it.

"Well," he says sagely. "She has a job to do. So I imagine if we ignore her, she'll go back to doing it."

"Sounds very wise," I agree, keeping half my focus on the dog and half on my favorite little guy.

When the dog flops down on the floor and closes its eyes, it seems clear she has no plans to leave. Shit.

Keeping one eye on her, I rub Iggy's forearm. "Listen, I need your help with something. But if I tell you, you can't tell Thea or Morgan."

"Anything!" he shouts, jumping up and down on the countertop. "I can keep a secret from Auntie Thea!"

"Perf," I chirp, still trying to watch him and the dog at the same time.

Behind Iggy, the dog opens one eye to look at us, then closes it again.

Gods, this is so nerve-wracking. I wipe my sweaty palms on my jeans as I fill Iggy in on my entire Halloween plan. He looks a little confused, but as soon as I mention candy and costumes, he agrees to help.

We retreat to my office to write up a quick flyer explaining what we're doing. I need to deliver them to each business and finalize the details of the glamour.

After swearing Iggy to secrecy for the fourth time, we take on our next task—getting around the hellhound so we can leave the shop. I hold him above my head and scoot around her, but she just watches from her spot in the middle of the floor.

The damn store is empty, every single monster having fled from the hellhound. I'm going to have to say something to the sylph about this, because she's obviously not doing her job, but what she *is* doing is scaring my freaking customers away.

I breathe a sigh of relief when she follows us out the door but heads across the street. Iggy settles on my shoulder, slipping his spade down into my tee.

"Okay, kiddo. You ready to help me tell everyone about the party?"

"Hells yes!" he shouts.

I slap his foot playfully. "Are you supposed to be using that kinda language?"

He chuckles. "Dad lets me sometimes. He says as long as I don't say it at school, he doesn't care."

I snort. That sounds about right.

For the next two hours, Iggy and I visit every business on Main. We explain the big Howl-O-Ween bash and my preparations. I've got a flyer with all the details. And we swear everybody to secrecy from Morgan and Thea. Wren has to help me with decorations, and I couldn't keep the secret from her anyhow, my sweet soulfriend.

After that's done, I comm Alo to let him know I still have Iggy. We return to the community garden to find Wren leaving it.

"Hey, you two!" She waves and joins us. "Mir, I was just coming to find you to talk about some stuff." Her green eyes flick to Iggy.

I laugh. "Ig knows; we just delivered the info flyers to all the stores on Main. Things are happening!" I singsong that last bit. I can barely contain my excitement over this sneaky, sneaky party.

Wren giggles, gesturing at the A-frame. "Want to dust us, and we can talk about it in your gourd? Morgan knows something's up, and she's been keeping a watchful eye on me. I'm hiding from her as we speak."

"I can't wait to surprise her!" Iggy hops up and down on my shoulder, jerking my body from side to side. Damn, he's getting big and heavy fast. It's hard to imagine him ever being as big as his dad, but it'll happen.

I dust them both, and a few moments later, Iggy and I help carry Wren up to the gourd since she's so pitifully wingless. Inside, Iggy dives for the plate of cookies Alo delivered earlier.

Wren waggles her brows at me. "Where'd you get these, Miriam?" She chuckles and snatches one up.

"You know where I got them," I mutter.

"Dad loves Miriam," Iggy announces.

Wren grins. "What makes you say that, honey?"

Iggy beams at her. "Because he's been cooking like, nonstop for the last week. And you know our motto is 'snack up, shack up'!"

Wren turns a barely hidden smile on me. "He ain't wrong, soulfriend!"

"Duh," Iggy snorts, slapping her shoulder with his tail spade.

We fall into a fit of giggles and spend the next hour talking about Howl-O-Ween. She wants the triplets to dress up as the Sanderson sisters. We convince Iggy to be Binx the cat while I debate the merits of being the cutesy girlfriend from Salem.

Wren, Iggy, and I play for hours in the kitchen. Around dinnertime, Alo comms me to let me know he's home. Wren gives me another knowing look and asks for help leaving the gourd. I take her and Iggy out and dust them to return them to their usual form, then we head home.

Well, to his home.

Not my home.

Except I want it to be.

When we leave the garden, Alo stands on the sidewalk waiting for us. His big wings are held aloft, flared slightly. His hair's getting long enough that he's got it slung up in a high man bun. Brown eyes sparkle as one corner of his lips curls up into a grin.

"Hey, you two," he says.

Iggy looks both ways then darts across the street, throwing himself in his father's arms as if they didn't see one another this morning. Alo crushes his son to him, squeezing him tight. Iggy crawls up to his shoulder, wrapping his tail around Alo's neck. My big gargoyle reaches a hand out for me as I cross the street toward them.

"Have dinner with us." His fingers curl toward me, and I can't resist taking them. Alo pulls me up onto the sidewalk, then leans down to plant a tender kiss on my forehead.

"Aww!" Iggy chirps, holding on to Alo's head with one hand. "Dad, you stole my girlfriend! I'm not mad though. Miriam said she's too old for me."

I snort and reach up to tickle him. "I am too old for you, but I'm just the right age for your dad."

"Yeah," Iggy agrees. "Can we have dinner now?"

Alo smirks but doesn't let go of my hand. "I've already got shepherd's pie in the oven, kiddo."

"My fave!" Iggy zooms off his father's shoulder and through the cottage's front door. She swings it wide, wiggling it back and forth at us in greeting.

Alo tugs me up the stairs but stops us just outside the front door. He pulls me close, running big hands over my ass to squeeze me tightly. Heat flares in my core at the way he's looking at me, like he can't wait to get a taste.

"I love you," he murmurs. "I've always loved you, Miriam, and I want to talk about what's next for us."

My heart stomps around in my chest like a herd of pegasi. "I love you too, Alo."

His sweet smile goes goofy and huge. "I wasn't expecting you to be ready to say the words so soon, but I hoped you would be."

I press up to my tiptoes, and he leans down to meet me. Our kiss is tender, but then he opens his mouth and slicks it more fully over mine, sucking my lower lip between his.

"Is it bedtime yet?" he growls into my mouth, licking at my top lip. "I really need it to be bedtime."

"Almost," I tease him. "Your bed or mine?"

He jerks his head toward the cottage. "My nest, pixie girl. I want you in my nest."

Gods. I've never even seen Alo's nest. A gargoyle's space is so personal, so private. "I can't wait."

Fifteen minutes later, we're sitting at dinner, and Iggy blurts out how he saw Dirk and the hellhound at school looking for portals. Alo scowls but fills us in on what the hunter team is looking for.

I sit there shocked, wondering how the hells Wesley could have built a fucking haven and attached it to ours.

"It's just a theory at this point," he cautions.

Still, it would explain how Wesley was able to attack us so many times in a row so quickly. Outside of Ever, it's barely been a day since the Hectors arrived. But inside our wards, it's been over three weeks.

"Well, me and Kevin are going portal hunting!" Iggy shouts, zooming around the room in a post-dinner carb rush.

"Absolutely not," Alo commands. "This isn't a joke, Ignatius; it's dangerous. The only reason I told you is because you already mentioned the sylph and the portal earlier. I don't want you to be unaware."

I bite my tongue listening to them. I don't want Iggy to be afraid; he's just a kid. But he's a protector species. He's wired to understand and respond to situations like this. I don't know how early gargoyle families begin to include their young in protector duties, but maybe five isn't too early to talk about it?

"I can help, Dad!" he shouts, landing in the middle of the table. The cottage shakes around us, and even I can tell she's saying no.

Alo points at the ceiling. "The cottage agrees. You can't go portal hunting, kiddo. But I'll tell you what. If you see a portal at school, let me know, okay? I'll tell Dirk and the hunters to check it out."

Iggy flutters around excitedly. "Me and Kevin can do that! He wants to be on a protector team too so we can look around the school for portals!"

I hold back a snort. Very few pixies are protectors. We're not fighters, and our wings are far more fragile than the giant leathery wings of gargoyles and dragons and such. Still, I know there are a few out there. They just have to invest in really stellar body armor.

Iggy crashes into me and wraps his tail around my waist, snuggling into my neck. "I'm tired, Miriam. Can you snuggle me in bed?"

My heart clenches tight in my chest, and I look over at Alo. He gives me a lazy smile, sipping a glass of wine.

"Of course, kiddo." I rub Iggy's back. I'll never understand how he can be zooming around the room one moment and passed out the next, but he's five, so I suppose that's reason enough. I wrap an arm under his body and another around his back, cradling his neck. Alo trails us up the stairs with our wine glasses. By the time we get to the top and down the hall to Iggy's nest, he's already snoring.

I lay him in the middle of the giant, plush oval, and he curls onto his side, grabbing his pillow.

Alo comes up behind me, his tail snaking around my ankle. His hand slides up my stomach under my shirt. "You're good with him. I love watching you together."

I sink into his chest, my head falling back against thick muscle. "He's such a good kid, Alo. You've done an amazing job, even though you had to do it alone."

"I've never been alone, though, have I?" His lips come to my neck. "I always had you, even when we were just friends. Except we were never just friends, either, were we?"

I turn in his arms, sliding both hands around his waist. "No, we weren't."

He grins and leans down, picking me up and tossing me over his shoulder like a sack of potatoes. One hand comes to my ass to hold me in place. I hold back an excited squeal for fear of waking Iggy.

Alo carries me out of the room, closing the door behind us. He stalks soundlessly down the hall to his nest and opens the door, setting me down inside.

I gaze around the room, my mouth dropping open in wonder. The angled ceiling is one gigantic window that soars high above us. A twelve-foot-wide mirror of Iggy's smaller nest sits in the center on a raised platform, making the whole "bed" about hip-height for, well, not me, but Alo. Sweat breaks out on my forehead just looking at it and imagining us doing *things* in here.

Three of the four walls are covered in intricate carvings. He comes to my side, grabbing my hand and guiding my fingers to touch the closest pictures to us.

"My parents," he murmurs. The carving shows a handsome, elegant male gargoyle and a starkly beautiful female. They stare at one another lovingly.

It's the same way Alo stares at me, and that takes my breath away.

He moves my fingers along the wall. "This one's Shepherd and I getting into trouble. This is Shepherd and I graduating from the Protector Academy. There are a lot of carvings of the two of us." He laughs.

I walk the walls, admiring every picture as Alo tells me the stories of why he chose to carve each memory. When we get to the third wall, I stop abruptly.

It's full of Iggy.

But not just Iggy.

Keira too.

There are happy carvings from the time when Alo and Keira were together, and even a few where she was pregnant, although she doesn't look quite as happy in those. The second half of the wall is all Alo and Iggy, and he shows me those carvings with pride, but I keep coming back to Keira.

Her face is everywhere on half of that wall. I gulp around a hard breath, turning toward him.

"Keira features very prominently here, Alo. You don't talk about her much. I'm a little surprised."

Alo turns me to face him. "She and I started this wall together. When we split, my father had these walls sent from Vizelle. He thought Iggy might want to have them, assuming that, as he grows older, he'll have questions." There's a sad look in his eyes, but it's there and gone fast. He pulls me into his arms, and we crawl into the nest.

Gods, it's so soft and perfect, and his heavy weight on top of me is comforting and hot all at once.

"I wanted you to see everything, Mir," he murmurs, kissing a path down my throat. "I'll carve you all over these walls too. Right beside Ig and me."

I roll my hips against his, loving the feel of him on top of me. When my folks passed and I moved to Ever, I made myself a few goals. Find a friend family. I've done that. Follow my dream to open a sweets shop. Crushed that one. The only thing I wanted that I didn't have was Alo, and he's mine now too.

But as he slips a hand up my shirt, I can't help but look around him at a wall full of carvings of his ex, and feel... discombobulated. It's not that I'm worried she's going to show back up and take him, exactly.

"Miriam!" Alo's deep voice breaks through my thoughts. He smiles. "I've said your name about a hundred times. What's wrong?"

I shove up onto my elbows. "I can admit to always wanting to see your nest, and it's gorgeous, but..."

He rocks up off me and back onto his heels, setting his hands on his big thighs. "Let me guess, it doesn't feel right to you because of Keira?"

"Yeah," I admit, biting the inside of my lip. "Her face is everywhere, Alo." I sit up more fully. "I'd never ask you to get rid of this, but I don't think I can mess around with you in here, even though I'd really, *really* like to. I just...I can't."

He huffs out a breath. "I totally get it. I've got to think of a way to fix that, Mir, because she's the past, and you're my future. I want our nest to be exactly that—ours. Not hers and yours and mine."

I lift the edge of his tee up, planting a trail of kisses that march down to his waistband. "I want that too, more than anything."

"I'll figure it out," he promises, rolling out of bed and pulling me with him. "For now, want to go downstairs, and I'll eat that sweet pussy in the kitchen? Or maybe we can hide in the closet and make out. Or maybe I'll put some whipped cream on you, pixie girl. Whaddya say?"

I lead him out the door. "Why not all three, Alo?"

He gives me a smirky smile. "I like the way you think."

CHAPTER SEVENTEEN

ALO

It's been four days since I had Miriam in my nest. Four days since I watched the happy light die in her eyes at seeing Keira depicted there. I fucking hate that. I'm a protector, a guardian. More than that, I'm in love. And it doesn't sit right with me that I can't bring my girl into my nest without her feeling like the other woman.

That won't do at all, so I need a solution, because I can't get rid of the nest. Iggy has never been too interested in Keira, but as he grows, I'll have to explain where she is and what she does. He'll probably want to meet her. So the nest walls can't go.

I want to see Miriam, to talk to her about things, but she's busy all day with Wren—they're setting up all the Howl-O-Ween decorations under a glamour with the Keeper's help. He'll unveil it all at once, and then the whole town will erupt into bats...or something. Miriam explained all her plans to me, but I'll confess to finding the whole Halloween thing a little odd. Still, I've done the primary duties she gave me by visiting each of the businesses to ensure they're good with their glamours for the big night. I also hauled basketfuls of her magical candies up and down Main while she kept the Hector triplets busy.

It's going to be amazing, and I'm so proud of her.

Heading out the front door, I take off on patrol. At least that way I can kill a few hours until Iggy gets home from school.

Miriam shows up at the cottage at five with Iggy in tow. Apparently, he flew directly to town for the party.

"Ig," I groan. "You need your costume glamour, remember?"

He leaps up and down in the front doorway, then snaps his fingers to pull his glamour down over his body. His horns and wings fade away, replaced by a very tall black cat who stands in front of me with my son's brilliant blue eyes.

"Gods, that's really something," I murmur, reaching out to scratch the top of his head. "You look great, Ig."

"Lemme see!" He leaps up into my arms, and I twist to show him his glamour in the mirror.

We've been practicing this for days. "All that practice was a good idea, hmm?" When I ruffle his pointy ears, he lets out a happy, adorable purr.

"Me next!" Miriam winks at me, then snaps her fingers. Just like Iggy, her wings shimmer and fade, and her hair goes long and blond until she's dressed like the teenage girl from *Hocus Pocus*. She bumps me with her hip. "Your turn, surly misunderstood teenager."

I set Iggy down and concentrate, calling on the ancient monster magic that allows us to glamour ourselves when we need to. My horns flicker first, then my wings, and finally my tail. My face drains of color until standing in the mirror is a—

"Really hot, Alo." Miriam laughs. "You're so hot in Max form."

"Grody…" Iggy moans, reaching out to slap her shoulder with his tail spade. "Are we ready?"

Miriam holds her arms open, and Iggy hops into them. "We're ready, kiddo."

Smiling, I open the door.

Fucking Dirk stands on the opposite side, one blue fist raised to knock.

I cross my arms and scowl. "What's up?"

Blue eyes cut down my body, then he gives Miriam a long perusal until I step in front of her and snarl.

"Seems yer ready for the party, eh, protector? I don't suppose yer planning to help us this evening then?"

"I patrolled earlier," I remind him. "And found nothing, not even at the spots you asked me to check out. You're on duty tonight; the entire town has a celebration. Remember?"

He chuckles, but it's not mirthful; it's cutting and sharp, like he's reminding me with his laugh that I have a job to do, and dressing up like a human isn't it.

"Well," he continues, "I managed to nab a feather off that pegasus at HQ like yeh suggested. The hounds are sniffing out the scent now. Could turn somethin' up, yeh never know."

"If you get a lead on Wesley, I'm there for you," I reiterate. "Ever's safety comes first. But if you just wanna patrol for shits and giggles with the hellhounds, I'm out of office."

I love that phrase, "out of office." Sounds so much better than "busy." Another humanism my new sister-in-law taught me.

Dirk glances at Miriam again. Iggy lets out a playful meow.

"Well then, I suppose I'll be out searching fer criminals while yer playin' dress-up, Alo. Find me later." He slaps the disk on his chest and disappears into thin air.

The moment he goes, Iggy's glamour falls, and he zooms in circles around us. "Oh my gods, Dad, he's so cool! How does that disk thing work? Is it like the comm disks? Does he turn into air, or is he just invisible? How come he keeps looking at Miriam?"

The questions go on and on, but Miriam manages to get him contained long enough for us to get out the door and head for Main Street.

Dirk's comments don't sit well with me, though, and my mood goes downhill fast.

But when Miriam slips her hand through mine, I remember this is her night. She's been working so hard to make this perfect, and I want to be there for every minute of it.

In the distance, the town bell rings, calling all the Evertons to Town Hall for a meeting. We drop our glamours, and I pull Iggy up onto my shoulder. The cottage flaps her front windows in farewell.

Main Street bustles with activity as the residents head up Main toward Town Hall. Iggy can barely keep himself still, hopping up and down excitedly.

Morgan and Thea cross Main and join us. Morgan's got her arms crossed, and she's scowling. She bumps me with her shoulder. "What's the scoop on this surprise meeting, Alo? You're always in the know, and Shepherd says he has no idea."

I give her my most innocent look. "This one is news to me too."

Her scowl falls into something a little more concerned. Gray eyes peer up at me. "You don't think something's wrong, like something with the hunter team, or...something worse?"

I reach out and pat her shoulder. "I haven't heard anything about the hunter team, so I'm pretty sure it's not security related."

Her focus moves in front of us. "Hmmm."

I resist the urge to look at Miriam, who's practically buzzing next to me. She squeezes my hand tight, and she and Iggy share a look. He is taking being sworn to secrecy very seriously. I'm proud of him. I was surprised she let him in on the plan. Keeping secrets is hard to do at five, but he's a champ.

The Town Hall gazebo is full by the time we arrive. The Keeper stands up front with Ohken. Wren leans against the railing. Green eyes flash with mirth when we join her.

"Wrennie, what the hell is going on here, and why do you look so gleeful?" Morgan narrows her eyes at her triplet.

Wren shrugs. "This is just my face, honey. I am fucking gleeful all the time."

Thea leans against the railing and pulls Morgan next to her, slinging an arm around each sister. "Whatever it is, we'll deal with it together, right?"

I hold back a snort. They're expecting the worst, and I can hardly blame them. Their time in Ever has been filled with drama.

The gazebo creaks and groans, its support beams stretching and growing to accommodate the last few monsters.

"Evertons, welcome!" The Keeper's voice booms throughout the gathering. He looks over at Miriam, who leaves my side and heads for him. "Thank you for joining us tonight for a big surprise. Mir, the floor is yours." He steps back, and Miriam stands at the front of the congregation with a huge smile on her face.

"Friends and family, thank you so much for coming this evening! A lot of hard work has gone into making tonight happen. Please join me in our very first Ever Howl-O-Ween in celebration of the Hector triplets' twenty-ninth birthdays!"

Morgan lets out a gasp next to me.

Thea shoots forward, blond braid swaying. "The what now?"

Miriam titters, pink dusting her cheeks. "Howl-O-Ween. Tonight we celebrate you three, and how blessed we feel to have you in Ever." She turns to the Keeper. "The glamour, if you please."

The Keeper smirks at her and snaps his fingers. Around us, dark craggy trees spring up out of the ground. They squeal and groan as they push out of the dirt and arch over the gazebo. Long rows of the gnarled trees march along the sidewalk toward Main Street. Broken orange and purple lights dangle from every limb, fireflies winking orange as they glide in and out of the branches.

Jack-o'-lanterns pop up out of the ground, lit from within and glowing softly. Magical firelight highlights their gruesome faces. Hundreds of them lift up off the ground to hover in the air.

"Holy shit!" Thea shouts.

Miriam laughs, addressing the crowd one final time, "Everyone, pull on your glam—err, costumes, please!"

Thea and Morgan whip around to watch. Wren hops up and down as if she's unable to contain her sheer joy.

Wings, horns, tails, and hooves disappear as the Evertons take on all sorts of costumes. Many of them planned to dress up like famous humans, but it's hilarious to see their attempts. Alba the centaur rocks an Ozzy Osbourne outfit, but her hair is still purple. Herschel looks like the Stay-Puft Marshmallow Man, complete with a little blue tie and cap. He's forgotten to remove his horns though, and they stick up into the air above the cap.

Ohken joins us dressed in an old-fashioned coat with a cravat and tight pants. He still looks like himself, just wearing clothes from hundreds of human-years ago.

"Who the hells are you?" I snark, pulling my glamour down.

He adjusts pale fabric tied in an intricate knot at his throat. It looks uncomfortable as shit. "Edgar Allen Troll, obviously."

"And I'm Mary from *Hocus Pocus*!" Wren chirps, gesturing

to her crimson dress. It's fitted around her bust and flares out wide to her feet, which are encased in pointed black boots.

Thea scoffs. "Wren, you were in on this? Is this why you and Ohken have been acting so weird?"

"Indeed," the big troll agrees, pulling his mate to his side. She leans her head into his chest and holds up a hand for a high five. He pokes her palm with one finger, a slight smile on his face.

Morgan opens her mouth to say something. Before she can, Miriam claps to get our attention.

"Okay, Evertons," she continues. "You know the drill. Head to Main for a crazy party, and don't forget to put out your candy for the kiddos!"

Morgan looks up at me with a barely concealed grin. "You knew about this, didn't you, you big sneak?"

"Of course." I laugh and jerk my head toward Miriam. "I've been her assistant this whole time."

A rousing cheer fills the gazebo, along with well wishes for the triplets. Morgan and Thea stand frozen as monsters wish them a happy birthday and leave the gazebo. On my shoulder, Iggy purrs and bats Morgan's hair with his black paw.

She jerks around. "Oh my god, Ig, you're a cat!"

"Binx!" he shouts. "I'm Binx from *Hocus Pocus*! And Dad is the rude guy, and Miriam is the smart girl, and you can be Winifred. And Thea can be Sarah!"

As the gazebo empties, Miriam and the Keeper rejoin us. Miriam's hands are clasped together in excitement. Happiness radiates from her, and it fills my chest with bright joy. I rub at my heart, wishing it was beating for her now so I could feel them synced together.

Soon.

Next to her, the Keeper smiles bigger than I've ever seen. He gestures at Morgan's tee. "May I glamour you? I prepared one with Wren's assistance."

Morgan's mouth opens and shuts, but she gives him a curt nod.

His smile grows bigger, exposing twin fangs. He snaps his fingers, and Morgan and Thea's clothes shimmer and fade, replaced with dresses that look just like the famous witches' from the movie. "That's better," he murmurs, dark eyes flicking back to Morgan's.

"You did this?" she whispers. "You did this for us?"

He jerks his head at Miriam. "Miriam is the mastermind behind this entire wonderful evening and Wren built all the foliage on Main. I simply reset the glamour to fit their ideas."

Miriam holds her hand up for a high five, and he slaps it with a laugh. "Well done, Miriam."

Morgan takes a step forward, her eyes shining with tears. She can't seem to tear her eyes from the Keeper. "Thank you," she whispers. "This is...unexpected."

"That smile is worth it," he murmurs.

The rest of us stand in silence. It's an oddly tender moment between them, and nobody wants to be the first to break it.

It's the Keeper who does it by snapping his fingers, his appearance shimmering until he stands in front of us as a bedraggled, rotted zombie. "Billy Bones," he quips. "At Miriam's request."

"This is fucking amazing," Thea shouts, tears streaming down her face. "You guys planned a whole entire Halloween for us? I am literally gobsmacked." She turns to slap Shepherd on the chest. "How the hell did you not spill the beans on this? I can't believe it!"

"Easy." He laughs and points at Miriam. "She'd have sliced my head off if I ruined this surprise."

"I kept the secret too!" Iggy shouts. "Aren't you proud, Auntie Thea?"

Thea opens her mouth to say something, but a jack-o'-

lantern whizzes past the Keeper's head. He ducks out of the way and laughs.

"Pumpkins don't typically fly on Halloween," Thea says, humor in her tone.

Miriam snickers. "Well, I might have put a magical twist on your holiday. Let's go party!"

Morgan stares over the Keeper's shoulder at Town Hall, a thoughtful expression on her face. "You know, Town Hall would make a fucking great haunted mansion if people like Halloween and want to do it again."

The Keeper smiles at her. "Noted, Miss Hector. Shall we?" He gestures toward the flood of monsters walking up Main toward the businesses.

Morgan grins. "Let's fucking do it."

CHAPTER EIGHTEEN
MIRIAM

Iggy purrs and leaps off Alo's shoulder when a group of kids runs by in costume.

I laugh as he sprints away from us with his fuzzy black tail straight up in the air, screeching wildly.

"Stay on Main, Iggy!" Alo shouts as his son disappears into the fray.

"That is wild," Thea says, smiling over at me. "How did you do all of this?"

"Well…" I shrug, pointing at the Keeper. "Wren gave me a book about Halloween a while back, and I knew I wanted to do something special for you three. I drew up a ton of plans, and Wren and the Keeper lent creative guidance. Then I gave everything to him, and, between the three of us, we got the glamour sorted yesterday."

"Thank you," Thea whispers. Shepherd wraps his tail around her waist with a soft smile.

We quickly reach the historical society, our first stop on this Howl-O-Ween tour.

"Oh God," Morgan moans. "Why do I feel like Halloween

in Ever is going to seem far more realistic than in the human world?"

I beam at her. "That's the idea, friend!"

We turn as a group to look at the low-slung building.

What's typically a cute little cottage with a row of orderly shrubs leading to a pink front door now appears abandoned. The wooden siding is moth-eaten and full of holes. The front door hangs from one hinge, and all the windows are cracked and broken. The interior is dark, but flickering candles wink at us from the windowsills.

"Holy shit," Thea blusters. "How is this—"

I shove her toward the front door. "Go yell trick-or-treat!"

"Oh god." Thea laughs and grabs her sisters' hands. "You're both coming with me." She looks over her shoulder at me. "Is someone in there?"

"You'll see," I say. "Just go." I squirm with anticipation for them to see my first surprise. Screams ring out from somewhere up the street, followed by raucous laughter.

"I'm so scared!" Thea shouts. She giggles hysterically and drags her sisters to the door.

Morgan raps on it, but nobody comes.

"You've got to say trick-or-treat," suggests the Keeper, shoving both hands in his pockets. He's grinning. Actually grinning. I haven't seen him look this pleased, well, ever? His ruby-red eyes sparkle as he watches the triplets.

Morgan clears her throat. "Trick or treat!"

For a long tense moment, nothing happens. Then the front door swings open with a big creepy groan. A faint light begins to glow from the society's interior. Thea yips and drags Morgan in front of her.

All of a sudden, three zombie apparitions spring through the entrance and land in front of the triplets, their bones jangling together. They pull to a stand and roar, and the Hectors scream and split, running in separate directions. Thea buries her face in Shepherd's chest with a high-pitched giggle. Wren doubles over with nervous laughter. Morgan runs toward the Keeper but jerks to a halt by my side at the last minute.

One of the zombies explodes, and paper-wrapped round chocolates fly all over the street, rolling in every direction.

I clap my hands and give the Keeper a look. "It fucking worked. Told ya!" Victory bells chime in my brain. This is so freaking exciting!

He laughs. "You are a wonder, Miriam."

The Hectors swoop down on the candy, picking up the rolling pieces to examine them.

Alo comes up behind me, wrapping both arms around my waist, his soft lips coming to my neck. "He's right, Mir. A fucking wonder. This is incredible."

I turn to respond but stop in my tracks. A dark figure slinks around the side of the historical society, blood-red eyes shining in the darkness. The hellhound growls at the zombie apparitions as they turn and march back into the building. The front door closes behind them, and the dog comes to a stop in front of me, sitting back on her haunches.

"That damn hellhound," I grouse, crossing my arms. It's the same one that came into the store and scared my freaking customers away. It's got a white star on its chest.

Her belly is huge and swollen; it looks horribly uncomfortable.

Not that I feel bad for her at all. I truly don't.

"Get out of here, Minnie," the Keeper commands. The dog lets out a soft whine but pushes up onto all four feet and jogs up the street toward the crowd, which parts as the hound stalks through. I'm not the only one on edge with the dogs, I guess.

Still, I'm not letting her ruin my mood. "Let's go, Hectors!"

I make the round-'em-up move over my head and point toward the rest of the businesses.

Pumpkins whiz back and forth across the street, chasing the children. Cackles ring out, and there's the occasional scream of terror. Main Street is full of beings in all states of dress. Some monsters drop their glamours, some keep them, and some change them depending on what they see others doing.

Giant gnarled trees grown by Wren hang over the buildings on both sides, creating a canopy of blackness above Main. Purple and orange lights dangle from their limbs. Every storefront looks destroyed with broken windows and shoddy siding.

Each business has its own unique glamour and spooky experience. I'm so grateful to the shop owners for how seriously they took my idea. The reality is that Evertons like a good party, and the community really came together.

Ohken jerks his head toward the General Store. "I've got pumpkin mead in the shop and I'm manning the store for the first two hours, so swing by if you get thirsty."

"Bye, honey!" Wren shouts. He kisses her and takes his leave.

"Wait till you see what I did with the storefront!" I'm practically cackling as I hop up and down next to my soulfriend.

She squeezes my arm. "I can't believe you wouldn't tell me your plans for your own store, you stinker."

I bump her with my hip. "I had to keep a few secrets."

She hugs me, leaving one arm around my waist. I grab Alo's hand, and we slowly make our way up Main, stopping at every business. I marvel at the twists the different shops have put on their storefronts. I gave them ideas for how to decorate with the mandate that they let the Keeper know what they wanted their glamours to look like by yesterday so he could put the magic together.

Fleur's storefront is a garden of withered sunflowers. A creepy zombie scarecrow hangs out in the window, holding a noose. When we pass, he cackles, and the Hectors all jump. Two centaurs tiptoe out of the front door, holding flagons of pumpkin beer. They keep a wary eye on the scarecrow as they leave.

I can't hold back a laugh when candy explodes out of the sunflower heads, covering the street and causing us and the centaurs to jump. Children flood toward us, screaming and laughing as they grab the candy and stuff it in pumpkin-shaped bags I designed for the occasion.

By the time we get to the sweets shop, the Hectors and I are all in hysterics. My Evertons have gone all out on their glamours. Every shop is a mix of candy and thrills, and I love that.

But my shop is still my favorite—the entire front is covered in a rainbow pumpkin arch. Pumpkins in every possible shade sit in neat rows up and down the door, candles flickering softly between and inside them. Burnt-sugar skulls float in the air around the door.

Morgan reaches for one, plucking it out of thin air to examine it.

I hold my breath. Will it work? Will it worrrrrrkkkk?

Morgan turns to me. "God, Miriam. This is fucking beautiful. How did you—"

There's a quiet pop, and where the sugar skull sat in her palm, a giant black scorpion now stands with a chocolate kiss in each claw, his dangerous tail held high to strike.

Morgan shrieks and tosses the scorpion. It hits the pavement and dissolves into a dozen wrapped jawbreakers.

I can't hold back a cackle as she turns an angry scowl on me. "Miriam Saihem, a little warning would have been nice!"

"Nope!" I manage between laughs. "I wish I could replay that moment every day. The look on your face!"

We dissolve into a fit of laughter. Alo and Wren come to my side, staring at the front of the store.

Aside from the surprise scorpions, my storefront is simply beautiful. Not spooky or terribly frightening, but stunning. Candies sit on top of every pumpkin, or they did. The kids probably snatched them already. Most of the candy is gone, although the inside of the store is crammed full of monsters trying out the specialty confections I made for the event. The store appears dark from out here, but once you step inside, it's lit as usual.

We follow the Hectors inside. The girls squeal at the blinking upside-down jack-o'-lanterns that hang from the ceiling. Sticky pumpkin insides drip from their cut tops, but by the time the seeds hit the floor, they transform into wrapped pumpkin fudge.

I stand in the middle of my shop, looking around. Candy bursts out of skull-shaped containers in every corner of the store. Children run from side to side, their joy nearly palpable each time they discover a new candy. Sugar-sweet happiness flows through my veins as I watch. This is my favorite place on earth.

The Keeper taps me on the shoulder. "Miriam, a moment?"

Alo joins us, a sly smile on his face.

When I see his devious expression, I put both hands on my hips. "What are you two up to?"

"Oh you just wait and see, pixie girl," Alo murmurs. "You're gonna love this."

CHAPTER NINETEEN

ALO

I've been waiting for this part of the evening all day. When I approached the Keeper with an idea to do something special for Miriam, he helped me take it one step further.

He smiles at her. "Go to your office, there's a surprise for you there."

She looks between us, barely repressing a grin. "What sort of surprise?"

My lips curl into a predatory smile. "The spooky kind, Mir."

The Keeper claps me on the back. "Have fun, friend." He gives me a knowing look before turning toward the Hectors.

I grab Miriam's hand and pull her toward the back of the store. Pausing in front of the door, I smile. "Drop the glamour and close your eyes."

She's practically beaming. I can't wait to show her what the Keeper and I cooked up. She dutifully closes both eyes and squeezes my hand tightly. I open the door and guide us through, careful not to let her bump into the frame. I pull her to my side, because I want to see the look on her face when she sees what we cooked up.

I drop my glamour and slide my spade between her wings, stroking the soft skin between them. "Open up, pixie girl."

Fuchsia eyes flutter open and she gasps, one hand flying up to cover her heart. She gazes around in wonder. I follow where she's looking because I haven't seen the final glamour yet either.

This room used to be her office. But all of that has been replaced by a giant midnight cornfield. Rustling stalks tower above our heads, swaying softly on a glamoured breeze.

"Oh my gods," Miriam murmurs. "You did this?"

I spin her to face me, tipping her chin up. "I held you at arm's length for years, Miriam. I'll always regret the time we lost because of that. But I will never stop trying to make it up to you. I need your smiles, my love, every single one of them."

Tears fill her bright eyes, but she smiles. I wrap both wings around her, holding her close. The only sound is her soft breathing. Silence stretches long.

"Alo."

"Yes?"

She giggles and pushes against my wings. "Let me outta here, I want to see what you did!"

I laugh and flare my wings wide, releasing her. She turns toward the field, clasping her hands together as her mouth drops open.

I bring my lips to her neck, sucking and biting my way down the slim column. Groaning into her ear, I step behind her and slide both arms around her waist. My bite grows more insistent, my wings held high behind us like a wall.

"Alo," she huffs, wriggling in my embrace.

"We're alone in here, pixie girl," I growl into her skin. "There's a treat for you on the far side of this field." I reach up and pinch one of her nipples playfully. She arches into my palm, her small breast filling it. I pinch again, rolling the hard tip between my fingers. "You can have it if you can get to it, Mir."

She whirls around in my arms, giving me a mischievous look. "Aloitious Noctis Rygold. Are you gonna try to keep me from that treat?"

I straighten and smirk at her, cracking my knuckles. When I pull my battle spines out along my shoulders, legs and tail, her eyebrows shoot up. She widens her stance, muscles tensing, her curiosity replaced with a ferocious look.

"I'm gonna do everything in my power not to let you get across that field," I say. I gesture toward the straight dark rows of corn. "Get going, Miriam."

She plants both hands on her hips, wings stilling behind her back. Her chest heaves, despite the bluster. "What if I feel like being a brat?"

I swing my right wing around her, grabbing her shoulder and spinning her to face the cornfield. I haul her against my chest, loving how the breath whooshes from her when her back hits my front.

Sliding my left hand up her neck, I grip her hair and guide her head gently away from me. A vein throbs just below the surface of her pale skin. I lick a path from her shoulder all the way to her ear.

She shudders and grunts, grinding her ass against my aching cock. I thrust against her, reveling in the tease. But more than anything, I want the chase. I didn't allow myself to chase her for years. I need it now.

I bite her neck, then bite again, and again, marking her up. I suck hard at her skin, pulling it between my fangs. She cries out.

I pull back and soothe the red skin with soft kisses before bringing my lips to her ear. "That's gonna leave a bruise, sweetheart. You don't want to know what you're gonna miss out on if you fail to make it to the far end of this field." I slide my right hand up between her breasts, holding her close.

"Run," I command.

She pops into small form and flits off between the rows. But my eyesight is excellent, and even in small form, I'm able to track her from a hundred feet away.

"I'll give you a ten second head start!" I call out. "Then I'm coming for you, pixie girl."

She darts toward the left as I break into a devious smile. This isn't *just* a cornfield. No. It's not immediately obvious, but it's a maze. Not only that, this maze is filled with a few creepy crawlies I got ideas for when I read Wren's Halloween book. I absolutely lied when I said we were alone in here.

A horrified shriek rings out from the left. Guess she discovered the first zombie. Nothing in here can hurt her, it's all a trick of glamour. But it's hard for your brain to tell your body that sort of thing. Especially when someone's chasing you in the dark.

Awareness prickles my nape, my horns flattening to my skull as I focus on the spooky scene in front of me. Wings wide, I crouch down then spring into the glamoured sky. I swoop left over the field. Ahead of me, Miriam runs in large form, arms pumping wildly as she flees a zombie. It shambles quickly after her, then hits a wall that springs out of the ground. Miriam whirls around, eyes wide. When I glide over her she screams again and pops back into small form, disappearing between the rustling rows.

Laughing, I glide down to fly above the stalks. They sway and move from side to side, their dry leaves rubbing together to make the most delightful creepy creaky noise. Gods, this is fun.

But I've lost sight of Miriam.

"Hey handsome," a voice rings out.

I swoop and turn, flapping in place until I find her.

There! She's perched on top of a corn cob, both hands playfully on her hips. Her wings flutter wildly at her back, her chest rising and falling quickly. "You sneaky sneak. You didn't tell me there were zombies in here."

I grin at her. "Got you pretty good, Mir." My shirt is battered and torn from the spines, so I rip it off and drop it to the ground in front of her. "This game would be a lot more fun naked, don't you think?"

She purses her lips in a barely contained smile. "You dirty dog. I think I see where you're going with this game."

I laugh as I slip my jeans down over my hips, dropping them with my shirt. My cock juts out in front of me, dripping precum onto the ground.

"Remember how I said you'd miss out on something if you don't make it to the end? This is what I'm talking about, sweetheart." I stroke my rigid length, thumbing the thick plate that extends over the top of my cock.

"Well," she sasses. "I guess I'd better get going!"

She zips into the darkness, her laugh echoing behind her. I swoop down a row of corn and land, tucking my wings at my back. Stalking up the row, I watch her turn, then whirl around as a giant spider appears in the next row over. She screams and takes off again. Predatory need rises and rises. I ball my fists, my breath coming in quick, measured pants. My battle spines lengthen, goose bumps covering my dark skin.

I close my eyes and twitch my ears, listening for the sounds of my spooked quarry. Up ahead, footsteps pound along the dirt. She's breathing fast, her heartbeat a wild, steady drum that calls every inch of my body to attention. The scent of her arousal and fear is a potent combination. My mouth waters, fangs descending as I prepare to hunt her.

I blink my eyes open, grinning like a madman into the darkness.

And then I take off at a run, long strides eating up the distance between us.

Miriam looks over her shoulder and yips, surging forward through the corn.

Need and possession rage in my system.

She's mine, mine, mine.

She slams to a halt when she reaches the end of the row and finds a dozen zombies standing there. Gasping, she whirls around only to find me bolting up the row toward her. She looks desperately from side to side, then takes off at a run toward a faint light—the prize.

Well, it's her goal, but that light isn't the prize. The prize is what I'm going to do to her as soon as I catch her.

The zombies roar in unison, lumbering quickly after me as I sprint past them.

Miriam rushes toward the light, but I'm close. So close. Almost there.

I barrel into her, knocking us both to the ground but shielding our fall with my wings. The zombies are on us in seconds, biting and snapping. Miriam screams and tucks her face into my chest. I slash out with both wings, eviscerating half of them. They fall to the ground and disappear in a puff of smoke.

Mir screeches as one reaches for her. I slice his arm off with my tail and laugh. This is so fucking fun.

I press up off the ground and burst toward the light, Miriam clutched frozen and trembling to my chest. The remaining few zombies lumber after us, their grunts and groans fading as we leave them behind.

She laughs nervously into my skin, her muscles quivering with unreleased tension. Good. Because that was my entire plan. Rile her up. Freak her out. Break her apart on my cock. Anticipation swirls deep in my chest, my body straining with need.

The light ahead grows brighter, revealing a giant see-through orb hovering thirty feet above the cornfield. I swoop toward it and push through the pliable outer bubble. Inside, a giant nest takes up the entire bottom of the bubble. It's a replica of the one in my cottage.

I set Miriam down in the middle and drop to my knees in front of her.

She looks around us in wonder. "A nest?" She looks up, eyes shining bright with unshed tears. "You made a nest?"

I stroke the underneath of her breasts. "I made *you* a nest, pixie girl. You're mine. You know that, right?"

She looks out into the cornfield, eyes scanning the swaying stalks.

"They're just a glamour, sweetheart," I remind her. "We're safe in here."

She turns back to me with a smile that melts what's left of the chill in my heart. Then she shifts onto her knees and throws herself into my arms, her mouth crashing against mine. Her kiss is rough and demanding, her desire the most potent of drugs. I hold her to me, one hand between her wings and the other gripping her ass.

I fall backward against the side of the orb, rubbing her sweet pussy all over my dick as we grind our hips together. She straddles me, rocking up and down my soaked length. My battle spines slip back into my skin as my focus shifts to pleasuring her.

"Get on me, Mir," I command. I grip myself as she rises, then lowers herself onto my cock. The tiny ruffles inside her pussy trill and flutter around me. My eyes roll back into my head, back arching as I rock my hips. "So godsdamn good," I grit out, grabbing the back of her neck. "You feel so good."

She groans and falls forward with both hands on my chest. "Gods, Alo. I'll never get over how fucking perfectly we fit together."

"Good enough to curse, hmm?" I laugh as I pull her forward enough to suck one taut nipple into my mouth.

She hisses, clenching around me. She grunts and rolls her hips. We rock together, slow at first. I relish the feel of her on top of me, knees pressed tight to my sides. She's so wet, so hot, sweet honey dripping down my cock.

"Ride me, woman," I growl, breathing the same air as her while she moves her hips steadily. Every time she pulls off me and rocks back down, her pussy clenches tight and massages me. A feral snarl rips from my throat as my lips curl back. She's everything I ever wanted, everything I dreamed of, everything I fantasized about.

The need to claim and keep her tightens my chest as her lips hover above mine. Her eyes are shut, her mouth open. Soft panting has my balls tightening to the point of pain. But I watch and revel in the way she fucks me. She's always been so open and honest about her love. I didn't return her openness for five whole years.

I can't wait to spend the rest of my days proving to her that she's what I need, that I'm sorry I delayed for so long.

"Let me, sweetheart," I command as a rush of desire spikes through me.

She opens her eyes, lips curling into a smile as she pauses her slow, teasing movements.

I drop my hold on her neck and slide my hand down to her ass, gripping it tight. Sliding both hands further down the voluptuous swells, I open her wide and guide her off my dick. Holding her spread, I thrust slowly, not taking my eyes from hers. Every time I fill her, her lashes flutter until her eyes roll back, her head falling to one side.

She's losing control, lithe muscles spasming with tiny shudders. A light sheen of sweat coats us both as I take her slow but hard.

I push her farther up so I can access her neck, biting my

way down her throat and shoulder, a tease of what I'll do when I formally claim her. Her soft moans morph into wild, desperate cries, her hips grinding hard.

I speed up, fucking her fast and deep. Pink steals across her cheeks and down her neck and chest. Every thrust jiggles her breasts. I can't stop staring at how fucking beautiful she is on top of me.

"I'm gonna fill you so full, Mir." I let out a purr of pleasure as her pussy clenches, choking my cock even as it strokes every inch of me.

"Alo," she cries out. "I'm, I'm—gah!" She screams and jerks in my arms, hips thrusting wildly as orgasm overtakes her. I'm so close to joining her. The scent of her arousal floods my nose and I tense. Orgasm strikes like a whip, unleashing a maelstrom of pleasure that blots my vision. I crush Miriam to me as our bodies clash together. Sloppy sounds fill the orb, her release and mine dripping down my cock to my balls. I want to imprint that scent on my body.

As orgasm fades, I stroke Miriam's wings. Her heart beats loudly against my chest. She's limp against me, her breath tickling my neck. After a long minute, she playfully nips my ear.

"I need more of that, Alo."

I slap her ass hard, loving the way she yips.

"I'm not done, Mir. Go small form for me."

She raises her head and gives me a curious look. "Why?"

I grin. "Because there's something I've fantasized about for a while, Miriam, and I'm gonna do it right now."

She narrows her eyes suspiciously, but sits upright. "Okay, I'll bite."

With a pop, she morphs into her tiny form, fluttering in front of my face.

Reaching up, I carefully grab her by the waist. Her hands

come to my fingers, holding herself steady. The look on her face is skeptical.

I bring her lower half just above my nose and suck in a deep breath, groaning when the scent of our combined release hits my senses. My horns flatten against my head, and I huff out a desperate breath.

She's candy and spice and cinnamon, but a darker scent underlies all of that.

My scent.

I nudge her thighs open with my nose. I had a dream about doing this one night, and I've never been able to forget about it. Her thighs fall wide as she pushes at my fingers.

"Are you…"

"Get on your hands and knees, Miriam." I growl softly into her pussy, vibrating her lower half.

She jerks between my fingers. I open them and lay my hand flat. Miriam drops to both knees in my palm. She shifts forward onto her elbows, pushing her ass up in the air. And gods, I'm lost staring into that sweet wet pussy. My cum leaks from her, dripping down the backs of her thighs.

I want it.

I bring my hand close and slip the tip of my tongue between her legs.

She grunts as my touch pushes her forward. "Alo, oh gods, you can't mean to—" Her words fall off as she releases a deep, throaty moan.

I lick a slow, gentle path from the front to the back, cleaning up the cream-pie mess we made. Miriam cries out and surges forward, wrapping her arms around my middle finger.

My balls pull tight against my body, my dick bobbing and dripping. Something about it feels so wrong, playing with her like this.

My next lick is more insistent, covering the backs of her

legs and that sweet pussy. Miriam rocks back and shudders, wriggling her ass against my flat tongue. I hold still as she grinds against it, working herself along my soft skin. Her flavor coats my tongue, seeping into my senses. My hips rock of their own accord, muscles tightening then going loose as I eat out her small form.

A groan rises from deep in my chest, tumbling from my throat as it gets hard to breathe. I just had her and I need her again.

She pants, her breath coming in rough rasps as her cries crescendo. Her legs quiver as I press my lips to her pussy and suck softly.

I'm going to fucking come again from the way she reacts to me. Growling, I carefully flip her over and lick her from the front. Every swipe of my tongue sends her thighs out to the side. I'm a cat and she's my sweet bowl of cream. Her back arches, tiny breasts punctuating the air with hard points. She cries out my name, throwing both arms over her head as her thighs fall open.

I lick and suck until she detonates beneath me, screaming my name as her hips jerk against my mouth. I stroke my cock with my free hand as I lick her through one orgasm and into the next. I join her, moaning as I spurt sticky cum into my hand with my lips between her tiny thighs.

When mutual pleasure fades, she lies boneless in my palm, groaning. I'm propped against the orb's side, chest heaving.

Mir pops into large form and flops against my chest, burying her face beneath my chin. "That was insanity. I could stay here all night," she mumbles. "Round two?"

I chuckle and stroke the back of her head. "Well, the Keeper has been distracting the Hectors while we're in here. They haven't seen Higher Grounds yet. We thought you might want to be there for that."

She shoots upright, eyes wide with apparent excitement.

"Oh my gods! That's right! Let's go!" When she tries to zip up off my lap, I grab both thighs and drag her back down, licking a path between her breasts and up her neck. When I reach her chin, I bite hard enough to remind her who the predator is here.

"Give me five more minutes, Mir. I can do a lot with five minutes."

One side of her smile tips up, her gaze going mischievous.

"You've got *five* minutes, Aloitious." Her laughter tinkles around us as I slide my tail up the back of her thigh.

I'm excellent under pressure.

CHAPTER TWENTY

MIRIAM

Five ecstasy-filled minutes later, Alo lets me go so we can show the Hectors what Higher Grounds did. Alessandro and Pietro had a truly wild idea and I can't wait to see how it turned out.

We pull our glamours back on and step out of my store to find Main Street still filled with monster families. Children run from one end to the other. The party is in full swing.

The Hectors are seated in rocking chairs on the sidewalk. Morgan grins up at me. "We've been waiting, Miss Saihem."

A hot blush steals across my cheeks. Gods, they know exactly what I've been doing.

The Keeper strides across Main and holds out three skullipops for the triplets. "As promised, ladies."

Morgan takes it with a soft smile, eyes focused on the Keeper. "You're still trying to distract us. Can we go into Higher Grounds yet or not? The outside is amazing!"

He smiles and turns to us, barely concealing a smile. "What do you think, Miriam?"

I laugh and grab Wren's hand, pulling her up out of the rocking chair. "I think it's time, Hectors. This is our last stop!"

Alo, Shepherd, and the Keeper trail us up the sidewalk toward Higher Grounds, except Higher Grounds is no longer. In its place, a huge black-and-red castle stands, complete with a moat and drawbridge. A sign over the front door says, "Welcome to Perkatory. Enter at your own risk."

A group of monsters leave, holding giant frosted black coffee mugs with pumpkin-shaped cookies stuck in the troll whip topping, which is now bloodred.

"Oh yes," Wren deadpans. "Ima need me one of those. Right fucking now." She rushes to meet Morgan, Thea, and Shepherd, who have already joined the group waiting to enter.

"This is amazing!" Morgan shouts from her spot in line.

The Keeper laughs. "Alessandro wasn't joking around. This glamour took me the longest of them all."

"Gods, that's fucking amazing," Alo says. "Look at that."

The Keeper pats my shoulder. "You did a great job, Miriam. Everyone is having an amazing time. I think there might be a revolt if we don't do this again next year."

I blush and tuck a lock of hair behind my ear. "You were an amazing partner. Thank you for the corn maze."

His grin goes wide and devious-looking. He opens his mouth to respond, but one of the hellhounds appears. It slinks up Sycamore toward us. Dirk appears out of thin air, following it. Irritation sparks in my chest and I cross my arms, glaring at them.

The big sylph stops in front of our group, licking his lips as he stares down my body. "Looking good, pixie. Humanity suits you."

"Fuck off," snarls Alo.

"Dirk I am truly not interested," I say. "Please stop staring at me like I'm a candy to eat."

One blue brow curls upward, but his focus moves to the

Keeper. "Patrolled again. Minnie seemed onto something by the skyball stadium, but we lost the scent."

Alo's comm watch rings. Iggy's name flashes above the band. He steps away and answers, "How's it going, kiddo?"

Iggy's teeny voice echoes out of the watch. "Dad! Me and Kevin found that portal you've been looking for! Are you proud? Can I go in it?"

All the blood rushes to my head, my vision blurring. The portal? He must be joking…right?

Alo freezes, his glamour falling as instinct takes over.

Shepherd jogs over from the coffee house line.

"Iggy, that's not funny," Alo says carefully, his chest rising and falling with rapid breaths.

"I'm serious, Dad," Iggy shouts. "It's blue and kind of shiny, and it's right here by the stadium! Minnie's here too, and she's growling at it. We found it, Dad; are you proud of me?"

Shepherd and Alo go into battle mode at the same time, spines slipping out of their skin.

Oh my gods, oh my gods, oh my gods.

I pop into small form and grab on to Alo's shredded shirt as he bullets into the sky. Below us, the Keeper shouts for Richard. Dirk barks commands into his comm watch.

Alo grabs a current and bursts through the air, questioning Iggy about precisely where he is. "Do not go into that portal, Ignatius; this is important!"

I pray hard, harder than I've ever prayed in my entire life. Please don't let anything happen to him. I don't know what I'd do without Iggy. I pray that he and Kevin are just playing, and this is some kind of a joke—because the other option is too fucking terrifying to entertain.

CHAPTER TWENTY-ONE

ALO

Get to Iggy. Get to my son. That's all I can think of as terror spurs me on. I climb through the sky to the ward's ceiling, grabbing the fastest current in town. Shepherd bursts ahead of me, battle spines out along his neck, shoulders, back, and tail.

Panic screams through me as I shout into the comm watch. "Do not go in, Iggy. I'm serious. Don't let Kevin go in; don't go anywhere near the fucking portal!"

"Okay, Dad," he grumbles back. "I'm just standing here; don't freak out!"

I'm too terrified to respond. Could it be true? He's found the godsdamned portal we've been looking for for days?

Miriam clings to one of my spines, and that terrifies me too. If Iggy's right, and there is a portal, I don't know what we'll find.

I push my muscles harder until my wings feel like they'll snap off as I claw through the current to get to my child. He finally comes into view, his cat glamour down. I shoot to the ground, landing with a thud and yanking him into my arms.

He snuggles against my neck, patting me reassuringly with

his tail. "Dad, I'm okay. But we found the portal! See?" He tries to shove away from me, but I don't let him go.

Miriam pops into large form beside me, grabbing Kevin and pulling him toward us. I flare my wings out wide to shield them all close to me. We're just past the skyball stadium, looking at the wards.

I give Iggy a stern look. "What are you even doing all the way out here, Ignatius?" I struggle to keep the terror from my voice.

He strokes my face softly. "Don't be mad, Dad, we were just following Minnie!"

I open my mouth to respond, but Shepherd drops out of the sky next to me, wings flared in warning.

In front of us, the ward shimmers a faint green. Except, right at ground level, there's a pale blue circle.

"How the fuck?" Shepherd leans forward and gazes at it. "I patrolled here this morning, and this wasn't here. Why am I seeing a godsdamned portal?"

I set Iggy down and look at Miriam. "Can you take the kids back to Main? This isn't safe. I don't want you anywhere near this."

Miriam's fuchsia eyes go wide, but she grabs Iggy and reaches for Kevin.

"I don't wanna go," the pixie kid grumbles. "We found the portal; I wanna see what's in it."

I drop to one knee as a truck comes screeching to a halt behind him. "This isn't a joke; this isn't playtime, Kevin. This is serious. Thralls came through last time Wesley attacked us, remember? You don't want to meet a thrall."

He squeaks and hops up into Miriam's arms.

I lean forward and press a kiss to her forehead. "I'll find you later."

The Keeper, Dirk, and Richard hop out of the truck. One

of the hellhounds leaps out of the back and joins the other, snarling at the portal in the fucking ward.

The Keeper hands Miriam his keys. "Here, take my truck back."

Wordlessly, she packs the kids up and heads for town. I'm desperate to watch them go, but I'm more desperate to get the people I love far from this thing.

Dirk stalks to the ward, glaring at the faint blue circle. "This wasn't fucking here earlier. Your people patrolled; I patrolled. The godsdamned dogs sniffed this spot."

"It's here now," I snap.

Richard crosses his arms and stares at the portal. "I wonder if the Howl-O-Ween glamour exposed it somehow. Glamours affect the entire haven, even the wards."

"Let's figure that out later," Dirk barks. The sound of hoof-beats announces the arrival of his pegasus teammate. The rock troll slides off her back, followed by the final hellhound.

All three hounds bay and snap at the portal.

Dirk opens a box attached to his belt and takes out a tiny orb. He tosses it at the portal, and it sinks through.

"Godsdamnit," Richard snaps. "The portal's active right fucking now. How is this possible?"

The sylph steps back. "Sent the camera orb through. It'll tell us what's on the other side. I think we can assume it's Wesley, and our theory was correct."

"What then?" I question.

He cuts me a sharp look. "Can't make a plan 'til I know what I'm dealin' with, protector."

Awkward silence stretches long between us. The camera orb zips back out of the portal and into Dirk's hand.

"Ah, lovely," he murmurs. He depresses a button on his side, and a picture hologram lights up the surface of the ward. "The orb'll show us what we can expect on the other side. Let's have a look, then."

We're all silent as the orb pans around. There's a gods-damned field of tents. Monsters of all species mill around in armor. Some cook over open fires. Some sharpen weapons. Off in the distance, there's a castle.

"Shit," I bark. "This screams Wesley. That's a mirror-image of the castle in Pouyet where he's from. I'd think it *was* Pouyet if I hadn't been there. The geography isn't right, but that's the castle."

"We need tae capture Wesley," Dirk commands, looking at his team. "Give me infiltration options."

"Wait," I say, lifting a hand. "What if we don't need to go in there?"

Dirk scowls. "Got a better idea, gargoyle?"

"Yeah," I bark, lifting my comm watch. "Call Catherine."

Our resident succubus picks up on the first ring. I quickly explain what I found and ask her to join us.

I glance at the Keeper. His expression is grim. "Are you thinking what I think you're thinking?"

"Yeah," I confirm. "I expect I am."

Dirk growls. "Anyone wanna let me in on yer thoughts, then?"

We've got a few minutes until Catherine arrives, so I point at the portal. "We don't know exactly how Wesley did this, but you already know Catherine painted the haven system into existence."

"Right," Dirk snaps. "Those paintings are behind lock an' key at HQ. So what?"

"So," I draw it out. "Catherine can paint a prison and put this portal inside it. We don't have to go in there."

"Oh, fook," Dirk yells. "Of course!" Then he gives me another look. "She doesn't like to use that magic, I'm told."

"She'll do it for Ever," the Keeper responds.

We fall quiet as the hunter team examines the portal. All three hounds scratch and whine at the wards, distressed. The one with the star on her chest paces back and forth, tongue lolling out of her mouth.

Long minutes later, Catherine pulls up in her tiny car.

I quickly fill her in. Her face goes drawn and pinched when she sees the portal.

"Catherine," I say gently. "We wouldn't ask you to use that magic if our safety didn't depend on it."

She lifts a palm to stop me. "Say no more, Alo. The only problem is I need to see inside. A picture isn't enough. If I don't grab enough of the details, the magic won't be strong."

I run both hands through my hair. "Fuck, I don't want you going in."

"I'll go with you," the Keeper says, stepping forward.

"Hells no," I demand. "You're the last line of defense for our town, you can't go in there. The hunter team can go, and I'll go."

"Not going without me," Shepherd growls.

"You need to stay here for our people."

"Fuck that," my brother snaps.

"Shep, I'm not asking," I say softly. "As your older brother, I'm telling you to stay in case this goes badly."

He scoffs in disbelief. "You're pulling age rank? That's bullshit!"

I nod. "It's my duty, brother. I'm older. I'm going in. It'll be fine."

He zips his lips closed, not bothering to argue with me.

Dirk makes plans with his team, and then we stand in front of the portal with Catherine. Nerves spike in my stomach, my senses screaming at me not to do this. But we have to get Catherine what she needs to protect Ever.

To protect my son.

To protect my mate.

If I get outta this alive, I'm not waiting another minute to bind Miriam to me. I love her, and she loves me, and she's already been a part of my family for five years. I was stupid and trying to be honorable and do the right thing. I lost that time with her, but I won't make that mistake twice.

Catherine lays a hand on my arm. "Come on, friend. In and out stealthily. We'll be back home in no time."

I nod. The hunter team steps through the portal. Catherine goes next, disappearing into the faint blue light. I give Shepherd a look. He growls but nods in agreement. He knows what I mean. If shit goes south, take care of Iggy.

Then, I step into the light.

Cool tendrils of power snake and wrap around me. Portal magic always feels so invasive, like the magic's trying to rip you apart and mash you back together. I struggle not to shrug off bonds that feel like a spider wrapping me up in sticky webbing.

Faint trees appear ahead. I rush forward, stepping out of the portal into a dark forest. Catherine steps aside as I come through. I flare a wing protectively around her.

Dirk turns to me, putting a finger to his lips.

I know this drill. His team will go first. Catherine goes in the middle. I'll bring up the rear and protect Catherine at all costs. My tail lashes from side to side, the spade pointed and long in my battle form.

We creep quietly through the forest. Twice Dirk stops us, listening for anything. After long pauses, we keep going until there's a break in the trees. In front of us, giant fields of tents confirm our suspicion—Wesley's building a godsdamned army here. Thousands of tents line big open fields in a semi-circle around the black castle. It rises like a cliff up out of the ground.

Wesley's in there. He's in there right now, I fucking know it.

It's hard not to leap into the sky and rush for the castle to tear it down brick by brick.

Catherine looks around, her expression distraught but focused. I can't imagine how she feels knowing her former mate is going to such lengths to capture her. She ventures out of the forest just enough to look down the hill toward the field. Pulling out a sketchbook, she draws quietly on it, noting some detail. After ten brutally long minutes, she tiptoes back to us with a quiet thumbs-up.

I'm on high alert, my senses pinging at the wrongness of this place. Still, we make it back to the portal without seeing another being. I don't breathe until we come out of it and stand on Ever ground once more.

Dirk looks over at us. "Got what yeh need, Cath?"

"I do," she confirms. "I'll go home and paint right now. I need to work quickly while it's fresh in my mind."

Dirk nods at the rock troll. "Go with her. Keep her safe and comm me when it's done. We'll stand guard here, and I'll call HQ now."

The rock troll is too large to get in the car, and jogs behind Catherine as she leaves.

Dirk reaches into his pack on the ground and withdraws a comm disk, tossing it on the earth. "Call Evenia," he commands.

Next to me, the Keeper shuffles, crossing his arms.

His mother's hologram pops up, dark eyes flashing as she eyes our group. She gives the Keeper a dismissive look before turning her focus to Dirk. "Hunter, what do you have for me?"

"Found 'im," Dirk says. "Our suspicions are correct. There's a portal here in Ever. Alo had the genius idea to have Catherine paint it into a jail at HQ. She's just gone to do that."

"Mmm," Evenia murmurs, giving me a dismissive look. "What else?" she questions Dirk.

"We'll stand guard until yeh confirm the painting did its job. After that, we return home, I assume? Unless yeh have another assignment fer us?"

Evenia cuts the Keeper a snide look. "Actually, Dirk, I'd like you to stay on in Ever for a while to keep an eye on things. I wouldn't put it past Wesley to have a backup plan."

Ugh. Just what I need—more of this fucking guy.

"Done, boss. Anything else?"

Evenia grins. "Please remind Catherine that a room will always be available here at HQ. I'd still like her to move here. Perhaps you'll have better luck convincing her than I have."

"Fat chance," I mutter.

When Evenia clicks off, Dirk turns to me. "Stand guard with me, protector?"

I nod as our group splits. Richard shoots me a quick look. "I'll patrol, but I'll stay close just in case." He jogs off into the pitch-black forest.

Despite Dirk standing there, I comm Miriam to give her an update. She's at the cottage with the kids, and everybody's fine.

They're safe, thank fuck.

When we click off, Dirk grins at me, blue eyes flicking to my watch and back up.

"Yeh're lucky, protector. Fecking lucky."

I cross my arms. "I know," I say simply.

His smile turns thoughtful. "Many'd give a wing to have what yeh have. A beautiful mate, a gorgeous family. I'm jealous, I'll admit."

Ugh. I don't want to talk about feelings and end up liking the big sylph. But damnit, I know what he means. I longed for Miriam for years, and now that she's mine, something feels complete in my chest.

But two hours later, I've had enough Dirk to last me for a lifetime. He pivoted from sharing emotions to softly humming. For two godsdamned hours.

Non-fucking-stop.

When Catherine calls to let us know the painting is done, I breathe an audible sigh of relief. Dirk and I watch as the blue ring in the ward fades until it's gone. The ward's surface once again glows a faint, healthy green.

Dirk comms HQ, and Evenia confirms the portal now leads to a jail cell at HQ.

"Thank fook she dinnae call me back tae HQ," he mutters when she signs off the second time.

I raise a brow in question.

"She's gonna go in there and rain hellfire down on Wesley, if I had mah guess, and I dinnae wanna be there for it. I fooking hate leading attacks. I'm much better as a hunter." He gives me a curious look. "There's a certain gargoyle female she'll probably pick. Something tells me yeh know that, though."

Keira.

My bloodthirsty ex-mate is the perfect monster to lead an attack on Wesley. Let her go do it. I want less to do with it than Dirk does.

My people are safe. My child is safe. My woman is safe. And all I want is to be with them. But there's something I need to do before I can go home.

I look over at Richard as he jogs back into view. "You got a few minutes to help me with something, alpha?"

Dark eyes spark at me. "Of course, Alo."

"Good," I mutter. "Let's get the fuck outta here."

CHAPTER TWENTY-TWO

MIRIAM

Alo comm'd me to let me know what happened, but I don't think I'll rest easy until I get him back in my arms. I try taking Iggy back to Main to keep us both occupied, but I can't enjoy Howl-O-Ween. Not while the rest of Ever goes on happily oblivious to the damn portal we've discovered. Just like a five-year-old would, Iggy goes right back to partying with Kevin, not another thought given to what he found.

The hellhound with the star appears again, trailing after us. Despite my reluctance, I can begrudgingly admit I feel safer having the dog right behind us. I might have a sordid history with hellhounds, but technically she's a protector.

Eventually, Howl-O-Ween ends, and Main grows silent and dark. Iggy slumps over my shoulder, snoring. Kevin has long since gone home.

And Alo still isn't back.

I resist the urge to comm him and check in, but he doesn't need me bugging him while he's trying to protect our home. Will it always be like this? Me being terrified when he has to go do his job?

I think so. But I try to remind myself that, in all the time I've lived in Ever, it's only recently that we've had any sort of safety issue. And if Alo's right, they found a fix, and Wesley will never be a problem again.

Heading back to the cottage, I thank her when she opens the front door for me. I pace through the quiet space as she flicks the lights on, illuminating my way. Iggy falls into his nest and grabs a blanket, curling into a ball in the center.

I retreat to Alo's room, but looking around at all the carvings, I can't sit there. Not with Keira's beautiful face staring at me from the backmost wall. Ugh.

Downstairs in the kitchen, I make a drink. Then I heat up a dinner I'm unable to eat. Eventually, I fall asleep on the sofa.

Sometime in the middle of the night, I wake up in Alo's arms. He's carrying me across the street from the cottage and into the garden.

"Alo." I grin. "You're back."

Relief crashes through me, and I lean into his chest. He smells as delicious as always, like a cedar forest and manly soap. I feel better than I have in hours.

He smiles down at me. "I'm back, pixie girl. And my favorite two people are safe." He stalks along the garden paths, stooping under the A-frame. "Dust us, woman."

Chuckling, I pop into small form and grab a handful of dust from the bowl just inside my front door. His glittering eyes close, and I toss the dust at his face. With a small pop, Alo morphs into small form and glides gracefully up to my porch. He stalks through the door, wings flaring wide behind him. They blot out pale light from the garden, making him look like a giant purple-gray demon standing in my doorway.

Alo's horns straighten slightly, pressing to his head. He shuts the door behind him with a wing and lets out a soft growl, eyes flashing with need. "I can't wait another minute longer to have you, Miriam."

"But Iggy—" I protest.

"Is currently being protected by a damn hellhound, who's parked herself on our porch. Guess you didn't notice it when we walked past her, sleepyhead."

I resist the urge to flit out the door and double-check.

"Go look if you need to," he encourages me, opening the door once more.

I should take him at his word, but the need to be sure Iggy's safe eats at me. I zip past Alo to the garden's entrance. There on the cottage's front porch, the hellhound with the white star lies in front of the door. Her blazing eyes are watchful.

The cottage waves her shutters at me.

I giggle.

He's safe, my little bestie. Safe and asleep, and I am so, so, so proud of him.

I return inside. Alo's at my pink kitchen island, pouring himself a drink from my bar. He lifts it to his lips and takes a slow sip. "Happy, pixie girl?"

"Very," I admit. I cross the room and slide my hands under his shirt, pressing my forehead to his chest. He's all rock-hard muscle. We stand like that for long minutes, soaking in the pleasure of being together. Finally, I look up. "What happened after you comm'd me?"

Alo strips his shirt off and rubs my hands down his abs and back up. "Catherine painted the portal into a prison at Hearth HQ, so it leads there now. Evenia's assembling a hunter team to infiltrate it and capture Wesley, and Richard's delivering the painting to Hearth HQ as we speak. They'll keep it behind lock and key, and then they've got to figure out how the hells Wesley was able to do this." He strokes my chin with the backs of his knuckles. "But that's their job, pixie girl. My job is done. For tonight," he tacks on.

I can't hold back a thankful grin. "You were so amazing

tonight, Alo," I murmur. "Watching you in battle mode like that was terrifying, but I never had any doubt you'd protect us."

"Good," he whispers. "Because I'll protect you every day for the rest of our lives. And one day, Iggy will hopefully join me."

I snort at that. "He missed you tonight, but we took Kevin back to Main, and he moved on pretty fast. Must be nice to be five, in that sense."

"He's resilient," Alo offers. "But we'll talk to him about it tomorrow. It scared the shit out of me for him to be near the portal, but he saved our town. He's a damn hero." Alo's expression goes soft and thoughtful.

"I'm so proud of him," I say finally.

Alo smiles. "Sorry it took me a while to get home, but I've got a gift for you, Mir."

"You're the only gift I need," I state, looking into those beautiful dark eyes. "I don't want anything else, Alo."

He reaches for his drink and takes another sip. "Oh, I think you'll enjoy this one though. I took a trip this evening to see your queen." He sets the drink down and drops to both knees. "I know it's traditional to ask for her permission to mate if I can't ask your parents."

My senses ping, butterflies rocketing around in my belly. My heart thuds in my chest, heat streaking to my cheeks. "You saw the queen?"

"And asked for your hand," he confirms, reaching into his pocket. When he draws out four delicate metal wing tips, my hand flies to my throat.

He reaches up, handing the beautiful metal tips to me. "Take me officially, Miriam, and allow me to claim you in the ways of my people. I don't want to go another minute without you being mine in all of the ways."

I stare at the triangular wing tips, designed to perfectly fit over the edge of each of my wings. They're significant, and so expensive that most pixies don't even bother with this tradition any longer.

"I can't believe you did this," I whisper.

Alo beams at me. "Is that a yes, mate?"

Mate.

My hands tremble as I take the tips from him and turn them over. They're beautiful scrolled silver swirls with inlaid aqua jewels the same color as my hair. Tears fill my eyes. "Alo, I—"

"Say you will, Mir," he commands.

A dam breaks inside me, emotion rushing to the surface as I pull him up off the ground. I throw myself into his arms, tears streaming down my cheeks. My legs go around his waist as I sob into his neck.

"Easy, Mir." He chuckles, rubbing my back. "Is that a yes?"

"Of course!" I cry. "Of fucking course it's a yes! I love you so much!"

"Good," he snuffles into my ear. "Let me place these."

I reluctantly slide out of his arms and turn, my body a live wire of anticipation.

Gentle fingers stroke down my spine. On a shiver, my head falls forward. Alo's body's not pressed to mine, but I sense his presence just behind me.

"Beautiful," he whispers. Deft fingers stroke the base of my wing.

I cry out at the streak of pleasure that shoots through it, sending me quivering as my knees buckle.

Alo growls softly. "I love how you respond to me, Miriam. I love knowing I'm the one who makes you shudder. Is that sweet pussy wet, pixie girl?"

"Gods," I huff out.

"Let me feel that honey." He slips one hand around my waist. Big fingers tug at my waistband, pulling my jeans down my thighs to pool on the ground. "I want to put my tongue here," he whispers in my ear, pressing his chest to my back. "I want to feel you shake when I suck on you, Miriam."

I'm panting with need, reaching down to claw at his forearm. "Lower, Alo," I demand. "Touch me, please."

He doesn't respond, but soft lips come to my shoulder. The wet swipe of his tongue follows the kiss. Teeth drag gently along my skin, goose bumps rising in their wake. My head falls to the side as Alo tastes and lavishes.

"Do you know how gargoyles mate, Miriam?" he asks the question in my ear. One hand comes to my left wing. He places the cap on it.

I shout as magic sears my wing bone, heat streaking to the tip before suddenly dissipating. When I flutter it, there's a new slight weight on the very edge.

"Magic?" I blurt out. "You got the magical ones?"

"Only the best for you." He reaches for the bottom of my left wing and slips the second silver piece onto the end. "I didn't want them to fall off. Because when I fuck you, Miriam, I'm not going to be gentle."

I cry out, arching my body into his. Alo grinds his hips against mine with a groan. He grabs my right wing and slips a third cap onto the bottom of it. The magic zings and pokes at my wing, and then the cap is permanent.

"Last one," he says, slipping the final tip on my top-right wing section. It clips into place. I flutter both wings, adjusting to the new weight. Turning in Alo's arms, I try to hold back another sob. Glancing over my shoulders, I admire the wing tips. They glint in the low light.

"They're so beautiful," I gush. "Thank you, Alo. I—"

He silences me with an unhinged, desperate kiss, like he wants to be as deeply inside me as he can. Hoisting me into his arms, he grips the back of my neck.

I'm caught in place, drowning under his onslaught. This

isn't a kiss; Alo's staking his claim over my body, mind, and heart.

He pulls away just long enough to murmur, "You are my everything, mate. I love you."

I attack him with my mouth, my tongue swiping along his. I suck at it, rolling my hips against him. "Bed," I command.

Alo turns and paces through the living room and into my bedroom. He lays me down on the bed and reaches for my shirt. Big hands rip it into two pieces, throwing them aside. Then he stands and unbuttons his jeans. The moment he slides the zipper down, his cock falls heavy out of them, jutting toward me.

Like every time I see him naked, I gasp at his size. He's long and curved and fucking thick. Add the flat protrusion over his dick and you've got the perfect cock. It takes everything I have not to fall onto my belly and show him everything.

Alo growls, and it sends goose bumps breaking out over my whole body.

"Mir, I'll ask again. Do you remember how gargoyles take their mates?" He slips his pants all the way down.

I'm too gobsmacked staring at his tree trunk thighs to answer. He puts a finger under my chin and lifts my gaze. "Need a refresher, pixie girl?"

I gulp. "I've been dreaming of this for years, Alo."

He smiles, horns flattening against his head as fangs peek out from his gray lips. "I'm going to slip inside you, Miriam. I'm going to make you come over and over, and when you're sobbing at the pleasure, I'll sink my fangs into you here." Big fingers snake down my neck to stroke a spot at the base of my shoulder. Dark eyes flick back to mine. "And when I bite you, my heart will start beating. Only for you, Miriam. Only ever for you, for the rest of our lives."

Tears fill my eyes again. Pixies don't have mating rituals like this.

"It's perfect."

Alo slides his hand down to my chest and pushes me backward. "You need at least two orgasms before I claim you, Miriam."

"I don't want to wait," I moan. But my complaint falls on deaf ears. Alo leans forward and licks a stripe up my pussy.

He's wet and soft, and the pressure of his lips has me arching my back to get closer to him. He groans, and that sound makes my pussy clench on nothing. Big hands come to my ass, and he holds me spread as he licks his way down my cleft and back up, nibbling my skin. His tongue slips inside, and he strokes a circle over that spot that drives me wild.

Growling, he grips my hips and flips me face down. He drags me back onto my knees and buries his face between my thighs.

Orgasm rips through me as his tongue dives in and out of my pussy. He moans, desperate sounds rising to a crescendo like he's so hot from doing this, he'll explode just from tasting me. A tidal wave of pleasure forces my legs shut as I scream. Stars burst behind my eyelids as I clench my teeth and shove my face into the soft sheets.

Pleasure fades, but Alo's not done. He pushes me forward onto my stomach and grabs my thighs, spreading me wide.

"Hold on to something, pixie girl," he commands.

I reach for the sheets. Alo covers me from behind, sliding into me one throbbing inch at a time. I cry out at a brutal snap of his hips.

"So full," I gasp. "You're huge, Alo. Gods!"

He chuckles. "You're good for my ego, mate. Tell me what else you like about this fat cock."

Oh gods.

He reaches between us, stroking me as something more

slips inside me. "I think this might be your favorite thing," he whispers. And then he godsdamn vibrates it, and it resonates against my G-spot. He laughs as I go off like a rocket, orgasm ripping through me a second time. Fluid soaks him as I clench around his impossible length.

A keening cry leaves my lips as I grip the sheets. Alo's everywhere. His scent, his filthy words. That godsdamned cock. He's not even thrusting; he's just teasing, and I'm undone by the entire thing.

When I come down, he lets out a pleased laugh. "Watching you come is my favorite activity. I need it again. Maybe a third time before I bite you, Mir."

"No," I groan. "Mission accomplished. I'm boneless. I'm near to sobbing, Alo." I look over my shoulder. "Don't make me wait. Please. I've waited so long for you."

That last bit does it. Alo grunts and flips us over so my back is pressed to his chest, and he's underneath me, still inside me, still fucking hard and slow.

"An apology then." He growls as my head falls back against him. "My deepest"—he thrusts once, hard, shaking me with force—"fucking"—thrust—"apologies."

I cry out at how he fills me. So fucking perfect. I'm going to fall apart again before he even says another sentence.

"You deserve everything, Miriam." A slow drag of his hips sends my pleasure sky-high. "You deserve every inch of me, pixie girl. Open wide while I fuck you." One hand comes to my slit, and he strokes my skin while his hips piston against me. "Show me your throat, Miriam." His voice is boulders tumbling from a rocky cliff, crashing into one another on the way down.

I clench around him, looking to my right to give him access.

"Beautiful," he croons. His fangs come to my neck, and he scrapes me, a hint of pain to drive the pleasure higher.

Then he strikes like a cobra, fangs sinking in where my neck meets my shoulder. Shooting pain and ungodsly bliss crack like twin whips against my consciousness. Alo bellows into the bite, and that unhinged noise sends me over the edge. Release squirts out of me, coating us both as ecstasy racks me. Alo's hips jerk fast, in and out, fucking me with wild abandon.

He unloads deep inside me with a choked roar. His movements lose their rhythm as he pants and grunts. I'm caught in his arms with his teeth buried in my shoulder, a tidal wave of emotion rolling over me, battering me against him.

We come together for so long, I lose track of time. I come until I'm ready to pass out. Only then does Alo release the bite, licking it softly to help it heal.

He growls, "Mine forever now."

A smile splits my face. Alo rolls us onto our sides, but I flip in his arms and press my ear to his chest.

Silence.

My smile falls.

Alo grunts, his body jerking as his back arches. Big hands grip the sheets, twisting them into knots. A scream falls from his lips, veins popping to the surface of his neck.

His scream becomes a deafening roar as cum spurts from his cock, coating his stomach. Alo's eyes are squinted tightly closed, claws ripping at the sheets as his body contracts and arches over and over.

Oh. My. Gods.

CHAPTER TWENTY-THREE

ALO

Sensation screams through me, blood rushing to my heart. It's been still since Keira, but I forgot what it was like for it to beat.

It was never like *this*.

It throbs in my chest, vibrating my whole body as orgasm crashes through me. I come a second time, and a third, spurting all over my stomach as my abs clench painfully. Miriam throws herself across me, shouting my name. She sounds worried, but all I can do is sob and groan as something yanks me from the inside out.

Thump. Thump. Thump.

The steady drumbeat of my heart.

"Alo!" Miriam shrieks. "Are you dying? Oh my gods, talk to me!"

I struggle to laugh. My heart feels like it takes up my entire chest, and there's no space for me to even breathe. I snake an arm around her and bring her ear to my pecs. "Listen, Mir."

She goes quiet. My chest rises and falls, that steady clock inside me calling to her, encouraging her beat to match mine.

She gasps, looking up at me. "I feel you! I feel you in here." She rubs at her chest and puts her ear to my pec again.

"This is the most incredible sound." Her voice quakes with emotion.

Grunting around the intensity of my own heartbeat, I push her back and press my ear to her chest. Hers flutters fast like a bird, but as I listen, it slows until it's beating in time with mine.

"Your heartbeat is the most beautiful music I've ever heard," I whisper, looking up at her. Emotion overcomes me, and my voice breaks. "I love you, Miriam."

She laughs, tears streaming down her cheeks. Leaning forward, she presses those soft lips to mine. "I love you too, Aloitious Rygold."

"Good," I murmur. "Come fuck me, mate."

And we do. For hours and hours, until morning sun filters through her gourd. Then I carry her to the shower to clean her up.

She yawns while I comb the knots out of her tangled hair. "I wanna go home. Iggy'll be up soon." She falls lazily against my chest, and I laugh, kissing the top of her head. I drag my lips down the side of her neck, nibbling at the mark that'll show everyone she's mine.

"Can't wait for Dirk to see this," I huff with pride.

Miriam laughs. "You really do not like that guy, huh?"

I growl, pressing fingers into her soft belly. "Mine. Everything about you is mine, and I don't want him lookin' at you."

She turns in my arms. "I love that you're a jelly toast, but it's always been you for me."

Grinning, I haul her into my arms and out of her gourd. She dusts us back into large form, and then we head to the cottage.

When we cross Sycamore, the cottage waggles her front steps at us.

Miriam freezes when she notices the hellhound still on the stairs. Its eyes are closed, but as we get closer, they blink open. She cuts us an assessing look before stretching out long, her claws contracting like a cat's.

"Looks like yeh've got a dog," Dirk's voice carries in the early morning quiet.

Miriam whirls around with a snort. "A what? No. Absolutely not. We can't have a dog, and not that dog. No." She crosses her thin arms and starts tapping her foot.

I give Dirk a fuck-off look.

He paces quietly up the street, both hands slung through his pants loops. "I don't make the rules, pixie. Hellhounds bond to one person in their life. I've been tryin' fer years to bond Minnie to me, and she never would. Now I know why. Plus she's pregnant, so there'll be more soon."

"Nooo." Miriam slaps a hand over her forehead. "You've got to be shitting me."

I know she's mad if she's cussing. She rarely does it.

I pluck at her wings, playing with the fancy new silver tips. She shudders. "We don't have to keep her, baby."

Miriam turns. "Bonded? Fucking bonded? I don't want it."

At that exact moment, the cottage door flies open. The dog leaps up and whirls around as Iggy barrels out the door, throwing his arms around the hellhound's neck.

I glare at Dirk, but he throws both hands up in the air and walks away slowly, laughing.

Dickhead.

"Come get your dog," I command. "Don't you dare leave this dog here."

Dirk sighs and turns as Minnie and Iggy join us. Minnie flops down at my feet. Iggy hops on top of her and rubs fervently at her ears.

The sylph lifts two fingers to his blue lips and whistles, patting his thigh with the other hand.

Minnie lets out a displeased harrumph but doesn't move.

Dirk shrugs. "Like I said, I don't make the rules. Congrats on yer new family member, protector." His eyes go to Miriam's rapidly fluttering wings. "Or should I say members, plural."

I laugh. Miriam scowls. Iggy lets out a whoop. Minnie stands and walks back toward the cottage with Iggy astride her like a horseback rider.

Godsdamn. I guess we've got a dog.

~

Three days later, I stand in front of the cottage waiting for Iggy.

"She's coming! She's coming!" Iggy zips up Sycamore from Main, shrieking at the top of his lungs.

"Best lookout ever!" Wren whisper-hisses, slapping him a high five when he gets close enough. The Hectors, Shepherd, Ohken, and the Keeper all stand in front of the cottage. I'm barely suppressing a grin as Miriam rounds the corner from Main and heads our direction.

As soon as she gets close enough to notice us, she gives me a sly look, waving at our friends. "Aloitious Rygold, you look sneaky as hells. What are you up to? And why are you all here?"

Wren laughs. "You're not the only one with sneaky secrets, missy. Although I don't think any of us will ever be able to top your Howl-O-Ween extravaganza."

Miriam's smile grows devious. "Nope. I can only top myself. Wait until you see what I have in mind for next year. Morgan's idea about turning Town Hall into a haunted house is gonna be, like, the ultimate awesomeness."

"Pixie girl," I break in, pulling Iggy up onto my shoulder. "Come here."

Iggy hops up and down with excitement, his spade slipping into my shirt to rest against my heart. He's fascinated with the way it beats now, constantly touching it with his tail and asking a million questions.

He leaps into the air, forgetting he's wrapped around my neck. Jerking to a halt, he laughs and flutters back onto my shoulder with a sheepish grin.

I give him the go-ahead look.

He clears his throat. "Miriam, me and Dad wanted to do something special for you." He looks over at the Keeper. "We're ready!"

I turn to face the cottage. Miriam comes to stand next to me.

The Keeper laughs and snaps his fingers.

The cottage shimmers and fades, and where there was just a story and a half before, it's now two full stories tall. A new addition covers the right side of the cottage. She waggles new pink-and-green shutters at us.

"Oh my gods," Miriam says. "You built onto the cottage?"

"Not just any old thing, either," Iggy says wisely. "We built you a nest so you'd have your own."

"A new beginning," Wren murmurs, resting her head on Miriam's shoulder. "Go in and see it, Mir."

Miriam looks around in disbelief at the group. "How did you do all this?"

The Keeper gives her a kind smile. "Iggy and Alo had the idea. I designed it, and as soon as Ohken built it, I hid it so we could do this today. Welcome home, Miriam."

She shoots me a gobsmacked look. Then she turns and sprints for the door. Iggy unwraps himself from me and zooms after her with a laugh. Minnie trundles quietly after them, her big belly swaying. Gods, we'll be covered in hellhound puppies soon.

The Keeper claps me on the shoulder. "Congratulations,

friend. I couldn't be happier for you. Go, be with your mate, and call us if you need us."

I give my friends a thankful look. "I appreciate you all so—"

"Get outta here, bro!" Thea shouts. "Thank us later after you, erm, experience the nest." She waggles her pale brows at me. Shepherd snorts.

I turn toward my home and my family. They're everything, and they're finally mine.

As I pace toward my front door, I hear the Keeper's quiet voice. "Morgan, have breakfast with me?"

I don't turn around to stare, even though I want to. Someone clears their throat, probably Morgan.

"Um, okay. That's fine."

Grinning, I enter my cottage and shut the door.

Another love story might be unfolding in Ever. But for now, I just want to grab ahold of mine.

CHAPTER TWENTY-FOUR

MIRIAM

I jog up the stairs with Iggy right behind me giggling like a madman. At the top of the stairs where there was a long hall with Alo's nest and Iggy's room at the end, there's now a door on the left. I whip it open and dive through.

"See!" Iggy zooms around as I stare at the room in awe. It's a two-story nest, twice the size of the other one. The entire roof is one big sheet of glass, letting the sun in. My gourd hangs from a giant branch that pokes into the room up near the ceiling.

Alo's lips come to my ear. "We can move the gourd back, if you want, pixie girl. But I thought you might like to have a private space in our home."

Our home.

Words I've wanted him to say for years. And he's finally mine. They both are.

A giant round nest rises up from the center of the room. The nest itself is the palest of pinks—my favorite color. Three of the walls are natural wood, and only one is carved. It's full of memories from when Alo and Iggy first came to Ever. I round the nest to trace the beautiful carvings.

There's the day the Keeper introduced me to Alo at Higher Grounds. Iggy was just a baby, and he was sobbing, but I offered to take him. I'll never forget the grateful look in Alo's eyes when his son fell silent and sleepy in my arms.

And there's the day Iggy went to preschool for the first time, and I took Alo to breakfast at the Galloping Green Bean to take his mind off it. We cried over breakfast and then hung out all day until Iggy got home raving about meeting a pixie named Kevin.

One entire wall is covered with our smiling faces. There's even a carving of Alo standing in the garden, looking at my gourd.

"That's when Dad was pining for you," Iggy says sagely.

I snort, but Alo comes up behind me. "It's true. I pined for a hot minute."

Turning around, I grin. "I've got something for you guys too. I ordered them last week, but they just now arrived."

Alo cocks his head to the side, fluttering big wings at his back. "Sneaky girl."

Iggy zooms in circles around my head. "Presents? I love presents! What is it? Lemme see, Miriam!"

I reach into my pocket and pull out two silver bracelets, holding them up. "They're the matching set to my wing covers." I shimmy my wings playfully.

Iggy grabs one of the bracelets and holds it out to me. "Can you put it on me, Miriam?"

I nod and take it, slipping it over his chunky fist. "Be very careful with this, Ignatius. This is important—it tells every-body you're my kid, okay? You can never lose it!"

He looks up at me as he hovers in place. Sapphire-blue eyes sparkle with tears. "Okay, Miriam. Thank you."

I gulp around the sudden lump in my throat.

I have a kid.

Brushing away happy tears, I turn to Alo. "Give me your hand."

He holds it out, and I slide the larger bracelet over his wrist, tracing the veins along the inside of his forearm. His heartbeat thumps visibly in the veins. It beats for me, and I can't imagine anything cooler than that.

My eyes move to Alo's as I tighten the bracelet. He's giving me a soft look, a look so full of love, it steals my breath.

"Love you," he murmurs. "So damn much, Miriam."

"You're stuck with me now," I say as I fasten the bracelet tight around his wrist.

"Me too," Iggy says. He grabs my hand and yanks me toward the door. "Come see what we did with the old nest! It's a playroom, and it's got all my toys and stuff, and Ohken built me a secret playhouse in the closet, and there's a slide that goes down into the kitchen! Come see!"

He zooms off without a backward glance.

Alo presses me to the wall, grinding his hips against me. "Iggy's been desperate to show you the secret library. But once we put him to bed, you're mine, pixie girl."

"Always," I agree, stroking the band around his wrist that marks him as my mate.

Iggy pops back into the room. "Are you guys coming or what? Eww, gross. Are you makin' out?!"

Alo turns and snorts. "*Making out?* Where the hells did you learn that word?"

Iggy shrugs. "Kevin told me it's how mommies and daddies make babies."

I laugh, shooting Alo a look. Time for a redirect. "Let's go see this library and slide, shall we?"

He trails me out of the nest and toward Iggy's room, but before we follow our kid in, he pulls me back to his chest. Rough lips come to my neck and nip at my mating mark.

"Speaking of making babies, Miriam, I want to do that with you. And I want it as soon as you're ready, mate."

A shudder racks my body. We've talked about kids dozens of times over the years. I've always wanted a big family.

I turn in his arms. "Deal. Practice later?" My grin widens as heat curls through me.

Alo presses his lips to mine. "Deal, mate."

EPILOGUE - ALO

Morgan paces next to me, the gas station at our backs. When she nibbles at her thumbnail, Richard sighs and crosses his arms. She's been pacing for the last fifteen minutes nonstop.

Dirk looks over at me with a sarcastic grin. "This is exciting, isn't it?" His glacier-blue eyes sparkle as she wears a line in the dirt beside me.

I roll mine and give him a shitty look. I don't know if I'll ever forgive his flirtation with Miriam, even though she was never interested. On top of which he saddled us with that damn dog, although she hasn't been nearly as awful as I expected.

Shepherd steps in Morgan's path, bringing both hands to her shoulders. She looks up, her expression almost distraught.

"Hey sis," he says softly. "I've got this, okay? This is literally my job. We'll get Lou to you safe and sound, okay? Besides, the map we used to call her, and you, as you might remember, has a protective spell."

She smiles, but it looks fake, falling almost instantly.

Thea and Wren stand by my side, staring at the faintly glowing wards.

Shepherd's comm watch pings and he glances up the road toward the ward edge. "Almost time. She should be coming around the corner in just a sec. Glamours on, every—wait." He looks over at me, his tone dropping an octave. "Thralls. Be ready."

"Thralls?" Morgan shouts. "Are you fucking kidding me? What's going on?"

I cast my senses around, and he's fucking right. That telltale tingle streaks down my spine, my horns flattening to my scalp.

"Hectors, behind me," snaps the Keeper.

Dirk disappears into thin air and Richard shifts into his wolf, sprinting toward the country highway that leads into town.

A beat-up truck barrels around the corner, tires screeching. A swarm of thralls follow it, one dangling from the driver's side window.

A woman is barely visible in the driver's seat, shrieking as she guns the truck toward us, trying to beat the thrall off at the same time.

Shepherd and I swoop into the sky and claw toward the ward.

The thrall yowls and swipes through the driver's side window. The woman screams and jerks the wheel sideways, the truck skidding. The thrall at her window goes flying and hits a tree. A swarm behind her takes its place, leaping into the truck bed and bashing their heads against the cab's back window. Long, claw-tipped arms scratch and tear at the truck cab.

Shepherd and I push through the wards. Thea's magic steals over me in a rush of heat, sealing them tight behind us. Terror is laced through the magic itself, but there's no time for me to stop and think about it.

We streak through the air, snatching thralls off the tiny

truck and slicing them in two. They don't turn to fight us. They seem intent only on getting at the woman inside.

Richard and Dirk join us, ripping thralls from the cab and dispatching as many as we can.

The woman screams when the truck hits the ward and bounces off. Thralls fly over the cab and hit the ward. It sizzles with Thea's magic as they hit it and drop to the truck's hood.

Shepherd, Richard, Dirk, and I are on them before they have a second to recover. In the span of thirty seconds, we dispatch every one.

The forest falls silent except for the woman's labored breathing.

I drop out of the sky next to the truck. Dirk pops into view next to me, one hand on the truck frame as he peers in.

The driver door is gone, and inside, a woman who could be Thea's twin grips the steering wheel, her knuckles white. She turns her head slowly toward us, amber eyes going wide as she grits her jaw tightly. Her gaze moves from me to Dirk and back again. Her muscles visibly tremble, her long-sleeved shirt ripped. Blood seeps from a wound on her shoulder.

Dirk's the first to speak. "Hey darlin'. Got yerself in a bit of a pickle somehow, but yer safe now, okay?"

Her eyes go wider. She's about to vomit, I can smell it bubbling up in her gut.

She needs a distraction.

"You're Lou, right?" I ask. "The triplets are waiting for you."

At my mention of the triplets she springs out of the truck and bashes her fists against my chest. "Where are they? Are they safe? Where are my girls?"

I fling both hands up and jerk my head toward the ward.

Magic snaps and pops as Thea drops her protective spell and rushes toward us.

Lou gasps with visible relief and runs to Thea. The women clash together, arms going around one another as sobs ring through the air. Morgan and Wren rush to join them, and the four girls fall to the ground in a sobbing pile.

Shepherd joins Dirk and me.

She was bleeding, did you see that? Think one of the thralls bit her?

Fuck. Fuuuuck.

I run both hands through my hair as Richard and the Keeper join us.

The girls stand, helping Lou up.

Thea clutches Lou's good hand to her chest. "What happened, Lou?"

It's then I realize not a single one of us still has our glamour up. Lou is literally faced with two gargoyles, a were-wolf, and a fucking sylph. At least the Keeper looks somewhat human, ruby red eyes notwithstanding.

Whiskey-pale eyes flick over to us. "I don't know. I was driving up the road and one of those...those things leaped onto the car. What the fuck was that?!" She points at us. "And what the fuck is going on here? Did I die? Am I dead?"

Morgan rubs a splatter of blood off Lou's cheek. "Honey, we've got a lot to tell you, but you're hurt. So let's get you to the doc and we'll go from there, okay?"

Lou lifts her arm, touching a long gash that runs from the top of her shoulder to her elbow. "Fuck," she grunts. "That godsdamn stings."

Shepherd gives me a look and speaks into our bond. *She says godsdamn? Gods, plural? Godsdamn?*

I roll my shoulders. Somehow, I suspect there's more to Lou than meets the eye. When we first dropped our glamours for the Hector triplets there was a lot of screaming and passing out. I don't know if Lou's just hyped on adrenaline or what, but she's taking this far better than I would expect.

The Keeper joins the triplets and introduces himself. He guides the girls through the ward and to Thea's old Honda parked in front of the gas station. They get in and drive toward town.

Dirk glances at Shepherd, Richard and me. "If that's a bite an' not a scratch, we're gonna have a problem. Yeh know that, right? What're yeh gonna do if she turns into one o' them?" He jerks his head toward the dismembered thralls lying in heaps around us.

Richard sighs and pinches the bridge of his nose.

"Fuck," Shepherd says aloud. "How the fuck did they even find her? The map is spelled."

None of us seem willing to answer Dirk's question. The idea of it is too fucking horrible. If the thralls did more than scratch her, if they bit her, she'll become one of them. And if she becomes a thrall...

Richard stalks to one of the downed beasts and drops to a knee, examining its back haunches. After a moment, he looks up, dark eyes narrowed. "Wesley's sigil is burned into this one," he growls. "But how? He's locked inside his haven in a cell at HQ."

I shake my head. This whole thing stinks of Wesley. But we beat him at his own game already. So how are thralls bypassing the map's magic? That's a question for another day, though.

The only thing I know for sure is that I've got my happily ever after, and I won't risk it for anything in the entire fucking world.

EPILOGUE - MIRIAM

I nibble at the edge of my thumb. Swear to gods I picked up this habit from Morgan, because she does it too. I visited the triplets and their Aunt Lou this morning. Lou is lovely. She reminds me so much of Thea, in particular. She's recovering from the thrall attack at Doc Slade's. As soon as he clears her —*if* he clears her—she'll stay next door at the Annabelle.

That's not why I'm nervous at this precise moment, though. Alo and Iggy sit at the kitchen island with our comm disk on the countertop. A name flashes above it.

Noctis Raven Rygold.

My father-in-law.

His name flashes for a few seconds before a striking male gargoyle steps into view. He could be Alo, or Alo's extremely handsome older brother. A straight nose leads to thick, angular brows. They frame sharp cheeks and eyes black enough to be cut from obsidian. His hair is the same shade and cut as Alo's, but sprinkles of white dot his temples. Beautiful horns sweep up and back from his forehead. They're longer than my mate's, and tipped in decorative silver points.

He's shirtless, a dagger strapped sideways to a holster

around his ample chest. He looks ready to go to war. He breaks into a smile, revealing twin white fangs. "Aloitious, Ignatius, hello my boys!"

I bite harder on my thumb. Oh gods, I'm going to be sick.

"Grandpa Noctis, we have huge news, like, it's so huge!" Iggy shouts at the hologram.

Noctis crosses both arms over his chest and gives Iggy a playful smile. "Huge news, hmm? Does your grandmother need to be here for this?"

Oh fuck. I grip the edge of the counter. Alo looks through the hologram at me, a smile curving his beautiful lips.

"Yeah!" Iggy says. "Call Grandma. Please," he tacks on at the end.

Noctis leans out of view, calling for his mate.

I close my eyes, focused on drawing deep breaths into my lungs. My heart beats so fast, it's all I can hear. Across the island from me, Alo rubs absentmindedly at his chest.

When a stunning female gargoyle joins Noctis, slinging one arm around his waist, I hold back an anxious scream.

Iggy glances over at me, looking concerned. "Miriam, are you okay? You look like you're having a heart attack."

Oh fuck, oh godsdamnit. I was planning to let them break the news before I stepped into view.

Noctis clears his throat. "Ignatius, who are you talking to?"

Alo reaches around Iggy's back, holding a hand out for me. "Come here, my love."

His parents stiffen.

But this is it, this is my moment to make a good first impression. I raise my chin and plaster a smile on my face, reaching around the island. Alo's fingers curl around mine, and he pulls me into view, settling me between his thighs, my back to his chest. Iggy hops up and down on the countertop in front of me.

Noctis's eyes narrow, but his mate clasps both hands and smiles.

Iggy's hopping intensifies as he throws both hands up in the air. "Grandpa Noctis, Grandma Seraphina, this is Miriam! She's my mom now! She was super nervous to meet you, but she's my best friend, and—"

"Hang on a sec, buddy," Alo says gently. He grabs Iggy's tail and pulls him onto his outside shoulder.

I resist the urge to bite my nail again.

Alo wraps one arm around my waist, settling his hand on my upper stomach. "Mother, Father, meet Miriam Saihem, my mate."

A single tear slides down his mother's face, and then another. She looks up at Alo's Father. "Oh Noctis, can you believe it?"

Noctis looks skeptical, dark eyes fastened to me. They're two glittering points I can't seem to look away from. "No, I can't. Tell me about yourself, Miriam."

It's a command, and I'm helpless against it. I probably go into far too much detail, but I talk about meeting Alo and Iggy and how much I loved playing with Iggy as a baby. And then I tell five years worth of story in sixty seconds, culminating with how much I love them both, and how grateful I am to be part of their lives.

Seraphina sobs by the end of it, and even Noctis looks a little misty eyed.

Alo rubs soft circles on my stomach, listening quietly as I speak.

When I finish talking, Iggy hops off his shoulder and climbs up into my arms, wrapping his tail around my neck. When the spade slips into my shirt, Noctis smiles.

"I—Miriam, it's lovely to meet you." He clears his throat. "You three certainly seem happy."

"We are," Alo states. "We are blissfully happy. Although it would make us even happier if you'd come visit."

"We'd love that," Seraphina gushes. "I'll look at the calendar tonight and comm you some dates, alright?" Her dark gaze flicks to mine. "Miriam, we can't wait to meet you in person." She elbows her mate in the stomach.

"That's right," he says in a rush. "We'll definitely visit soon and welcome you more formally."

"Okay," I say brightly. "Looking forward to it!"

We fall silent, and it stretches long and awkward until the back door slams open, and Kevin lets himself in.

"Alright, are you done with this stuff yet Iggy? We have shit to do!"

"Kevin!" Alo and I bark at the same time.

Kevin turns to us and shrugs. "Oops? I shouldn't have said shit."

"Twice," Noctis barks from the comm hologram.

I give Alo's parents a nervous look. Noctis scowls but Seraphina gives me a knowing look.

"Little boys can be a handful," she says with a wink.

I pat Alo on the shoulder as I smile at his mother. "Big boys too, in my experience."

She laughs, then I laugh, then the kids join in, even though they probably didn't get that.

We disconnect with Alo's parents and Iggy leaves us to hunt bad guys with Kevin. When he's gone, Alo spins me in his arms, bending me against the island countertop.

He bites my chin softly before trailing harder and harder nibbles down to my shoulder.

"Pixie girl, we've got a while before Iggy shows back up for dinner. I'll give you a ten second head start. Get to our nest. Be naked when I get there. I'm bringing up a surprise."

"A surprise?" I grab his horns and drag his face back into view. "You know I love surprises."

"This one's tasty. And sexy."

"Just like you."

Alo laughs. "Ten."

When I don't move, he sighs and pushes one thigh to the side to give me space to escape. I remain firmly planted between his enormous thighs.

"Nine. Eight. You're not moving, Miriam."

I cross my arms.

When he gets to three he slips off the stool and crouches, big wings flaring behind him. His pupils dilate, overtaking the chocolate brown of his iris.

"This is my favorite game," I admit.

"Two," he grits out. "You better run, woman."

I examine my nails. "I'm faster than you give me credit for, Aloitious Rygold."

"One," he snaps.

I pop into small form and zip past him toward the stairs.

Toward heaven.

Toward happily ever after.

++

Wanna know what happens when Miriam and Alo go skinny-dipping at the mermaid grotto? Sign up for my newsletter at www.annafury.com to access the spicy bonus epilogue where all that (and more) transpires.

Book four, Waltzing With Witches, is coming soon! Keep your eye on the Amazon series page HERE. Alternatively, if you're on my newsletter, you'll get updates straight to your inbox!

BOOKS BY ANNA FURY (MY OTHER PEN NAME)

DARK FANTASY SHIFTER OMEGAVERSE

Temple Maze Series

NOIRE | JET | TENEBRIS

DYSTOPIAN OMEGAVERSE

Alpha Compound Series

THE ALPHA AWAKENS | WAKE UP, ALPHA | WIDE AWAKE | SLEEPWALK | AWAKE AT LAST

Northern Rejects Series

ROCK HARD REJECT | HEARTLESS HEATHEN | PRETTY LITTLE SINNER

Scan the QR code to access all my books, socials, current deals and more!

@annafuryauthor
liinks.co/annafuryauthor

ABOUT THE AUTHOR

Hazel Mack is the sweet alter-ego of Anna Fury, a North Carolina native fluent in snark and sarcasm, tiki decor, and an aficionado of phallic plants. Visit her on Instagram for a glimpse of the sexiest wiener wallpaper you've ever seen. #ifyouknowyouknow

She writes any time she has a free minute—walking the dog, in the shower, ON THE TOILET. The voices in her head wait for no one. When she's not furiously hen-pecking at her computer, she loves to hike and bike and get out in nature.

She currently lives in Raleigh, North Carolina, with her Mr. Right, a tiny tornado, and a lovely old dog. Hazel LOVES to connect with readers, so visit her on social or email her at author@annafury.com.

Printed in Great Britain
by Amazon

32634204R00145